Flames at Twilight

Also by
Fachtna Joseph Harte

They Shall Bear You Up

Flames at Twilight

The Novel of St. Patrick and Ireland

Fachtna Joseph Harte

Images courtesy of Mayo County Council.

Cover Art by
Jill Burkee
Artida Arts Inc.
56 Ludlow Street
NewYork

Additional Art by
Giancarlo Biagi
Germana Pucci Biagi

Archway Publishing books may be ordered through booksellers or by contacting:

Archway Publishing
1663 Liberty Drive
Bloomington, IN 47403
www.archwaypublishing.com
1 (888) 242-5904

ISBN: 978-1-4808-5834-3 (sc)
ISBN: 978-1-4808-5832-9 (hc)
ISBN: 978-1-4808-5833-6 (e)

Library of Congress Control Number: 2018901645

Print information available on the last page.

Archway Publishing rev. date: 2/19/2018

Dedicated in Memory of
Thomas P. Moran,
Friend and Counselor
"Always There"

Contents

Preface

Dear reader,

This novel is written to convey the life of Saint Patrick (Pátraic) and the times and culture in which he lived. The story is based on history, legends, and myths. Please keep in mind it is a novel, but after you have read it, you will hopefully have a better understanding of the saint and the work he achieved in bringing Christianity to the Emerald Isle.

Now read on …

Fachtna Joseph Harte

Acknowledgments

I express my deep gratitude to the following people:

Sharon Mayer, who edited this book and worked tirelessly and with dedication in the editing process

Father Brendan Hoban, County Mayo, Ireland

Father John E. McMullan, Orlando and Belfast

Brother Bonaventure Frain, FMS, County Dublin, Ireland

Jim and Monica Fitzgerald, County Dublin, Ireland

Ann Jackson, County Cork, Ireland

Donal McCormick, County Mayo, Ireland

John Maughan, Mayo County Council, County Mayo, Ireland

Marie Ring, County Cork, Ireland

Lucy Jennings, Belfast, Ireland

Fachtna and Mary Harte, County Mayo, Ireland

Aidan and Margaret Harte, County Mayo, Ireland

Patrick MacNeil, Florida

Daniel Freedman, New York

Michael Moran, Florida

All have contributed in one form or other toward the publication of this book, and I express my deep gratitude.

Map of Ireland

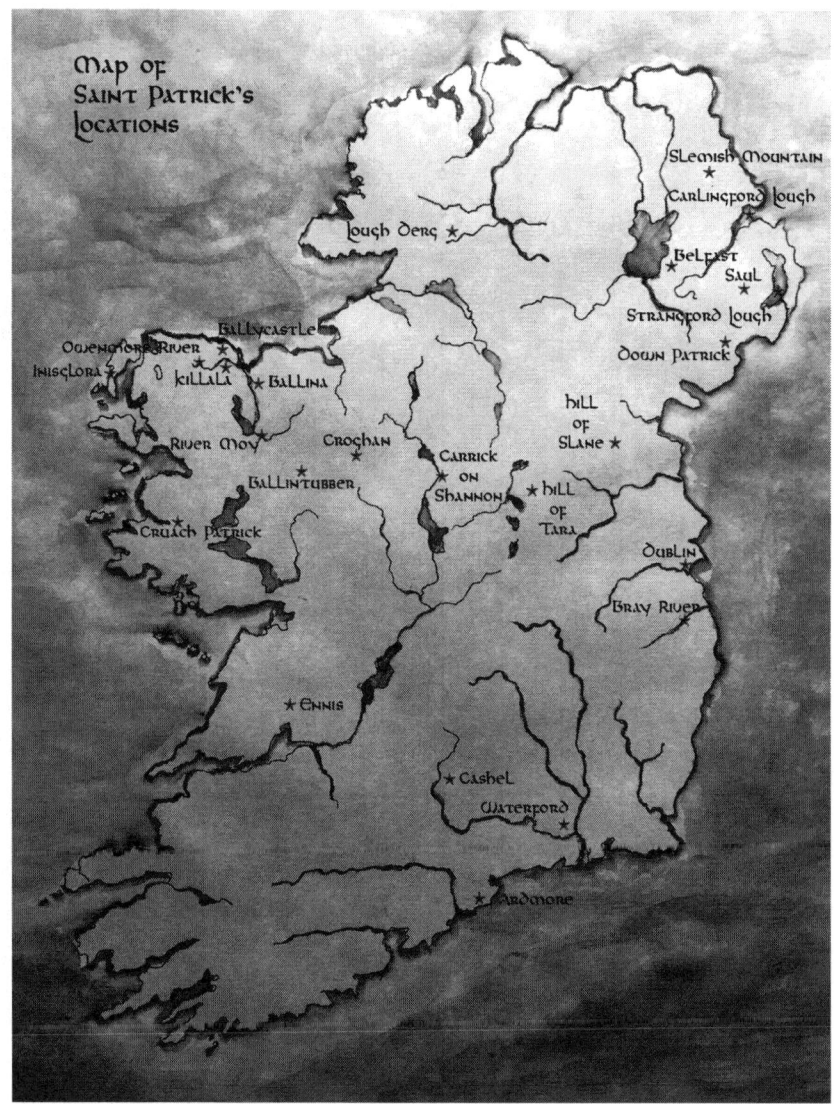

Chapter 1

An Imperial Order

But every house where Love abides,
And Friendship is a guest,
Is surely home, and home-sweet-home:
For there the heart can rest.[1]

Ablatum Bulgium[2] had become home for Calpurnius, a Roman officer. He was contented there with his wife and son. The farther from the emperor of Rome, the better! Life in Southern Caledonia[3] was mostly peaceful. Roman rule had been for the most part accepted by the people living here. That was because the area was so much closer to Britannia[4] than the other parts of Caledonia that had shrugged off Roman imperialism over the past fifty years or more. In the south the majority kept the peace because it seemed a lost cause to rebel. Any kind of opposition brought higher taxation or perhaps even eviction from their property. The amount raised from each property owner depended on the person's relationship with the tax collector. Calpurnius knew that as an officer of the

[1] *A Home Song* by Henry Van Dyke.
[2] Dumfries, Scotland.
[3] Southern Scotland.
[4] England.

Roman army and a tax collector for the emperor as well, the locals showed him nothing but respect. There was good reason for that. The people were mostly farmers! There were some Christians in the area, too, and as a deacon of the Christian faith, Calpurnius took part in the liturgies for the scattered and minute population of Christians who wanted to practice their faith to the full.

As he rode his horse from his comfortable estate home to the Roman compound, Calpurnius was reflecting on his many duties. There were soldiers to be overseen on a daily basis. There were taxes to be collected from his constituency, some of them now outstanding. At the weekend there were church duties if he decided to attend, though most of the time he found reason to stay home. Since Rome's conversion to Christianity, Sunday was regarded as a religious holiday, and even the army had only the most necessary duties. It was a good time for him to be with his wife and young son, and frequently he failed to show up at the local church ceremonies.

"What are we planning for Sunday, *mon cher*?"[5] his wife had asked as he mounted his horse that afternoon.

"Well, I haven't thought about it yet."

"Oh, I see. But we haven't been to church for several weeks. And you haven't participated in the ceremonies or been of any help to the *prêtre*.[6] I thought perhaps on Sunday we might go to church first and then plan to be together for the rest of the day. It would be good for the boy too. And I am sure the prêtre would be delighted to have you with him at the Messe.[7]"

Conchessa wasn't happy with her husband's constant reneging on his church duties. Nor was she happy that her young son was not getting the Christian teachings—or example of religious fervor—that a young boy should have.

"You well know, Calpurnius, that your prêtre father would be

---

[5] My dear.

[6] Priest.

[7] Mass.

greatly upset about the situation if he were alive today. We need to educate the boy in his Christian beliefs and obligations."

By this time Calpurnius had mounted his horse and was already on his way as he responded looking back at his wife.

"The boy is young still. I promise I will find him a teacher who will educate him in everything Christian, and when I come home, we can talk about Sunday."

In short time, he was close to the compound. It was surrounded by impregnable wooden fences that were unassailable to an ordinary citizen. The turrets on either side of the entryway carried an unwritten message to the passerby to keep out. The sentinels at the gate knew him well. No need for a password to be allowed inside. The men saluted.

"God be with you, sir."

Calpurnius returned their salute and silently rode inside. The officers' quarters were toward the center of the compound. Calpurnius dismounted and walked in. Only one officer was present, sitting at a rough-hewn wooden table. The tabletop, however, was very smooth, and the officer had both hands resting upon it.

He stood now and saluted his fellow officer.

"I have a script for you," he said.

"A script?" replied Calpurnius.

"Yes, the emperor's emissary left here a short time ago. The order was to give you this script today."

For the first time in many moons, Calpurnius now had an anxious look on his face. A message from the emperor could mean dismissal from the army, a demotion, or a reprimand. His brain ran wild with improbable rebukes to himself. His fears mounted. He hadn't done anything out of order that he could remember, and he had always reported for duty according to schedule. He had collected the taxes as far as he was directed and had forwarded the demanded amount to Caesar. He was working on overdue taxes, but those were hardly enough to warrant a censure or for a demand from Caesar to pay up immediately. Could it be that the taxes fell short of the emperor's expectations? If so, he would have to make up the deficiency out of his own pocket. There was a noticeable shake in his hand as he rolled open the script.

His eyes automatically went to the signature at the bottom. The script was indeed from the emperor of Rome, and the signature left no doubt. The seal of the emperor was there just below his signature. The name Flavius Honorius Augustus was written with a flair. Calpurnius was fearful to raise his eyes to the beginning of the script, but there was no choice.

> Calpurnius Potitus, you will honor your emperor and Leader of the Western Holy Roman Empire by transferring to that part of Britannia alongside and north of the Bristol Alveo.[8] You will take with you a hundred men needed to reinforce the Roman army in order to protect the population, especially those citizens who are Roman. You will protect against hostile marauders, especially those uncivilized Celts from Hibernia who so frequently invade the coastlands and murder or capture Roman citizens. You are hereby given authority to move your family from your present estate in Caledonia to another that awaits you at the town of Leucarum[9] along the Carmarthen Bay.[10] Your present estate will be taken over by the Roman legionnaires and bestowed on the officer appointed to replace you. Your emperor expects you to lose no time in moving your men, along with your wife and son, to the designated area heretofore named.

---

[8] Bristol Channel.
[9] Now located in the city of Swansea, Wales.
[10] Southwest of Swansea.

Then followed the signature of the emperor and the date—
July 384.

Calpurnius was visibly stunned. His fellow officer saw his com-
plexion change from its previous affable and relaxed countenance to
pale and disturbed with traces of anger beginning to show themselves.
He handed back the scroll to the officer so he could read it for himself.
As he turned his eyes to the scroll, he heard Calpurnius mutter in a
low voice, "How did the emperor settle on me? I have enemies."

"No, sir, you do not. You are a good officer and a great leader,
and the Roman authorities want you to protect what is becoming an
unsafe place along the Bristol Bay. You have been judged the very best
officer for that difficult task. I have no doubt the Roman governor in
London recommended you for this position."

"Sometimes one pays for his abilities," replied Calpurnius, accepting his fellow officer's comments and beginning to calm down.

"They chose the right man," said his companion officer. "Now
you need to get ready for your future journey, sir."

"It will be bad news for Conchessa. She is so happy where she is,
and she is very settled into the area as if she had resided there forever,"
Calpurnius responded.

"She will get over it," said the officer.

"I hope she will. Now to my last tasks of this present location.
How are the men?"

"Everything is fine, and I am sure we will be receiving another
messenger any time now to give us news of your replacement. But no
doubt there will be sadness at your leaving. You are a popular legionnaire, and your men love you. Perhaps the best thing to do now is
to sit down and choose the legionnaires who will accompany you to
your new station."

"Yes. I suppose you are right. Can you let me have the lists of all
soldiers under my command? This is going to take time. First I need
to choose a messenger to carry a script south as to the approximate
time of my arrival."

"Eusebius will carry out that task for you. He is brave and dedicated to his duties and indeed to you."

"Try to locate him and send him to me. Meanwhile, I will write the script myself here and now, and he can start his journey early tomorrow."

"How soon do you think you can start *your* journey to Leucarum?"

Calpurnius thought for a moment. "Well I have a few chores to take care of that may take a couple of weeks. So let's say I will start the journey south with my family in two weeks' time."

Later in the day as he rode home, Calpurnius felt a sadness he had not experienced in a long time, not since the death of his prêtre father. He reflected on how his life was about to change. He was being sent into dangerous territory; he would have to say quick goodbyes to his friends and neighbors, and how would Conchessa receive the news? What about the uncollected taxes? He would have to get all that done before his departure—sometime in the next ten days. By the time he dismounted his horse at his family estate home, he still hadn't decided how exactly to break the news to Conchessa. But time was up! Conchessa came out to greet him. She watched him dismount and saw the concern on his face. She knew her husband well enough to know that something might be wrong.

"Is everything all right, *mon amour*?[11] You don't look happy."

There was only one thing to do—break the news as gently as possible and hope for the best.

"Let's go inside, *m'amie*,[12] and sit down for a while. I would truly like a drink of water."

Conchessa rushed to get the water, and within a few moments she had handed her husband a flagon full of fresh water. He accepted the water as his wife awaited whatever he was going to say.

"Well, *ma chérie*,[13] there is some news that may upset you."

---

[11] My love.

[12] My love—as addressed to a woman.

[13] My dear—as addressed to a woman.

Conchessa listened intently as her husband continued.

"There is a big change coming in our lives. I had a script from the emperor today. We have to move south to Britannia to a place called Penarth on the Carmarthen Bay. It is a long way from here, and the emperor has notified me to lose no time in getting there with a hundred legionnaires. We have been well settled here, and now we have to leave."

"Why did the emperor pick you out? There must be hundreds of others who could have been appointed."

"Well, one of my fellow officers at the compound believes that the emperor chose me because of my ability to lead. I should like to think that is the real reason."

Conchessa was thoughtful before she uttered her words. "He is probably correct, but I truly wish we had been left alone." Tears were beginning to roll slowly down her cheeks. "We were so happy here in this peaceful place. Now we face a long and dangerous journey to the south, and we must leave behind our beautiful estate. I will lose all my friends, and we really don't know what lies ahead."

It was time for Calpurnius to make an effort at consolation. "You are a wonderful person, always have been. You make friends easily, and I am sure that when we are settled for a while on our new estate, you will have a multitude of friends. And I will do everything within my power to make the journey easy for you. We will be accompanied by a hundred soldiers, and they will easily ward off any intruders on the way. We will place your wagon in the middle, and the boy will be with you. I will ride up front, and with fifty soldiers to the fore and fifty more at the rear, he and you will be very safe. Indeed, I will get you a chariot and four horses so that the boy and you will be comfortable on the journey."

"There will be a new estate for us at journey's end?" asked Conchessa, who appeared to her husband to be calming down somewhat.

"Yes, there will."

"I hope when we get there we can find a good teacher for the boy, both in Christianity and classic education," replied Conchessa.

She was now looking ahead. She had very obviously moved her mind forward from her present situation to what would follow in Penarth.

"Certainly we will. I promise you I will live up to my duties as a deacon better than in the past, and the very first thing I will do is find a teacher for the boy. Tomorrow I must go out and find the landowners who have not yet paid their taxes to Caesar. It will take the entire day and probably several days more. I don't want the word to get out that I am leaving before the taxes are paid. Meanwhile, you can take a look at what is valuable to you so that we may begin storage for the journey. Indeed, I need to look at my list of men again. The *praefectus castrorum*[14] recommended that Eusebius carry the message to Britannia as to when I will arrive, and it occurs to me he should not go alone. It is a long journey, and he will need a companion on the way. It will take four or five days at least, perhaps a week, and someone should accompany him."

[14] Senior military tribune, third most senior commander of the Roman legion.

Chapter 2

The Messengers

Eusebius had been given the news. He had a long journey in front of him. He needed to pack his things, not least of all food to take him a good part of the way. When he ran out, he would purchase more from farmers along his route, as well as visiting an inn occasionally. There would be need for arrows as well to protect himself from possible highwaymen who were not uncommon in any area governed by Rome. And of course his long spear would help defend him in any close encounter. That long spear, a feature of the Roman self-defenses, had shielded him many times in man-to-man engagements. It was longer than the normal spear commonly used and was indeed a particular feature of the Roman army. He would leave as soon as possible and report to the praefectus castrorum—the officer in charge of the compound. But before he had finalized his plans the praefectus sent for him. Eusebius reported immediately.

"Eusebius, it is best that you have a companion on the way. It is a long and arduous journey. You will be accompanied by Lucus, a cavalryman of no little reputation. He is an *alaris*[15] who has distinguished himself in many an encounter, and he will be a good companion for you as well as affording you better protection on your tedious journey."

---

[15] Prestigious horse soldier, noncitizen of Rome.

There was a nod of the head from Eusebius.

"Yes, sir," he replied. "I am grateful. I am ready to leave as soon as possible. I have preparations made."

The praefectus was satisfied with Eusebius's reply.

"Lucas is also readying for the journey," he acknowledged. "He will make himself available to ride out of here with you the day after tomorrow."

That was later than Eusebius had planned, but he nodded his head in agreement. One did not challenge the praefectus castrorum, one of the most powerful officers within the compound.

"That will be fine," he responded with a salute. "Long live the emperor."

Two days later they were on their way: Eusebius, a somewhat heavy man with Eastern European features, and Lucas, more gaunt, athletic looking, and apparently ten years or so younger, the sort of person who would make a good companion in any kind of skirmish. Their bags were packed, the letter to the praefectus castrorum in Leucarum securely enclosed in the inside pocket of Eusebius's bag, food for at least part of the journey, and sufficient denarii[16] to help his fellow traveler and himself return back to their Caledonian base.

As they left the stockade at the break of dawn, the sun was beginning to peer over the distant Cheviot Hills, quiet reigned, and only the notes from the early-morning birds cheerfully broke the restful silence. Since the path they were taking was not really a road, rather a green grass pathway through the upcoming mountainous regions, not even the sound of horses' hooves made an impression on the auricular muscles. Both men quickly found they were going to be intimate companions: Eusebius, with wisdom gained from his longer membership of the Roman army, and Lucas, with his fine record as an alaris and eager to converse about the history of Rome. As they rode south, Lucas was curious about the journey his senior officer had mapped out.

"Where will we be entering Britannia?" he inquired. "I'm sure you have the journey well planned."

---

[16] Roman coin.

"We will go southeast to Hadrian's Wall,[17]" Eusebius replied, "and enter Britannia close to Aballava.[18] We will be keeping an eye on the late sun and the evening star, which will let us know a westerly direction, but we will first travel southeast to avoid the ocean inlet to Aballava. The midday sun will also help us in our southward direction."

Lucas was reflective for a few moments. He was thinking about the journey as well as taking in the first real appearance of the sun as it crept above the Cheviot Hills to the east, beginning to throw its light on their immediate area. It seemed to Lucas the surrounding countryside was dressing itself in its morning glory. The gorse with its yellow petals was crying out for attention, although Lucas reflected to himself that its attractiveness and its peaceful appearance betrayed its sinister plan to insert its thorns in any unfortunate who might happen to fall or stray into its hostile surroundings. On the other hand, the heather with its varied shades of purple seemed at peace with the world, was more humble in its presentation of itself, and combined with the yellow of the gorse made for a glow of peaceful stillness that affected the psyche and gave promise of a beautiful day in the making.

Lucas brought his thoughts back to reality.

"You mentioned Hadrian's Wall," he said to Eusebius. "You know I came straight to Caledonia from Rome, and although I have heard of Hadrian's Wall, it will be good to see it."

Eusebius responded with a smile.

"It's an old setup like myself," he said, "but I guess age makes history!"

"Come now, you surely are younger than Hadrian's Wall," his companion replied. "Isn't Hadrian's Wall a long time past Hadrian's

---

[17] Extended from present-day Newcastle on Tyne on the east coast of England to Carlisle on the west coast on the Celtic Sea.

[18] Roman fort, a short distance south of Solway Firth, now Burgh By Sands, England. The first phase of the wall seems to have been between present-day Newcastle Upon Tyne and Burgh By Sands. The wall was completed from there to Carlisle.

time, and he built it. I wonder what you will look like in more than two hundred years!"

"A skeleton!" replied Eusebius jokingly. "Most of the wall still stands, but my old skeleton will be under ground. The wall is still above ground and even at this time can be a hindrance to marauders who might like to get beyond it. Indeed there are fortifications here and there along the wall, and if we are lucky, we may be able to stay in one overnight when we get there."

Lucas's curiosity was aroused.

"Forts along the wall?" he inquired. "I suppose they were built by Hadrian also. Those must have been rough times in this part of the empire. Were the peoples of these parts a dangerous breed?"

"Yes, Hadrian included the forts in his plans. Did you know that he also built a ditch all the way along the wall so that it would be much more difficult for a would-be marauder to get across? First he had to somehow climb the wall that was about forty feet high, then he was faced with a deep drop, and if he got across that, he was met with javelins and arrows from the Romans. In addition, Hadrian ordered a gate through the wall to be built every mile or so. Sometimes that gate led to nowhere as the wall went over hills and mountains, and some of the gates built were useless, as all they did was open the way to an impossible entry with a deep fall on the Britannia side."

"Then why were the gates ever placed there if they were that dangerous?" asked the curious Lucas.

"Because nobody wanted to challenge the emperor. That would be more dangerous than the fall over the cliff!" responded Eusebius. "Now let me tell you why Hadrian built the wall and the mystery of the ninth legion."

"A mystery? Tell me," said Lucas.

"Well," said Eusebius, "the ninth legion was stationed in Luguvalium,[19] south of where the wall now stands. Hadrian was

---

[19] Town located within present-day Carlisle, northwestern England on the Celtic Sea. The mystery of the disappearance of four thousand Roman legionnaires is historically documented and has never been resolved.

emperor. It was around the year 117 after Christ. One morning the ninth legion left to march north, mostly on a military expedition to let the natives see Roman might. They never returned to their fort."

"Where did they go?" asked the younger absorber of a part of Roman history that he was just learning.

"Where *did* they go?" Eusebius replied. "That's the mystery. Over four thousand men and their officers disappeared off the map. All in one day. No bodies were ever found. No trace of what might have happened."

"And of course Hadrian established an inquiry?" asked the young learner.

"No, he did not. He was afraid the whole thing would cause him to be dethroned as emperor. So everything was hush-hush. Then a wall began to be built from Pons Aelius[20] to Aballava at the quiet command of the emperor. It took a long time, probably a couple of years, to build the wall. But there was no inquiry into the missing troops. And it would appear to me that Hadrian feared the damage was done by the Picts in the area north of the wall, so he not only had the wall erected, but he established forts along the wall to protect the whole area."

Lucas was reflecting again. This time on the piece of history he had just heard.

"You mean over four thousand men disappeared from the earth in one small area in one day, and nobody knew anything about it?"

"Yes indeed. That is one of the great mysteries, as I said. Somebody must have known something about it, but it wouldn't be good for them to report the matter. And perhaps Hadrian didn't want to know. He feared the loss of his power."

"So how did they build the wall?" asked Lucas.

"You'll see before too long," said Eusebius. "It was mostly of large stones with layers of sod running at particular heights. Keep in mind

---

[20] (Latin: Aelian Bridge) or Roman Fort very close to present day Newcastle Upon Tyne. For more information go to https://en.wikipedia.org/wiki/Pons_Aelius.

that cement was discovered in Rome, too, long before Hadrian's time. Rome is a walled-in city. The cement helped to bind the rocks together so that any Roman wall will last for ages and ages. You know, Lucas, we are still the greatest builders in the world. Our people don't live in huts, and we have running water that can even be brought into our homes. We have heated floors in our homes too. The Picts around here are still painting themselves and are thieves and robbers; the Celts, especially those over there" (he pointed west), "keep looking for a fight and like to make raids on us even from their own country. That is why Calpurnius is being sent to Britannia. He is a strong leader who knows no fear. I won't be surprised if he is to become the praefectus castrorum."

"Well, I guess I know now why Caledonia really never fell fully under Roman rule," the younger man replied.

"It never did, except in areas here and there," responded Eusebius, "mostly the southern portion not far from the wall. The emperors found it impossible to control the Celts and the Picts, and I don't think it will be too long before we withdraw south of the wall entirely."

Their discussion of historical Rome helped to make the journey and the hours speed by. The sun had already advanced in the sky and seemed to have been progressing on its own journey as they continued to discuss the might of Rome and its many conquests.

Soon the sun was high in the sky. The travelers saw no sign of civilization. Forests of trees and low-lying furze lined their way, as if by some bizarre event the forces of nature had created a pathway. It was time to dismount and bring a little food from their saddlebags. A shady tree a short distance away looked inviting, and soon they were there allowing their horses to do a little grazing of the heath while they sat and enjoyed the lunch that restored their energy to journey on.

As they mounted their horses, Lucas asked, "How far do you think we are from Aballava?"

"We should be there before too long," replied Eusebius. "We will know long beforehand because that high wall of Hadrian shows up from a good distance away."

They were still heading in an easterly direction, but it was time to veer southeast. Eusebius had judged that dry land for the rest of the journey must now be a certainty. They had long crossed the Annan River, and he felt the Solway Firth was well behind. Now it was almost a straight ride to Hadrian's Wall. Once through the wall, all that lay ahead was simply to follow the wall right into Aballava. The sun had moved west but was still high in the sky, and Eusebius judged that the time must be somewhere in midafternoon. It had been a pleasant ride; they stopped here and there to water their horses and thoroughly enjoyed the peaceful aurora of the Caledonian uplands. Suddenly Lucas spoke with a tension in his voice.

"Look to the east. There are about ten horsemen riding at a fast pace toward us, and it looks to me as if they are all without clothing."

Eusebius glanced, saw the horsemen, and shouted loudly to Lucas, "They are Pict warriors. When on the warpath they wear no clothes, but they are heavily armed, and it's ten of them against the two of us. Let's gallop away from them."

The men urged their horses on, but the heavier loads their horses were carrying tended to slow them down somewhat.

Eusebius urged his companion.

"It's a ride to the death," he exclaimed. "We cannot outrun them."

The Picts were gaining ground in the race, as the Roman officers, now sweating from the exertions of the chase, were breathing heavily.

"Look," said Eusebius, "a goodly clump of trees in the distance. Let's see if we can get into them. The Picts will most likely spread out within the clump searching for us, and we may be able to make it a one-on-one fight. It's a long shot, but it's the only chance we have."

The two officers, encouraging their steeds, headed for the very large clump of trees, probably five acres or so of bald cypress and spruce. They reached the trees. The ground was somewhat soft, but in reality that was better for the situation they were in. It muffled the sounds they were making and made it more difficult for the Pict warriors to hear.

"Let's stay together," said Eusebius. "Most likely they will spread out to search for us, and that will give us the opportunity of a fight with a smaller group or even possibly dispatch them one by one."

"Good," agreed his partner. "It will give us a chance to make them pay."

The Picts had reached the wood, and just as Eusebius had surmised, they spread out among the trees trying to locate their prey. The Romans could hear their loud conversations, but it didn't mean much since they were speaking a different language.

"Just stay quiet, and we may be able to make a run for it," Eusebius whispered.

It was not to be that simple. Right then they heard the sounds of a horseman coming toward them.

"I think he is on his own," whispered Eusebius.

Lucas reached for his long sword. The horseman had not seen them before it was too late. He lunged at them, sword pointed at Lucas. Lucas was quick to react. First he struck the sword of the onrushing enemy with his longer weapon. The warrior saw immediately that it was two on one, and he had an inferior sword. He screamed for help at the top of his voice, but the force of his own onrushing horse carried him closer than was safe and directly into Lucas's blade. In a moment his life was ended. He fell to the ground, his frightened horse vanishing into the forest.

His lifeless body had barely hit the ground when two more warriors arrived on the scene screaming words the Romans could not understand.

"Charge!" shouted Eusebius.

This time it really was one on one, each legionnaire taking a separate opponent. The result was a skirmish that lasted less than a minute. The Picts were gallant warriors, but they were at a big disadvantage with their shorter swords and lack of armor. The legionnaires defended themselves well, never allowing the enemy to get within close distance, and when that happened their fighting art drove back the assailant. Suddenly one warrior reached into his saddle, and in moments a hatchet was flying toward Eusebius's head. He saw it coming and was able to dip his head so that the hatchet flew over and stuck in a tree behind him. Now it was Eusebius's opportunity to make a sudden advance with his horse. His sword finished off the opposing Pict in a second or two.

Meantime, Lucas was exerting his skills with the other attacker. It was a mismatch really. The younger legionnaire excelled in hand-to-hand fighting and had his would-be assassin dead on the ground almost at the same time as Eusebius had ended his own fight.

The men looked and listened for the sounds of the enemy. What sounds they heard brought them to a conclusion that the remaining seven were at a distance toward the far side of the wood.

"Let's make a run for it," exclaimed Eusebius. "If they catch us, and they are all together, we have little if any chance of survival. The wall may not be far away, and once through it, those remaining seven would hardly follow us through. They know there are forts with Roman soldiers on the south side."

Lucas was listening to the sounds of the forest as Eusebius spoke.

"If we go toward Aballava," he replied, "they will cut us off before we reach the wall. Let's head directly south."

Eusebius agreed. The men turned their horses toward the point of entry, and soon they were galloping in a southerly direction that would prevent an ambush had they taken the shortest route. It was somewhat uphill, and the horses seemed to be losing speed.

Then Lucas shouted, "Look, they have seen us, and they are on our tracks."

Both men raced to the top of the hill.

Eusebius saw it first. The wall! It was straight ahead, less than a quarter of a mile. Lucas had seen it too.

"Look for an open entryway!" shouted Eusebius. "Let's go east along the wall until we find a Hadrian entrance."

Lucas looked around. The Picts were having trouble with tired horses, too, and were far back. There was time to escape. They were racing along the wall and keeping their distance from their pursuers. The Picts now understood their intentions and suddenly changed their pathway to try and cut them off before they could escape into Britannia.

"Look!" shouted Lucas. "There's an opening about two hundred metres ahead. Let's get there to freedom."

They galloped on. They saw the large opening just ahead. It was wide enough for two horsemen to go through together.

"We are just about there," shouted Eusebius.

They looked around. Their pursuers were still a long way behind. The evening was in twilight, and the sun was setting far away to their right. As they reached the opening and galloped through, the horses froze and tried to stop. There was a fall of most likely three hundred metres that came right to the entranceway. The unexpected effort of the horses to stop threw both riders out of their saddles and pitched them forward over the deep slope. They were in the air for a short few seconds, and then their bodies smashed into the hard surface below.

Eusebius and Lucas would journey no further in life.

Hadrian, were he still alive, would not have been disturbed.

Chapter 3

A New Post

Three weeks later, Calpurnius and his ala[21] rode into Leucarum. It had been an uneventful but tiring journey, especially for Conchessa and their teenage son Succat. They had traveled steadily for almost all of those three weeks, overnighting mostly at Roman fortifications and occasionally at an inn where only a few persons could be hosted—Calpurnius and his little family and some of the higher-ranking officers who were escorting them south. The rest had to make do with sleeping outside in whatever shelter they could find. And there were no hostile incidents along their way.

It was not hard for the party to find the Roman quarters. These were located on a height and were easily visible from the populous town. As Conchessa looked from their special carriage, she saw the mud-wall homes of the inhabitants, with the odd timber home here and there. The roofs were made mostly of something that looked to her like rushes, with a thatched roof of straw looming occasionally. The homes were small and detached. Children were at play on the gravel and stony streets that had evidently been created by the Romans. Her thoughts flew miles away to her happy estate home in Caledonia, and she hoped she would never have to inhabit a home such as those she saw before her.

---

[21] Roman cavalry unit.

In a short time they had arrived outside the high walls of the camp. The lookout in an entry tower had seen the *tablifer*[22] holding high the standard with its insignia of the serpent highly visible. He was well aware of the cavalry uniforms and the magnificence, not only of the Roman steeds but the ability of the riders to display their own training and gifted genius to guide their horses in military unity, making it almost appear that the horses were marching like foot soldiers. Immediately the call went to the gateman to open up. Calpurnius and his men entered in formation, going toward the middle of the fort, knowing that it would be in that area they would meet the praefectus castrorum and report to him. Meanwhile, Conchessa and her son sat side by side in their carriage and surveyed the surroundings. This was where Calpurnius would serve the emperor in the coming years.

Now they had arrived at journey's end. The praefectus was standing at the entrance to his compartment with his *adiutor*[23] by his side. Calpurnius saluted, and his salute was returned in similar fashion. It was the praefectus who spoke first.

"We have been awaiting your arrival for some days now. You did not observe protocol and send a messenger to announce your arrival."

There was something cold about the praefectus's remarks. Calpurnius noted the coolness in his voice. This was the first time they had met, and this new acquaintance did not seem very friendly. Calpurnius thought he had misunderstood.

"What did you say?" he questioned, partly to put the praefectus through his paces again, partly to see if there might be any shift in tone.

"I said we have been awaiting your coming," the praefectus replied, this time in a little friendlier tone, "but you did not send any word as to the time of your arrival."

Now Calpurnius was ready to reply.

---

[22] Standard-bearer.

[23] Deputy.

"Yes," he said. "I sent two messengers together about three weeks ago. They should have arrived here a few days afterward. Are you telling me they did not arrive?"

The praefectus was beginning to understand. His voice was softer as he said, "No sir, your messengers did not come here. I have been moved to Londinium,[24] but I could make no arrangements until I heard from you. I am to replace the praefectus in Londinium, but I could not leave here until your arrival."

"And may I ask why?" Calpurnius retorted, his mind taking on a flight of fancy he felt could not be true.

The praefectus looked him in the eye.

"Well, sir," he responded, "you must know the fort cannot be left without a praefectus. When I didn't hear from you, I sent a messenger to Londinium to inform the praefectus there that I would come as soon as possible, but I was awaiting word from you. You are to replace me here, and it surprises me you have not been informed of that."

Calpurnius's head was spinning. He had been promoted without being informed.

"I wonder why that message was not conveyed in the brief from the emperor," he said.

"I don't understand that either," said the praefectus. "Most likely it was an omission by the emperor."

He paused.

"You know too that it might have been deliberate. Perhaps the emperor wanted to surprise you. This is a very important post. It's possible the emperor didn't want you to know that even with promotion he was placing you in a very responsible position. This is a very busy fort. And it has a big problem. The Celts from Hibernia[25] have been making raids along the inlet and frequently capturing and taking hostages, especially the younger boys. I am glad to be leaving and going to what appears to be a quieter post. The people of

---

[24] London.
[25] Ireland.

Brittania are submissive, but those Celts"—there was a pause in the statement—"well, they need to be taught a lesson. However, we will have time to talk about that later, and I invite your family to dine with my family this evening. By the way I am Cletus, and I welcome you to your new post."

Calpurnius noted the complete change in tone. Obviously the praefectus felt insulted that he had not received a message as to his arrival. He was beginning to be distracted in his own mind about the missing messengers.

Then Cletus spoke again.

"I presume that is your wife and son in the carriage. They must be tired. It is still a couple of hours to our meal, but I will immediately send a message to my wife that you are on the way to our home. Your wife might like to rest a little before we eat. I will also send a guide with your carriage to take you to my home. Cecilia, my wife, will welcome you. I will follow on as soon as I finish some business I was attending to here on the post."

Calpurnius thanked the now friendlier praefectus and walked back to his wife and son. Conchessa had not been able to catch the conversation. Her curiosity led to her question "Is everything all right?"

"Well, yes and no," her husband replied. "The bad news is that the messengers we sent never arrived, and nobody seems to have heard of them or from them. The praefectus was upset because he thought I had not sent a message about the time I expected to arrive, and I suppose rightly so. He will leave for Londinium shortly, probably in two weeks or so. He hasn't told me yet where we will reside in the meantime. You see, ma chéri,[26] I am now praefectus castrorum. No more tax-gathering, and I am in charge of the fort. We have been invited to dinner this evening, and we will stay overnight with the praefectus, whose name is Cletus. And when he departs, we will move into his place. Cletus is sending a guide with us now to take us to his

---

[26] My beloved.

home where you can get a little rest, and I am sure Succat will be glad to lay his head down too."

Conchessa was silent for a moment. The news was almost too much.

"You are praefectus castrorum," she said, climbing quickly out of the carriage.

In a moment she embraced her husband with a tear trickling down her face.

"This is wonderful!" she exclaimed. "I was so unhappy leaving Ablatum Bulgium, but now, see how God has blest us! You get a wonderful promotion, and I am sure we will make new friends. We are close to the bay, and the sea air will be so healthy for all of us."

In the excitement of the moment, the fate of Eusebius and Lucas had been forgotten. The accompanying infantry had been given the order to be at ease and were now being addressed by the adiutor. They would be staying at the fort and would be shown to their quarters.

Chapter 4

Unexpected Crisis

onchessa and Calpurnius were happy. Cletus had arranged for them to temporarily reside in a neighboring home presently vacated by another Roman officer. It was a comfortable place to live, sitting as it did right over the bluff with a beautiful view of the inlet. The homes were large and built in Roman tradition, with running water even within. The estates were smaller than Conchessa was used to in Caledonia, but now they had the ocean breezes and a nice beach beneath that gave ample opportunity for children to play and for all to swim in its salty waters.

Calpurnius was relieved of gathering taxes, something that took away the stress of his former Caledonian home. Cletus would be leaving for Londinium shortly, and they would inherit his estate and still continue to live in the same oceanside area. Cletus would take with him the usual security units to protect his family and him on the journey.

Most pleasing to the newly arrived family was that a small Christian community had existed in Leucarum for quite a while, and as deacon, Calpurnius could take part in church services every Sunday. Within a few days of their arrival, he had found a Christian tutor for Succat—a young man who taught well and befriended his boy in every way. Through his guidance young Succat was learning

exceptionally the tenets of his Christian faith even in the short time
since they had arrived. He was now fourteen years old, and was making friends with boys of his own age, all of whom somehow appeared
even now to look to him as their leader. In groups they spent much
time along the shore. Conchessa was especially pleased when she
noticed the amount of time her son spent in prayer. She frequently
remarked to Calpurnius how satisfied she was with the tutor he had
acquired, and together they wondered if Succat might later become a
legionnaire, or perhaps a prêtre like his grandfather.

Life was good for the newly arrived family. Calpurnius had taken
over the responsibilities of his office and appeared to be well liked by
his legion. They had moved into their own home, still overlooking the
beach where they could watch the rolling waves, the waters lapping,
and the trader galleys coming and going far out in the open sea waters.

A year had passed. No piracies had taken place on their side of the bay, although they were aware that the Celts had taken spoils of grazing animals
on the south side and had damaged homes while doing so, but there were
no human casualties. Succat was growing and developing into a healthy
young man, and he spent much time with his companions on the shore.

Without warning, the world came crashing around their feet.

Succat and his young friends were swimming in the waters of the
bay when they saw at a distance an unusual-looking boat approaching. It was large with a red sail, and it was obvious that it had many
oarsmen. Succat was the first to spot it.

"Look!" he shouted to his companions. "That's a Celtic galley.
Let's get out of here as quickly as we can."

The boys saw the galley and recognized the danger. They raced
from the water not even taking time to put on their clothes. None had
far to run as in Roman style the homes were all close to the seafront,
separated from their lands.

Conchessa was at home and was greatly surprised by the arrival of her out-of-breath son, who could barely speak through his gasping. She looked at him uneasily as he tried to announce what was taking place. It was obvious to her something was amiss.

"There's ... a Celtic galley ... it's coming ... into the bay. It's very large ... I'm frightened ... they will raid us. Whe ... where's father?"

Conchessa saw the fear in the boy's eyes, a fear that somehow was beginning to transfer itself to her own heart.

"Are you sure?" she asked. "And how do you know it is a Celtic galley?"

Succat was still recovering from his run and trying to overcome his fear.

"It has a big sail," he said, trying to find his breath. "It is ... a large ... boat and ... we could see the oars on the sides, ... a lot of oars. It has ... a big sail ... that was red ... and it was ... coming ... very fast. We all ... ran. We left our ... clothes on the beach. Where ... is ... father?"

Conchessa now saw the reason for the boy's fear. The Celts were coming again, to raid for cattle and anything else they might find, even young men. And these Celts were from Hibernia.

"Father is with the troops at the stockade," she replied. "By this time I am sure the military lookout will have seen the galley and sent for reinforcements. Don't be afraid."

In reality though, Conchessa was becoming fearful herself.

"I hope they will keep sailing up the bay," said Succat.

"Last time they did that I am told they had a bad experience with our legionnaires who were waiting for them and had watched them arrive. The same will most likely happen this time too. So don't be afraid, Succat," his mother replied.

There was a loud knock on the door. Conchessa recognized the accompanying voice. It was a neighbor.

"The Celtic marauders are landing down on the shore!" he screamed. "We all need to run to safety! There is no sign of help from the fort. This has all happened so quickly. These bullies will take or kill everything that comes before them. Nobody is safe from them."

Conchessa was confused. Yes, it was unexpected, but so was every Celtic raid. She wondered if the army was coming to help. Their horsemen would cover the ground very speedily. She looked at her young son, now growing toward adulthood. Could this be really happening? Those Celtic invaders were now only a short distance away. She spoke to the neighbor.

"Where are we going?" she asked.

"As far away from here as possible," he replied. "They can have my cattle and anything else they want, but not my wife and children. Run; let us run."

"Run, Succat, run!" screamed Conchessa. "Let us go with all the others. Let us stay together for safety."

Neighbors were gathering in a hurry. The voice of a man could be heard.

"This way, away from the shore and as far inland as we can get. Let's go toward Clydach.[27]"

For Conchessa it was an unimaginable scene. Families were running from their homes; babies in arms were being held closely by their parents; older people were being helped along. There was only one aim. Get away from the danger as fast as possible. It was a scene of frenzied fear and turmoil as some fell back, unable to keep up with the others, with the leading party lengthening the distance between themselves and those aged who were less energetic. Some fell back to help, but many kept running as fast as they could. It was survival of the fittest. Conchessa noticed an older man and his wife almost out of breath and beginning to lag far behind.

"Look at that poor couple!" she shouted. "They need help. Succat, let us go back to help them."

The young boy immediately replied, "Mother, you go on ahead. I'll go back and do what I can for them."

---

[27] A small village not far from Swansea.

"Leave them," another voice screamed. "The Celts won't harm them even if they catch up with them; they are too old."

But Succat was already on his way toward them with the speed of a youngster. Conchessa saw what was happening, and without hesitation she, too, turned back to help.

"O God," she prayed, "please help us out of this situation. Don't let the Celts catch us. Bring us help and save us."

Succat had placed himself between the two struggling older people. He was helping each of them arm in arm as their breathing became pronouncedly faster and heavier. Conchessa joined with him in his efforts, noticing at the same time that the main body of the escaping neighbors was getting farther and farther from them.

"If they disappear from us," she whispered to Succat, "we will be left on our own. All we can do then is try to hide."

There wasn't time to hide. The Celts had seen their quarry. Six or seven brutish-looking men were bearing down on them as they rounded a blind corner that had a clump of trees destroying forward vision. They were less than one hundred metres away. There was no escape. All of the invaders carried round shields and short spears, and two or three had clubs as well. The clubs looked to have sharp pointed pieces of wood sticking out of them.

"Succat, run!" screamed Conchessa. "Don't worry about me, I will be all right."

Succat looked around. He didn't want to leave his mother behind.

"We can't leave these people," he shouted. "And I can't leave you."

Conchessa was wavering between helping the old couple and running with her son. Her heart was torn. Meantime the Celts were closing in, only about fifty metres away. Fast-moving pursuers were chasing down a stationary object. Conchessa froze as she heard one of the Celts scream wildly. She had no idea what he was saying, but her instincts told her it was something to be frightened about. Within a few moments Succat was in the grip of an invader. Now there were two of them, and her young boy simply had no chance. He was being hustled away.

"Let go of my son; let him go!" Conchessa screamed.

Through her tears, her screams could now be heard a long distance away. But there was no one around except the old couple. There was nothing they could do, and the attackers had no interest in them. They dragged the boy forward despite his futile resistance. Conchessa kept following and begging for her son's release. Suddenly an invader turned around and forcibly pushed her to the ground, where she lay in a faint.

She would not see her son again.

Succat stole a glance backward, and his last recollection of his mother was of her prostrate form stretched on the ground with two older people bending over her.

The Celts were ruthless.

Whether Succat liked it or not, he was being dragged forward roughly toward the waterfront. His screams of dissent earned him a blow of a fist on the head that left him very nearly unconscious. When he had fully recovered, he was being hustled onto the invaders' galley, as they pulled and dragged him onboard. His hands were tied behind his back, and then a strong thick rope fastened him to the hull of the ship. Cattle were being loaded also—fourteen or fifteen animals that in the morning had belonged to a Roman officer or a local farmer.

Then Succat got a surprise that drew his attention away from his own plight. Two other young boys who had been on the beach with him that very afternoon were now also in shackles like himself. They were separated from him at the far side of the boat with the cattle in between. Tears flowed as he recalled the awfulness of this day. Not in his wildest imagination could he have thought that by nightfall he would have lost his parents, his comfortable home, and his companions, and find himself in the grasp of a brutal gang of thieves who treated him with less care than they rendered to the animals. The two unfortunates on the other side of the galley had seen him now and were looking mournfully at him as he tried to put on a brave face.

Now it appeared as if everybody and all booty was on board. The oarsmen assumed their positions, three to an oar—in all, twenty-four oarsmen on either side. With a signal from the coxswain who sat at the rudder in the middle of the boat, the oarsmen began to work in harmony, slowly at first and then with a fast, rhythmic form. It was still bright evening with the sun beginning its downward journey far to the west. Succat looked back at the land he was leaving, his thoughts roaming to his parents, his last sight of his mother lying on the ground, and wishing his father had been around to save them all. He saw the beach on which he and his companions had been together earlier in the day. He remembered where he had put his clothes as they all went into the waters totally unaware of the close advent of his captors. As he skimmed the coastline, there was no sign of Roman soldiers or of any vessel that might have come to the rescue. That simply was not to be! The galley was now gliding smoothly over the waters, increasing the distance between him and his home with every stroke of an oar and bound for a destination he knew not where.

The waters were calm, the sea at its friendliest, the cattle between his captors and himself not making much of a stir. Then the oarsmen began to sing in unison, their notes seemingly in tune with the movement of their oars. He had heard that the Celts, especially the Hibernians, were accustomed to singing while they rowed their boats. Now he had firsthand experience that he wished he didn't have! The lilt, however, had a calming effect on his nervous system as he listened to singers in a strange language pouring forth lyrics that were in harmony with their oars and the movement of the waves. The coxswain at the rudder appeared to be enjoying both the journey and the singing. It appeared to Succat also that this man was the captain of the galley. And as they sang, the galley gathered speed and appeared to be turning somewhat to the north and far, far away from his parents and his home. To the west was the setting sun, still with its bright rays throwing light on the prison galley, perhaps trying to send a message that all was not yet lost.

Now they were an hour out to sea. The waters were beginning to show signs of rebelliousness. The calm of the Alveo Bay was quickly dissipating. The Celtic Sea was beginning to show its disenchantment with those who might try to subjugate its power. By the minute the anger of the sea grew more and more intolerant, and mighty waves began to throw their power against the galley and its oarsmen. The coxswain shouted, and the singing stopped momentarily. Now the oarsmen were rowing harder and harder, almost with twice their former effort. Succat saw the sweat dropping from their brows. But the heartless ocean had no intentions of withdrawing its force. The oarsmen retaliated by singing now all the louder. Suddenly a mighty wave struck starboard. The ship rocked and swayed to larboard, and Succat watched as the galley appeared as if it might be overwhelmed by another wave coming from the same direction. Cattle were looing as the vessel tilted to larboard again, and water washed in from the defiant sea.

Succat looked across at his fellow captives and raising his eyes to heaven indicated they should join him in prayer as the crisis grew ever more severe. He lowered his head in prayer, noting the other captives were doing the same. Darkness had now fallen, and the moon in a dark and cloudy sky shone its dim rays over the angry sea and their bobbling galley. The crew on board did not appear to be afraid as they continued their singing, and the coxswain tried to steer through the storm without showing any concern. Succat thought to himself, *"These men have been through this before."*

Without warning an overpowering wave struck starboard. The galley was almost lifted above the waters as it rolled to the opposite side. The cattle braced themselves against the floor of the boat, fear resonating from their throated calls. Sprays of water drenched the vessel and its occupants, and for a moment it appeared as if it was ready to capsize. Then Succat saw a mountainous wave coming the other way, a wave that not only righted the vessel but threw it to larboard. Tied as he was to an iron ring at his back, he felt the pain on his wrists as the boat lurched side to side. The Celtic Sea was defiant and showed no signs of wavering in the imperious consummation of its original designs. But the sea appeared at odds with itself, or perhaps it was adding a new front to its war, as the galley was attacked by waves hurling themselves against it from both sides, something that actually helped the boat survive and stay afloat in the midst of the raging waters. Then suddenly the winds began to grow with an apoplectic display of antipathy to the galley and all within it. Someone shouted, and all rapparee heads turned upward toward the vessel's large sail. It was catching the winds and tugging the boat from side to side in one interminable movement.

The coxswain looked up and then looked around. He issued an order in a gruff manner and voice. He was looking at an oarsman, and his command obviously was to go up and take down the sail.

"How dangerous," Succat reflected within himself.

He watched the sailor climb the rigging as the vessel swayed to either side. Now the winds had joined forces with the ocean in one solid pact of destruction. All hands on board watched as the climber tried to keep himself from what might be a fatal fall. Without warning an unmerciful wave rolled into starboard, instantly sending the galley and all its occupants to the opposite side. There were no oarsmen to starboard. They had lost their balance and were tossed across the galley among the rest of the crew. At the same time the individual on the rigging lost his grip and was thrown into the ocean, disappearing beneath the waves for a few moments and then resurfacing for a few more moments before going under again. By this time all oarsmen were back in their positions except the one now in danger of drowning. The coxswain shouted an order and another oarsman jumped overboard to rescue his companion in distress.

Both men disappeared beneath the waters.

Chapter 5

Land Ho!

The Celtic Sea had exacted its vendetta on the booty vessel. Now it appeared to be satisfied. The storm began to subside. The Celtic plunderers had amassed their loot across the ocean, but the sea that carried their vessel had exacted its own toll. It had taken two of the crewmen.

Succat had been offering his prayers for all on board and for his own personal safety also. Just the same, he found himself unable to put away the distraction that two of the rapparees had met an unexpected end. He was among the booty they had claimed several hours earlier, as were his two friends across the deck. Indeed, one of the two now lost at sea was the one who had struck down his mother at his capture. He was able to forgive and to include the two in his prayers that they might receive a merciful judgment.

His thoughts were straying to what might lie ahead for his two companions and himself when the coxswain bellowed again. It was obviously an order, and it concerned him. One of the steersmen came lunging toward him, released the chains that bound him to the steerage, then caught him roughly and seated him in the position given up by one of the drowned men. He was being signaled to row in unison with the others. Then he caught sight of what was happening on the other side. The companion who had been with him on the beach was being forced into the same chore as himself. The meanness and ferocity in the eyes of the captors showed there was no doubt it was useful to be cooperative.

Succat did his best. He tried to pull the oar in harmony with the crew. It was difficult at first, the length of the oar overpowered him, and until he found a way to protect himself from being struck by the oar in his chest again and again, he had to endure the resultant pain. In a short time the storm was completely over, and as the waves settled back to a restive repetitive rhythm, Succat began to master the oarsman's craft. His other companion was similarly employed across the keel. Succat couldn't help wondering what fate had in store for all three hostages, but he reminded himself constantly of God's goodness and love.

As the galley turned in a more westerly direction the morning sun was beginning to illumine the ocean, its rays revealing dancing waves skimming and shimmering along the waters in rhythmic excitement welcoming the arrival of a new day. The brightness of dawn brought another revelation too! Quickly a cry went out that Succat could not understand—until he saw the crew all looking west together. Land loomed in the distance! The sights of home obviously gave new heart to the crew, and the singing of the oarsmen intensified with the knowledge that the end of their journey, and the awful plundering they had accomplished, would soon come to a fruitful end. They would be at sea again, but for now it was "mission accomplished."

Succat looked toward the rising sun, but the only thing to be seen were the waters of the Celtic Sea. With sadness in his heart, he wondered when his father got home, how his mother had fared after his capture, and whether she had survived the rough treatment she had received at the hands of the brutal Celts. His mind was in a maze. Where was he being taken? What did the future hold for him? How soon would he be able to return home, if ever? He felt himself among a group of brutes who cared little for man or beast. The temptation to despair and throw himself overboard presented itself, but Succat was aware of the presence of the Lord and placed his future in the hands of that Divine Providence he had so recently learned from his tutor at his new home. He remembered, too, his mother's zeal that he might learn of God and the participation of his deacon father in the Christian ceremonies. Besides, he knew that two of his friends were on board and faintly hoped they might all be together wherever their new destiny lay.

The galley was quickly closing in on land. It was a wooded land with high hills that extended way above the trees with gradated slopes that had an abundance of sheep grazing here, there, and everywhere. What struck Succat also was that the land was green with varieties changing from emerald to teal to lime to sateen in a continuous pattern that befriended the eye. Somehow or other the colors reflected what Succat most needed at this time—hope! His future now rested in hands other than his own, and it appeared to him that the galley holding him prisoner was fast approaching a land carpeted in green that held out the news that life, though continually changing, was filled with future promise.

The coxswain bellowed an order. The oarsmen stopped their singing and made adjustments to their rowing that began to bring the galley into dock. There was no sign of life around; it was still early in the morning. The dock looked a makeshift landing spot, formed by bringing together rocks and smaller stones bound together in some fashion or other with a sort of promontory that reached a hundred metres or so into the ocean. Quickly the landing gear was set up, and the crew began to drive the cattle onto the land. Then it was time for the captives to be moved. They were brought roughly to shore and then tied together with ropes around their waists that allowed them to walk but left no room for escape. Succat had hoped that once in this foreign land they might be treated as humans again, but his first steps to shore brought the knowledge that nothing lay ahead except a very dim future.

The crew tied up the galley to posts alongside, and then an order was given to go forward. The cattle led the way, followed by the tied-up captives, who were ushered forward with the animals as if there was no difference in kind. Forty minutes later or thereabouts, they reached a hamlet consisting mostly of small mud-wall homes. Smoke was coming from the homes through what appeared to be a hole in the roof—a far cry from the Roman civilization to which Succat was accustomed—and apart from the doorway there was no other way for light to enter. Here and there someone stood in an opening to view the activities, but indeed there wasn't much interest in the commercial goings-on. To Succat's way of thinking, this was not an unusual sight and was one that created little interest to the inhabitants.

A further ten minutes, and a small square in the village was reached. This was very obviously a marketplace. Small groups of people were standing around in conversation, all of them men. They became very interested when the cattle were driven in and conversed with each other in an apparent evaluation of the animals. With the arrival of three youngsters tied together, the conversation grew even louder. Not for long though!

A burly individual, his face covered with a full beard, stepped forward, his long hair flowing over his shoulders. He immediately approached the leader of the rapparees, pointing to the three young men in ropes. He was holding a horse whip in his hand and without warning lashed the whip severely across the young boys' backs. Succat and his companions winced in pain; they had no idea of what was being said, but the burly individual was very animated. Heads nodded and shook; vigorous conversation continued until finally the hand of the rapparee met the hand of the burly individual in a firm clasp.

Succat knew a decision had been reached on his fate, a decision that was confirmed when he and his companions were unloosed from the ropes that bound them together. Then a large amount of coins was passed over to the coxswain—now a business entrepreneur. Succat and the other young man who had helped row the galley were taken together and placed in a horse-drawn cart, their wrists again tied in a way that made for no escape. The man who had made the purchase sat on a cross-board in front accompanied by the driver, who took the reins. As the cart rattled forward, the burly one turned around, pointed to himself and repeated a few times "Meelco." The boys understood that he was telling them his name and that he was in charge.

They were now his slaves. They had a new home, wherever it was!

Sitting in the back of a rickety horse-drawn cart that rumbled and clattered along, Succat and his fellow slave tried to estimate where they might be. It certainly wasn't Caledonia. The galley had taken them first in a northerly direction and had then veered to the west. The inhabitants were speaking a language that was entirely foreign to them. The brutishness of their captors had disappeared somewhat, although the man who signified himself as Meelco seemed unfriendly and with an uncouth personality. He seemed discontent with the world and frequently appeared to be abusive in his demands of his reinsman. Succat and his companion—Blasius[28]—whispered their comments to each other at the rear of the cart noting that in front all did not seem well.

It took several hours to reach their destination. It was well into the afternoon, and both boys were hungry. Eventually they came to a long hedgerow without a view of what lay within. The cart turned through a gap in the hedge and there, about two hundred metres in front, the boys saw a large turf or clay house that had a couple of straw-roofed buildings of the same materials nearby. The home, they noted, had an opening in the center, but the prisoners could not see any door attached. Meelco turned and signaled the young men to get out of the cart, while with the same gesture ordering his driver to release their wrists. Then he signaled them to march in front of him to what was the open entry. They didn't need to understand his language to know the wishes of their new master. They had barely entered the home when a lady dressed in a red shawl rose from where

---

[28] Anglicized Blaise.

she was sitting with a smile on her face and a gesture of welcome for the captives. It was the first sign of humanity they had experienced since being taken. But it was not to last.

Meelco barked an order. The woman immediately went to a pot hanging over a broad fireplace below a hole in the roof that took away the smoke. She took a ladle and a couple of earthenware bowls and filled them with stew from the pot. At the same time, Meelco and his driver sat at the roughly hewn wooden table and ravenously swallowed down the stew. The bowls were empty in a few minutes, and then replenishment was demanded. The men ate their second helping less greedily and took time to clean their plates with the pieces of bread that the woman had provided on the table. When they had finished, the woman spoke to Meelco apparently asking if she should feed the young men still standing in the room. Meelco glared at his new possessions and then nodded to the woman to do so. However, no place at the table was offered, and when the bowls were handed to the starving boys, they were ordered outside by a gesture from Meelco, without spoons or any kind of cutlery. Succat and Blasius obeyed. The scent of the stew had already raised their epicurean sensitivities, and even without cutlery they had consumed their portions in a short length of time. Unfortunately for them, nothing further was offered except a container of water from which they both drank. For now at least, and possibly for the day, the boys were aware that was that.

Meelco stood up from his seat at the table, sardonically staring at the captured, and gestured them to follow him. He walked to one of the thatched outhouses they had seen previously on their arrival. It was a storage place used for hay and straw. There were rafters overhead to keep the earth and sod in place, and the area was apparently very dry. Meelco's signs to them were clear. This was where they would spend their time for the rest of the evening and night, and they could make themselves comfortable any way they wished. He then disappeared through the door, and they heard his footsteps on the gravel yard as he walked to his own quarters.

Succat and Blasius looked at each other in silence for a few moments, still trying to make peace with what was happening in their lives. They had no covering for the night except the clothes they were wearing. They could of course cover themselves with hay that was around in plenty, but that was a far cry from the comforts of their homes and the love they had routinely received.

There was no undressing to be performed. Succat invited Blasius to pray with him. They both fell to their knees—two captives in unknown country, their families lost to them, exhausted after a terrible capture and an enervating journey, treated like animals and roughly signaled to make this their sleeping place for the night. They had much for which to pray. Succat led the prayer.

"O Lord, please keep us in your care. We need your help now. Bless us and help us to deal with this awful situation. We have sinned, Lord, but we know that you died for us and that you love us. Can you get us free? We will try to sleep now, Lord, but we commit our sleep and our lives to you. Thank you for listening to our prayer."

Succat went silent, and so did his companion. They both remained on their knees for ten minutes more. Then they arose and tried to make themselves comfortable in the hay, even covering their bodies fully with it and burying themselves down as far as they could in an effort to make themselves a sleeping place. After a few moments Blasius whispered, "Look at the big rat on the rafters overhead."

Succat looked in the direction Blasius was pointing and saw the rat too.

"It will be difficult for us to sleep," he said, "knowing there are rats around us. If there's one, be sure there are lots more. Oh, look. There's another one just a few feet over. Let us pray together that the Lord will protect us as we sleep, "The Lord is my shepherd, I shall not want; in verdant pastures he gives me repose; beside restful waters he leads me; he refreshes my soul. He guides me in right paths for his name's sake. Even though I walk in the dark valley I fear no evil, for You are at my side with your rod and your staff that give me courage.

You spread the table before me in the sight of my foes; You anoint my head with oil; my cup overflows. Only goodness and kindness follow me all the days of my life; and I shall dwell in the house of the Lord for years to come."[29]

"May the Lord be our shepherd," said Blasius, "and may we sleep in His peace."

Despite their anxieties, the fatigue of an overpowering calamity finally took its toll. Within minutes the boys were asleep. Their dreams that night were interspersed with a herd of cattle taking over a galley, a man jumping overboard into the ocean, a woman smiling, and a burly and ugly slave master throwing them and other people around. But the dreams dissolved into peaceful sleep, and the rats stayed on the rafters.

It was early morning when a rough voice made a command. When they opened their eyes, Meelco was standing over them urging them to get up and follow him.

---

[29] Psalm 23, New American Bible (Catholic Book Publishing Company, New York).

Chapter 6

Shepherds in the Hills

Meelco walked to his dwelling, the boys following, and barked an order to the lady they had seen yesterday—apparently his wife. He did not allow his captives to follow him within but rather signaled that they stand outside. They could see yesterday's cart driver sitting at the table supping from a bowl. Very shortly thereafter the lady appeared with two bowls of oatmeal, handing a bowl to each individual as well as a wooden spoon. She smiled as she handed them the spoons and then retreated inside to return with a large bowl of milk.

Succat and Blasius were then left alone and found a couple of rocks as seats while they enjoyed the bowls of food that had been handed to them. They contended with the chill of the morning and had a few minutes to banter before Meelco arrived on the scene again, this time followed by his horseman. The two men spoke to each other, pointing to their new arrivals. Eventually the driver came and made signs to Succat. He was apparently asking, "What is your name?"

"Succat," was the reply.

Meelco and his driver looked amused at this name, strange to them. "Su … cat … a" he repeated. Then he signaled his driver to tell the young man to repeat the name.

"Succat is my name."

"Su … cata," said Meelco. He nodded his head that he was satisfied. Now there was a gesture as to the other young man's name.

"Blasius," he replied.

"Blawse," said Meelco. "Sucatta and Blawse is how they will be known," he uttered.

Very quickly the driver went toward the outhouses and came back with the same horse and cart in which they had ridden yesterday. The captives were ordered to get aboard. The cart rattled its way forward on a journey that seemed to take a couple of hours. Both young men noted a fair supply of hay in the cart as well as an ax, pickax, a kind of wooden shovel, and something the equivalent of a spade that was also hewn in rough wood with a sharp edge. When they reached their destination, they were in for a surprise. They were at the bottom of a mountain that was just like those they had seen from the galley. It had trees stretching a distance up, and beyond the trees they could see a much steeper rise to what was a relatively flat top. Seemingly countless sheep grazed the area.

They were beginning to get the message—they were shepherd slaves. There was no tomorrow for them.

The driver dismounted from his cart, ordered them to remove the hay and the implements, and pointed to the sheep above. He intimated they were to carry the hay forward through the trees. It was, of course, too much for them. They knew they would have to come back and get the rest. Having arrived at the end of the tree line, the hay was dropped and an indication came that they were to return to the cart. The driver accompanied them the three hundred metres or so back. He took the implements from the cart while they carried the rest of the hay. The climb was becoming harder the second time, and when they got to the destination, they dropped the hay wearily. Then their subjugator handed them the instruments and made signs they would need them for digging.

Seeing the curious look on their faces, he placed both hands together to the side of his face with his head on the hands as if in a sleeping position. They would be staying up here! Here would be their home, and they would have to build shelter for themselves. They would sleep under the stars until they had completed some kind of habitat.

Not only that ... there was no sign of food! The driver reached within his long coat and pulled out a snare. They weren't sure what this meant until a rabbit skipped in front a short distance away. The driver pointed to the rabbit, then put his hand to his own neck indicating the snare was to catch rabbits. He then pointed to the sheep, gesturing with his hands and making it clear that they were in charge of the sheep and would remain on this mountain permanently. He expressed a word that sounded like "Sleeve mish"[30] but they had no way of knowing what he meant. Then he turned and left, and they could hear the sounds of the cart as it made its way down the hill.

Sliabh Mis as it is today—where Patrick spent upwards of seven years in cruel slavery

The newly named slaves Succata and Blawse stared at each other with blank faces. For them the situation had worsened beyond all imagination. They sat on the ground for a while in the most despondent mood they had ever experienced, looking mostly down and nowhere in particular. After a time Succata looked at Blawse and spoke.

---

[30] In Gaelic, Sliabh Mis.

"Here we are, shepherds on this mountain. When we spent time by the ocean at home, the thought of being a shepherd never crossed our minds. We heard about the shepherds in the gospel when Jesus was born, but we thought little of them. They were poor men who lived in the wilderness with their sheep. That, we thought, would never apply to us. Now it does. But Blasius, remember the other verse from the Psalm—'The Lord is my shepherd, there is nothing I shall want.' We are going to be all right. Let us commend ourselves to the Lord and ask for His angels to be with us while we are here."

Blasius looked at Succat.

"I wish I could be as confident as you," he said. "We are now owned by Meelco, a man without a heart. Where was the Lord when we were being captured? Where were the angels then?"

Succat was silent, but not for long.

"Blasius," he replied, "there is always a good end to what God allows. We will pray together, and the Lord will be with us."

Blasius was not about to be consoled.

"Yes, and we will snare rabbits together, too, so we can stay alive. Meelco is a brute, and we should try to escape."

Succat thought for a moment before replying.

"Perhaps yes, we should try to escape, but not yet. We know nothing about this wild country. Most likely if we were to be caught we would be returned to Meelco and be lashed severely. Thank God we are away from him, and we can try to make our own life here until the time is ripe for us to try to get away."

It was now time for Blasius to be reflective. Then he responded, "But how are we going to live? We will starve in this place."

Succat replied, "God will provide. Remember, 'The Lord is my shepherd.' In time we will come to know God's will for us. Right now we need to take a look at the sheep and see if there is anything we need to do for them."

"We know nothing about sheep," Blasius replied sulkily, "and Meelco has told us nothing."

"Ah, yes," said Succat, "but you can be sure he will be back, or his man who drove us here or somebody else who will crack the whip to make us pay if we have shown no interest in the flock. We can at least try to count them, and as we go around we may be able to find a stream of good drinking water. There should be good clean water up here on this mountain."

While numbering the sheep, Succat and Blasius found there was an abundance of rabbits all around them. They were not only in the woods but out in the open, frequently around the sheep, who did not take any interest in their presence. Now all they needed was to find out how to set the snare, and there would be meat aplenty for both of them. Of course they had to be able to get a fire started, but they both knew necessity would eventually bring that about too. They spent many hours checking around, looking for sheep that were scattered all over the mountain, even down to the tree line. It was difficult to ensure they were not counting the same sheep twice, but having spent several hours walking the mountain they both came up with a figure of just over two hundred.

They found a stream of onrushing water cavorting over the rocks as it made its way to the bottom of the mountain. The particular locality was not too far from the woods, and once they would find a utensil to hold the water, they could easily supply their needs. But that could hold for another day. There was still a lot of work ahead for them. They needed food. The day was becoming somewhat chilly. Obviously they would have to sleep in the open tonight. They decided the trees would provide some kind of sanctuary through the overnight hours, and even if it might rain, the overhanging branches with their heavy foliage would afford some protection. They placed the hay in a suitable location, and now at least they had made their sleeping arrangements.

Next they would see what success they might have in catching a rabbit. They were both hungry, and more than a little exhausted from their wanderings on the mountainside.

Succat spoke thoughtfully.

"Before we begin the hunt, let us kneel and pray that the Lord will help us to find food," he said, as he went to his knees.

Blasius followed suit, and both young men spent a few minutes in silent prayer. Their prayers were answered in quick fashion. They were going to have a tasty rabbit for dinner—if they could find a way to light a fire and learn how to use the snare. They looked around for sticks to rub together.

Then the unexpected happened!

Chapter 7

Aogán

They were examining the snare to see how they might set it in place for the catch. It wasn't going to be easy to manipulate the wires, since they had never seen anything like this before. They examined and discussed and were absorbed in scrutinizing the implement when they heard twigs breaking farther down the woods.

"The sheep must be in there," muttered Blasius. "Those sheep cover a lot of ground."

The sounds continued and came closer and closer.

"Sounds like a person trampling through the woods," said Succat.

He was right! It was a person, a youngish man, not much older than themselves with fair hair, seemingly sunburned facial appearance and a smile on his face. The new slaves had not seen too many smiles recently, and as they looked at him curiously, making an effort to smile themselves, the visitor greeted them in his own Gaelic language.

"Mise Aogán,"[31] was what they heard. To them it was meaningless until the young man pointed to himself and repeated, "Aogán."

Now they knew he was telling them his name. He was still smiling, and they recognized he was a friend.

---

[31] I am Aidan.

"Succat"—in imitation of the newcomer, pointed to himself with his name.

"Blasius"—reporting his name, smiled.

Aogán took the snare. He walked a short distance with his hosts following him. He found a rabbit burrow not very far away, set up the snare to entrap the outcoming rabbit, and made gestures to them to try to help them understand. Then to make sure, he handed the snare to Blasius and had him repeat the operation. After a few tries, both young men had learned, and Aogán clapped his hands in approval. They all returned to the place that had been established as their living quarters, and Aogán sat with them.

It was a learning experience, and through signs they understood that Aogán was no friend of Meelco, nor indeed were many of the neighbors. Aogán signaled that he would teach them how to speak in the Gaelic language and that he would come frequently and be their friend. He repeated his own name, saying "*Mise* Aogán" and encouraged them to speak their names in Gaelic.

Succat was first to respond. "Mise Succat."

Aogán nodded in delight.

"Mise Blasius."

Again more approval from Aogán.

Succat remembered the missing water utensil and made signs to Aogán. Quickly Aogán understood and uttered a word that caught their ears as "a-máw-ruck."[32] Eventually they understood that Aogán would bring the vessel to hold the water, next day.

"A-máw-ruck," they said good-humoredly to Aogán as he trundled back through the woods. Waving to them, he disappeared in the distance with the same smile with which he had introduced himself.

"Too bad he didn't bring us any food," said Succat.

"And a few coals of fire," added Blasius. "Let us check the snare anyway." Blasius sounded optimistic.

They walked to the snare. And there, for the first time in their

---

[32] "Tomorrow"—from the Gaelic Amárach.

young lives, they witnessed a dead rabbit, his eyes wide open, his body still warm but stiffening. They took their dead prey from the snare and reset it again.

"Do you think," said Succat, "we might be able to rub sticks together to light a fire?"

"Let's try," said Blasius, "but first we must find kindling that will enable us to get the fire started."

"Yes, and a pair of suitable dry sticks too."

The required sticks and kindling were easily found. As Romans the boys had been taught how to rub the sticks in order to set them alight. It took a while, but they finally succeeded, and a nice blazing fire was shortly ready for their cooking purposes. Cutting the rabbit in pieces was another problem, but eventually it was done with the little equipment they had been given. They were hungry young men, not master chefs, and the rabbit was cooked fur and all. But their hunger was satisfied, and they were able to get ready for the night with comfortable stomachs.

The evening was moving on, and the temperature began to fall. A slight wind from the Celtic Sea added a chill to the air. With only the clothes they wore, the slaves knew they would experience a cold night ahead. They arranged the hay they had been given, placing it under a tree, some for bedding and some for cover, and lay as close together as they could to try to share their body heat. Darkness fell quickly enough throughout the wood, and it took little time for them to fall asleep after another of the strangest days they had ever experienced in their lives.

They were awakened by an intense rain that seemed to be aiming pellets of water the size of peas in their direction, so much so that the leaves on the tree above them were soon leaking water on the hay that covered them as if coming through a sieve. The chilly night added to their misery, and in a short time they were covered with sodden hay that eventually allowed the dampness to invade the light clothes they wore. Sleep was over—at least for now—as the cold night air pervaded and chilled their young and unready bodies and placed them in a crucible of never before experienced excruciating bodily agony. As the rains continued to fall and the leaves dropped more and more water on their night shelter, the young men huddled closer to the tree trunk, a move that helped a little but did not bring any relief to their already saturated situation.

Succat spoke through the silence created by their sodden condition.

"We can't sleep any further," he said, "and there is no sign of the rain ending. We are frozen through and through; we can't light a fire now because there are no dry sticks, but we can and should pray. Let us address our troubles to the Lord and seek His help and mercy."

"Prayer is beyond me now," exclaimed Blasius. "I am so cold I can't do anything."

"Then I will pray aloud, and you can join me in your mind," said Succat. "I know God will help us. He is not far from us."

Succat began to recite the "Our Father." He repeated this prayer over and over again, and after a while Blasius joined in. They both prayed for a long time, so much so that when they began to concentrate again on their surroundings, the rain had stopped, the trees were no longer dripping water on them, a cool breeze was blowing, and even though they were chilled to the bone, their discomfort was giving way to hope for better times. They slid down to the bottom of the tree, hunkered up, closed their eyes, and slept. It was dawn when their soggy clothes awakened them to the world of reality again.

It appeared to them that the day was going to be good, and their first task was to get a fire going and get their wet clothes dry. Getting the sticks to light took a little longer than before, but they eventually succeeded and had a crackling fire in minutes. Then they crept close to the flames and were ecstatic when they felt heat creep into their bodies. In half an hour or less, their clothes dried as they wore them. Blasius, however, had suffered the effects of the rain and chill, and his nasal tone alerted his companion that he had caught some kind of cold as a result of the night chill.

There was work to be done. They needed to count the sheep, a task that wasn't easy, as many of the sheep had scattered into the woods during the night, both for shelter and perhaps through habit. Then when that task was completed, the young slaves went looking for food. That was the easy part. Another rabbit had entrapped itself in the snare, providing a good breakfast for two young men who had previously felt frozen and were really ready for nourishment. They gave thanks to God for the blessing of food and sat to relax a little bit by the fire.

"I wonder," said Blasius, "is this going to be our life here, counting sheep and trying to stay alive?"

"There must be more to it," said Succat. "I wonder what will happen when winter comes."

"We need to build some kind of covering for ourselves, something that will shield us from the weather. That is why they gave us the wooden pickax and the shovel," Blasius replied.

"Let's get started today while the weather is good," Succat offered. "Perhaps we can find a spot in the woods that might be free of tree roots, or at least have fewer of them."

Blasius was coughing a lot, but through his coughs he agreed with Succat.

"Let's get the implements and begin," he said. "Let's do that, and may God bless our work."

It was still well before noon, and the sound of cracking twigs reached their ears again. It was Aogán, and he was carrying a wooden bucket and an iron pickax. Aogán had anticipated the tasks for the day. The slaves now really knew they had found a good friend.

Chapter 8

The Seanchaí

Aogán came again and again. He helped them erect an earthen hut that had a roof of sods supported by strong branches they had broken from the trees. He brought them food frequently, and above all he taught them to understand and speak the language. From him they learned that Meelco was an unfeeling and vengeful individual who cared little for his slaves and punished them severely for their mistakes. It was not unusual for a slave to be tied to a post and lashed until he almost bled to death, and lashings were administered sometimes for the slightest of reasons. Meelco was a ruler who governed his tenant farmers with an iron fist and upped their rents whenever he wished, which was unfairly recurrent for productive farmers. Aogán told his two friends that Meelco was despised throughout the area and that he and people of his ilk were encouragers for the capturing of slaves for their estates and keeping the slave traders in business.

From Aogán, too, Succat and Blasius got a perception of another side of their slave master. Although Meelco's attendant came to supervise the slaves almost on a weekly basis and attempted to count the sheep, Meelco himself rarely if ever appeared, and they saw him about once a year when the sheep had to be gathered in spring for shearing, and their lambs taken away for sale as food.

Time passed. It was a dreary existence. Their friend continued his visits. Then one day Aogán announced that the *seanchaí*[33] was coming to their neighborhood not far from the bottom of the mountain and that there would be a gathering at a home that evening. Aogán explained that the seanchaí was a professional storyteller—of whom there were many—who traveled around various parts of the country telling wonderful stories and enthralling his listeners with tales of days gone by—tales of Na Fianna[34] and their heroes Fionn McCool and Oisin and their wonderful companion soldiers whose motto was "Cleanliness of our hearts, truth on our lips, and actions according to our promises."

"You must hear of Oisin," said Aogán. "I'll tell you a little here. Oisin was a member of Na Fianna and a great friend of Fionn, who was the leader of the great Fianna. One day didn't Oisin meet a beautiful lady called Niamh? She was gorgeous, and Oisin fell in love with her. Now, as it turned out … wasn't the lady from the country of the Celtic gods? And both of them rode away together on a magic horse to *Tir na nÓg*.[35] This is the place where the gods reside. Well … this was a magic place too, and Oisin saw some of his Celtic gods, and he was very happy. Indeed, he wanted to stay there forever, but after three years he got a little homesick for his people, and he wanted to go back and see them, especially Fionn. Niamh agreed and told him to take the magic horse for a short visit but that he must not touch the ground while with his people back on earth.

"So … when Oisin arrived back he became very excited. He would visit with Fionn McCool and all the warriors he had left three years ago. He couldn't wait to meet them. Ah! Sure we are all like

---

[33] Professional storyteller.

[34] Na Fianna, according to tradition, were a group of warriors who were entirely ethical. They probably did exist at some time or other, but in the passing of the years their exploits were almost certainly enhanced in traditional storytelling.

[35] The country of the Celtic gods would be a faraway place, unreachable for the ordinary person unless a god decided to allow a particular person in, as was the case with Oisín. The direct translation means, The Country of the Young.

that! Now I am going to disappoint you in the rest of the story. You see, Fionn was dead and all his warriors!"

"How did they all get killed in three years?"

"They didn't," said Aogan. "They had died from old age."

"I don't understand," said Succat. "How could they have gotten so old in three years, or were they very old when Oisin left them?"

"True," said Aogan, "some of them were old enough at the time of Oisin's departure, but Oisin was away three hundred years. He had enjoyed himself so much he didn't feel the time passing."

"Was he disappointed," asked Succat, "and what happened to him?"

"For sure he was disappointed, but he wasn't sure he should believe what he was hearing. Worse was to come! He was riding around on his magic horse being careful not to touch the ground as Niamh had directed him. He saw four men trying to move a stone. He watched them struggle and not make much headway. Being an old member of the Fianna, one of his principles was to help all in need. He rode over to the men and spoke.

"Looks like you need a little help," he said.

"We do indeed," replied one of the men. "But who are you, and where did you get that lovely horse? We haven't met you before."

"Well, I am belonging to Fionn's men. We always try to help out. I am Oisin. I am just visiting for a short while."

The men looked at each other. Where did this man come from? How did he get such a lovely horse? Even his speech was a little different to theirs.

"Well, Fionn is gone for three hundred years," said the man, "so you don't belong to Fionn."

"I heard that Fionn is dead a long time but I don't believe it. I left Fionn just three years ago, and now I have come back for a visit."

The laborers with the stone were now totally confused. The visitor must have a failing mind. He was a young-looking man, and he thought he belonged to Fionn's warriors. Poor fellow.

"Three hundred years is how long Fionn is dead," replied one of the men.

It was now Oisin's turn to be confused. He was realizing his worst fears. He had been away three hundred years, not just three! Just the same he was still a member of the Fianna. He knew he had to help. These men were not friendly, but he had helped unfriendly men before.

"I came here to help you," said Oisin.

"Well, then help us," said another of the men with irritation in his voice.

"Oh, now, I want to tell you," continued Aogan, "that Oisin was aware of the orders he had received not to touch the ground. He forgot the rock was part of the ground. He knew how strong he was! He didn't have to get off his horse to help move that stone, and move it for them he would.

Succat was intrigued. "What happened?" he asked.

Ah, this is the sad part! Oisin stayed on his horse all right and reached down and got a grip on the stone. And as soon as his hand touched it, his horse bolted and disappeared into thin air. Oisin was thrown to the ground. Poor Oisin! He immediately became a very old and wrinkled man, and although he had time to tell some real stories of the *Fianna* to an enchanted audience, he died in a very short time.

"But," continued Aogán, "you must hear the story from the seanchaí himself, and perhaps he might talk about it tonight. Anyway, I assure you he will have some good stories."

"That's a great story," replied Succat, "and I would like to hear more. But how can we leave this place? If Meelco finds out, we will be lashed."

"When was the last time you saw Meelco?" Aogán asked.

"A long time ago indeed, but if someone tells him …"

"Well, for one thing," said Aogán, "Meelco won't come to listen to the seanchaí. His workers won't come either because they would be afraid, and the likelihood of his finding out is very small indeed.

Why don't we count the sheep? We will all go to my home for a meal, and then we will go to the seanchaí."

Blawse was coughing heavily, but he agreed. The thought of a possible good meal was his chief incentive, and if Aogán's parents were anything like Aogán, then a good meal was assured.

Blawse was correct. It was indeed a good meal of lamb stew and vegetables. It was the best meal the young men had eaten since their arrival on the shores of Éireann.[36] Not only that, but Aogán's parents were wonderfully welcoming, and it was obvious they pitied the slave friends of their son. Their home was indeed modest, erected mostly from sods with some kind of wooden roof that was covered with a thatch of straw. There was a wide opening in the roof allowing the smoke of the fire to escape. This and the unclosed entryway provided the only light that came into the home. Through the entryway, Succat and Blawse could see the odd rain shower but did not allow the phenomenon to distract them from the pleasure of their food and the hospitality that was being afforded them. It was getting late in the year, and darkness had arrived when Aogán's parents announced it was time to go across the fields to the house that was hosting the seanchaí.

The journey was short, but despite that an unpleasant shower brought some discomfort. Arriving at their destination, the newcomers were welcomed by about twenty people, all of whom had gathered for the entertainment promised. A fire glowed in the little one-room home, but there was no sign of poverty! Everybody present held a drink of some kind in their hands. Succat and Blawse were welcomed warmly and each handed a jug that tasted like apple cider. With little furniture, the majority sat on the floor and waited expectantly for the seanchaí—sitting on a stool near the fire—to begin his stories.

The seanchaí looked an elderly man whose face showed the weariness of his travels. He sat firmly on the stool with a long stick in his hands, and as he leaned over the stick, he began his story. The

---

[36] Gaelic for Ireland.

seanchaí wasn't just a storyteller. They were about to find he was an actor as well, with special movements of his body to emphasize the tale he was telling.

"Is everybody here?" he asked.

"I think so," said the householder.

"Well, I have many stories to tell you, but I am here for two nights, so what you don't hear tonight you will hear tomorrow."

Applause from his audience!

"Now … last night I was coming along the road, and as I was rounding what must have been a *sí rath*,[37] there sitting under a tree what did I see but a leprechaun?"

The seanchaí suddenly moved his stick to his left and leaned the same way.

Dead silence among the listeners.

"Ah … sure I wasn't ready for that at all. In fact it gave me a sort of fright first, but I watched the little fellow for a moment, and then he started to run. I was so surprised I was stuck to the ground. He turned around and pointed to the top of the tree, and didn't I look where he pointed? That was it. I never saw him again, he was gone … disappeared … and me the fool."

Seanchaí hits a hard wallop on the ground with his stick, then moves the stick back to center.

"I learned the hard way that if you see a leprechaun you must keep your eyes on him. This little fellow was no more than two feet tall, but then … sure they are all small. I'll tell you why! A long time ago when Éireann had only a small population, it was invaded by a tribe called the Fir Bolg.[38] They were all small men with a very big stomach on them, but they were a hardy little crowd and managed to take over the country by dent of numbers. They spread here, there, and everywhere, and soon the land was filled with these little fellows.

---

[37] A fairy mound, sometimes called "the home of the little people."

[38] Pre-Celtic invaders of Ireland who held sway for hundreds of years. Tradition says they were smallish in stature with a large stomach.

But keep in mind they were very strong. They ruled the roost for a few hundred years, but then in came another tribe called the Tuatha De Dannán,[39] and they wanted Éireann for themselves. But first they had to get rid of the Fir Bolg. Now the Tuatha were very good fighters, but still the Fir Bolg were not afraid of them."

Seanchaí moves his stick again, turns slightly toward the fire.

"There was many a battle, and would you believe it, the Fir Bolg held their own against the big monsters of Tuatha. In the end, however, the Tuatha were too strong, and they succeeded in driving out the Fir Bolg to an island off the west coast of Éireann. The little men, because little they were, managed to build a major fort[40] on that island where they held off the Tuatha for many a year, but in the end they lost out. Now ... they had a certain amount of magic, too, so those who remained made themselves smaller still, and back they came to the land they loved, except this time they had to make mounds for themselves, and they lived inside. You'll recognize their dwelling places to this day because there are pathways on them that spiral to the entry at the top. The little fellows had to climb up those circular pathways to get into their dwelling. And most times there's a level field close to the mound because often they come out in the moonlight and play a game of hurling.[41] The Tuatha didn't have the same amount of magic and couldn't stop them. And they didn't try very hard either because 'the little people' didn't really bother them. Ah ... but there's another side to it!"

Seanchaí whispers—moves his stick dead center between his knees.

"You see, they had to die, as all of us will. They had no belief in the gods of Éireann, and the gods didn't want them either. So the gods

---

[39] Occupied Ireland after the Fir Bolg and before the arrival of the Celts. Like the Celts, they were a warring tribe.

[40] Dún Aonghasa, historical and archeological site in Inishmore, Aran Islands, County Galway, Ireland.

[41] Gaelic game played in a large playing field where the players use a specially made stick to strike a ball.

told them they could never get to Tir na nÓg, but that they could reside forever as 'the little people' in the raths[42] they had created. They gave them a few tons of gold, took away their big stomachs, but told them the only time they could come out was at night, and if a human laid a hand on them they were caught and would have to hand over a pot of gold. You never see a leprechaun in the daytime. Some people will tell you they did … but I'm telling you they did not."

The seanchaí was only getting started!

He moved his stick again to one side and leaned over on the stick as if to make a big announcement.

There was complete silence, and the audience watched every move he made and listened with great intent.

"We call them Na Sí,[43] because they are not normal people at all. The gods took away their humanity. They normally don't hurt anyone, but they can make noises, especially when the wind blows, and you can hear the high pitch like a scream traveling on the winds. That's the Sí, and they are celebrating and probably letting everybody know they are still around. They love Éireann. So, if you hear that sound when the wind blows, you can be sure there's a leprechaun around somewhere or maybe a dozen of them, but of course you won't see anything. The best place in the world to hear them is to pass by a mound on a stormy night. They are celebrating inside. Some people are afraid to pass in the dark, but I'm telling you they won't touch you, and if you see one, grab him and keep your eyes on him. You can be sure he will try to fool you, to have you look away, and of course then he is gone. Keep your eyes on him and get some of that gold."

"Now," continued the seanchaí, "I must tell you something else, and this is sort of the bad side of Na Sí. As you know, they have a habit of exchanging babies."

Seanchaí moves his stick to center, leans forward, tilts his head to the side, and takes in the room to make sure everybody is listening.

---

[42] Underground forts with mounds above ground.

[43] Fairies—mythological small people who can only be seen by moonlight, if at all.

"Last week I was about a hundred kilometers from here, much farther to the west, and I heard this story. There was this man and woman who had a lovely newborn baby girl. She was sleeping in her cradle when these two smallish people, a man and a woman carrying a baby, arrived at the entryway to their little home. They told the residents they were just asking for a little bit of food so they would be on their way. Well, of course, in Éireann we never refuse to welcome people. The house was small, and the husband went out to fetch wood for the fire in order to make soup for the visitors. Meantime the lady of the house had her back to the newcomers as she prepared the food. A good meal was rendered, and the visiting couple left.

Well … when they had gone didn't their baby in the cradle start bawling! Now that was the very first time they ever heard their baby cry like that with a high screech. The mother lifted the baby in her arms to console her and remarked that the baby didn't look like herself at all and she must be very ill. The poor mother was right on both counts! Her baby didn't look like herself because she had been stolen by the visitors, and the baby left behind died in two weeks. Sometimes when passing the nearby rath, the couple think they can hear the crying of their own child from within. So, of course, the lesson is if you are visited by a couple you don't know, keep the baby in your arms until they have left. The Sí will have nothing to do with a sickly baby."

The seanchaí was now in his element.

"It's time for a dance," he said as he reached for his fiddle. He thought for a moment.

"Well … I suppose I should finish about the Sí first. There's a lady called the beansí.[44] You've all heard of her, and maybe some of you *heard* her too. She's known by her wailing. I can't boast I ever saw her, but I met a man who did—not very long ago either. His description of her frightened me. He said she had a strange head that was sort of hanging on to her neck and bobbling every which way. And it was

---

[44] In English, banshee—a preternatural spirit associated with death who mythically cries with a loud wailing before a member of a family dies.

long like a pig's head. Her arms were stretched out and blowing like clothes hanging on a clothesline in a high wind. Her eyes were sunken into her head. Her appearance was frightening. On seeing her you'd want to run for your life after you got over the shock. This poor man couldn't run, he was so shocked, and then the thing he was seeing started to wail at the top of her voice. He was frightened to death, but he couldn't move. She kept up the wail for a long time, twisting and blowing in the wind, and then she was gone."

Seanchaí moves his stick to the front as if he was carrying a heavy weight.

"Well … a few days afterward the brother of the man who saw her died! You see … he was a sailor and drowned in the Celtic Sea. It was during a storm, and this man jumped in to save another worker who had been blown off the galley. The beansí wails before an Éireann person dies. Indeed, I hope you never hear the beansí at all.

"Now, before we do the dancing—I brought my fiddle … There's one more story I'll tell you tonight because someone asked me to tell the story. It's a story of Fionn McCool. You remember I have told you a lot of stories about our great Celtic hero. Well here's another …"

Seanchaí shuffles around a little coming full face with his audience …

"As you know Fionn was such a great man and so very tall that he was regarded as a giant! As I told you, too, he was a peaceful man, as were all the Fianna. He fought only if there was a reason, and that was when he was under orders from his king …"

Another shuffle. Seanchaí moves left to get the heat of the blazing fire.

"Well … sure another fellow in Alba[45] was very famous too. Now this fellow whose name was Feargal heard about Fionn. He wanted to fight him hand to hand … Didn't he come over the sea to Eireann looking for Fionn? … Well of course, the word got around that Feargal was looking for Fionn. Now as I told you … Fionn was

---

[45] Scotland.

a peaceful man, and he wanted to have nothing to do with Feargal ... Ah, but Fionn's wife was very smart. She knew Fionn was worried about this stranger looking for her husband ... so she said to Fionn, "Would you go and make a cradle for yourself?"

"A cradle," said Fionn. "Whatever on earth for?"

"Well," said his wife, "when the Alba fellow comes, you can jump into the cradle; I'll cover you up like a baby, and I'll say you are away, and I am minding our baby."

"*Mo grádh thu*,"[46] said Fionn. "We can try that."

So one day shortly afterward here comes the big fellow from Alba peering his head into the opening of Fionn's home. He saw only the woman and the cradle.

"Where is your husband?" he inquired. "Because one of us is going to die this day."

The woman replied, "Fionn is away for the day. He will be home late."

When she said that didn't the child in the cradle begin fussing and crying. Feargal looked at the huge baby as the woman went over and stroked his head. But the howling continued.

"Our son is getting hungry," she told Feargal. "You don't mind if I feed him, and you can sit down and wait for Fionn."

Feargal was rethinking the issue! If the baby son was this large, how large would the father be?"

"I have other things to do," he replied. "Just tell Fionn I was here."

"He was gone as fast as his legs could carry him."

The seanchaí winked at his audience.

"That's a true story! Fionn could have killed him anyway, but as I said, he was a peaceful man. And the message is ... 'Don't trouble trouble until trouble troubles you!' Ah, sure like that Alba fellow we can all make fools of ourselves at times!"

Applause from all!

"Now let's dance! I'll be back tomorrow night with more stories, and I hope you will be generous to me at the end of it all."

---

[46] You are my love.

Seanchaí takes his fiddle and plays merry music. All begin to dance.

It was "the wee"[47] hours of the morning when the celebrations came to an end. The house was small, and those who had no room to dance within overflowed outside. The moon shone brightly on them, and it appeared to Succat and Blasius that here was a people who made little of their problems and took time to celebrate to the fiddling of the storyteller, and whether they believed the seanchaí or not, they took full delight in celebrating life and neighborliness.

It was time for Succat and Blasius to make the trek back to their own little hut. Aogán told them he would accompany them to the beginning of the woods. As they walked and discussed their evening together, there was a sudden change in the weather. The moon was covered by a black cloud that shrouded its light from the walkers. Suddenly the rain came thick and heavy, and with the wind blowing into their faces, all three were drenched in a couple of minutes. Aogán suggested they return to his home to dry out, but Blasius was determined to continue, such was his fear of being caught away from his place of work. At the beginning of the woods, with the rain coming in sheets and soaking their flimsy clothing through and through, Aogán invited them to his home. Blasius was not receptive to the idea, fearing a whipping from Meelco. They bade each other farewell and struggled forward through the autumnal storm. The hut was but a short distance away, but when they arrived the rains had quenched the fire they had left smoldering early in the evening. The hut itself was damp on the inside as the blistering rains had pierced its cover.

"Our sleeping places are very damp," said Succat, "and we will have to sit up for a while. There is no point in trying to light a fire since there is no dry wood. All we can do is undress from the

---

47 Earlier hours before dawn between 1:00 a.m. and 4:00 a.m.

soaking clothes we are wearing, and perhaps they will dry in the winds tomorrow."

"I don't feel well," said Blasius.

"Nor me either," said Succat. "It's from those wet, soggy clothes we must get off us. We will be cold, but we will at least be dry."

Blasius coughed quite a long time, and agreed Succat was right in what he said.

The young men tried to find a dry area within the hut and sat together, their bodies shivering, their arms and legs almost quivering in and out with the shock of the cold on their nearly numb bodies. They found a spot where at least they could sit, and Succat suggested they take time to pray and offer their sufferings to the Lord.

"Let's try," said Blasius.

Succat repeated his fervent "Our Father" time and time again, and tried to let Blasius hear him praying in his own language for their safety and future comfort. Succat's prayer went on and on. Blasius had become silent long before Succat ended his praying. In a short time, he fell back and seemed to be sleeping. Succat noted his breathing was somewhat abnormal, but he associated that to the trauma that they were still enduring. Eventually, Succat leaned back beside his friend, both chilly and undressed. Having shivered for a while, nature took its course, and a fitful sleep separated them from their agony.

The morning light was creeping into the hut when Succat's eyes were opened to reality again. He glanced over at Blasius. He was in the same position as when he had last seen him. There was no movement.

Succat reached over to awaken him, but there was no response.

Blasius was dead.

Chapter 9

Death and Thoughts of Escape

It was Aogán who first learned of the death of Blasius. He took a risk and went to deliver the bad news to Meelco, knowing that if he were questioned as to how he knew Blasius in the first place, it would place him in a precarious position. He would have some explaining to do. Fortunately for him, Meelco's wife greeted him on his arrival and on hearing the news she shed some tears. It was evident that Meelco was not home.

"My husband is too hard on his slaves," she said. "This is sad news you bring. I will tell Meelco what has happened as soon as he comes home, and he will make arrangements for burial. How is the other boy?"

"Taking it badly," replied Aogán. "His companion and he were great friends, and from the same area in An Bhreatain Bheag."[48]

The lady wiped tears from her face, thanked Aogán, and watched him disappear through the opening in the hedge some hundred metres away.

Meelco's reaction was apparently not quite the same as that of his wife.

---

[48] Wales.

That afternoon Succat watched him and his foreman come through the trees. There was no sorrow and no expression of regret. Succat wondered if Meelco could know or feel anything of regret in his life.

Meelco spoke with his usual gruffness, "One of my slaves has died. Where is the body?"

Succat made signs to his owner, bidding him to follow him to where the body lay.

Meelco looked at the body and then turned to his workman.

"How are we going to get him out of here? We can't get the cart this far up the hill."

The foreman replied, "It would be best for us to go back and get another helper to carry the body downhill, and perhaps bring a bier on which to lay it."

Meelco nodded.

"We can do that."

Then looking at Succat he said, "We will be back before too long. Meantime you make sure to take care of this flock of sheep. You will have more work to do now, and I don't know when the next shipment of slaves will arrive."

Succat acted as if he did not quite understand what was being said. He knew he had to protect Aogán, who by this time had taught him fluent Gaelic. He said nothing, pointed at the sheep and then at himself, with an inquiring gesture.

Meelco gave him an aggressive look, and turning on his heel, with his foreman accompanying him, disappeared through the trees in quick time. Succat looked at his dead companion with tears in his eyes. Then he knelt and prayed for a long time.

In his prayers, he found himself distracted by the thought that the sheep were surer of their meals than was he. He got up from his praying posture, and the noise of some sheep rustling through the trees alerted him that there was work to be done, and he had better get on with it. He counted the sheep and fed them the hay previously provided by Meelco, as well as cabbage and turnips.

He had barely finished his chores when Meelco and two other men arrived, put the body of his dead friend on a bier that very obviously had been quickly put together for the purpose, and without a word to Succat, as if he did not exist, they moved away through the trees to the cart that awaited farther down the hill.

Succat never heard of his friend again, nor did he know anything of his burial.

For the very first time in his life, Succat now felt alone in the world. He was a prisoner in solitary confinement trying to endure the hardships of wind, snow, and rain on the side of a mountain a long, long way from home. His future was as clouded as the skies in the north of Éireann before the rains or snow began to fall. He kept up his spirit with thoughts of the God who had died for him, and time and again simply conversed with his Lord.

He had no notion of time, but he knew the seasons by the temperatures and the falling leaves, and then the return of life to the mountainside. He knew, too, when it was spring because he would always see Meelco and his men come to shear the wool from the sheep. It seemed strange to him at first that sheep should have their warm coats removed, but his friend Aogán educated him on the necessity of the practice. The spring rains would lodge in the wool, and eventually the weight of water would bring the sheep to the ground, causing its death in due course. The wool was valuable and would be profitably sold by Meelco. When shorn, the sheep would take refuge under the trees, and occasionally Succat would see them shivering in the same way as himself. He noticed also that, on the more chilly days, the sheep would huddle together exchanging with each other the warmth of their bodies.

The winter snows were a major challenge for Succat. As the snows covered the ground, sometimes up to nearly the length of his elbow, it was hard to find the rabbit burrows unless the rabbits came out and left a visible sign. The rabbits were apparently able to do without food for a number of days whereas Succat needed food every day. He found some solution in taking a turnip or two, as well as some cabbage that had been supplied for the sheep, and boiling them in his water can. He also crushed some of the oats designated for the sheep using a couple of small rocks, tried to pick out as much chaff as he could, and then boiled the remaining oats. It didn't taste bad, and in this way he was able maintain his strength until the rabbit burrows were exposed again.

Sometimes snowdrifts caused severe problems. The snow, as it began to thaw a little, slid down the sides of the mountain. Since his little living place had been put together a very short distance into the woods, there were times when he found his habitat drowned in snow, and the fire extinguished. He had to be content with exposure to the chill of the night, with no covering for his body while he slept. Aogán would bring an occasional blanket or perhaps a piece of clothing, and this comforted him greatly. However, there were occasions, too, when he found the body heat of the sheep huddling together, combined with Aogán's blankets, to be a soothing relief to the cold. On such an occasion the sheep were his best friends. They, too, would move in among the trees, huddle together to keep themselves warm, and since they knew their shepherd, they did not scatter when he took himself among them, allowing him to use their body heat to get him through the night.

With the passage of the years, Succat found a way of keeping his fire alive. He built a little cave of stones from the hillsides, placed an opening toward the woods and away from the snow, so that the fire within was protected from the major snow assaults. The plan worked most of the time, but more than once Succat had to seek the relief of trying to mingle among the resting sheep to keep heat in his body.

Aogán remained his friend but was careful not to be seen by any of Meelco's men whenever they came to bring food for the sheep in winter. Meelco himself showed up rarely, and probably would not have been able to recognize Succat at all since he had now grown a thick beard.

The years passed. Succat knew not how many. In his solitude time stood still. Yesterday, tomorrow, next week all convened into one. The future was always now—a hopeless congestion of nothings and nowheres.

He had accompanied Aogán once to visit with the aging seanchaí. It was a good session, with just a few stories, but this time the seanchaí had brought his harp and sang sad songs that Succat assumed were part of Éireann's culture.

As usual Aogán accompanied him most of the way back to the mountain that night. The sad songs had not raised Succat's spirits, and he began to reflect on the texture of his life.

"How long more can this go on?" he remarked to Aogán. "What *is* my future?"

Aogán thought for a moment, or perhaps two or three. Then he was forcible in his reply.

"You were a teenager when you came here. You must now be nearing twenty. You are a man like myself. There are things a man can do that a child cannot. How about making a dash for freedom? It will soon be spring, the weather will have improved, and you will be able to survive, I'll bet. The main thing will be to get away from Meelco and his pursuers because they will surely be out looking for you."

Succat didn't hesitate in his reply.

"You know, I have been thinking the same thing myself. Obviously I am not going to be released from slavery unless I escape from it."

By this time they had reached the edge of the woods.

"You are right," said Aogán. "Come spring, and that is just a short time away, you should make a run for it. I'll tell you what, let me think about it, too, and when I return we can sit and make some plans. See you very soon. *Slán leat.*"[49]

Next day, Succat heard a rustling through the trees. He thought it would be Aogán, but to his surprise it was Meelco. Succat greeted him with a smile. Meelco grunted an indistinctive reply.

---

[49] Good-bye.

"How are the sheep doing?" asked Meelco.

Succat understood the words perfectly, but he did not want to pretend he had any knowledge of what was being said. He looked at Meelco quizzically..

Meelco mumbled with an indistinctive gesture, nothing new to Succat. He had grown to know the antics of this bully for almost six years now.

"Are you keeping them fed with all the food we send up for them? So why are their troughs empty now?"

Meelco looked angry.

"Your job is to take care of the sheep!"

Suddenly he drew his horse whip and lashed at Succat. The cords of the whip tore into Succat's back. The nerves of his frame were unsettled from head to toe.

"Fill those troughs now."

Meelco swung his whip again. This time he tore the skimpy clothing on Succat's back, and the whip went through to take blood and skin. Succat screamed as his body became alive with pain, and he felt the blood running down his back.

Meelco shrieked.

"So now you think you are a man! Well, I've had a few like you, and they learned their lessons. They tried to escape when they were about your age. But let me tell you, they paid the price. Don't you try that. Believe me, if you do I will catch up with you, and then you will have reason to scream. Now go fill the troughs for the sheep."

Meelco wheeled around and headed for his horse. Succat looked after him, the pain in his body still throbbing in his limbs and threatening his consciousness.

His mind was made up. He *would* fill the troughs again, but not for long.

Spring was almost here, the evenings were lengthening, and he and Aogán would work out an escape plan.

Chapter 10

Escape

Meelco had ridden away but a few minutes when Aogán arrived. He had seen Meelco's horse and had hidden himself among the trees. He had also watched the atrocity that had taken place on Succat's body.

The young man had tears in his eyes as he greeted his friend.

"Succat, I saw what happened. How can I help you? Let's go over to the stream and put some cold water on your back. It might help the pain."

Succat nodded in agreement. His voice had not quite returned as he tried to breathe air into his lungs. He was still gasping, with shoots of pain paralyzing all parts of his frame. They walked in silence toward the flowing steam. Succat winced as the cold water flowed over his wounded back.

"Your clothes are destroyed," said Aogán. "That will be the first part of the escape plan. I will bring you some protective clothing as soon as I can. You couldn't get across the country in this condition. It will take a couple of weeks for those wounds to heal enough to allow you to walk."

Succat was recovering by now. He found his ability to speak returning.

"Thank you," he replied. "I am so glad to have a friend like you."

"Let's go among the woods and discuss the plan," said Aogán. "Here is how I see it. Spring is almost with us. Some morning Meelco will find out he has no shepherd for his sheep. Meelco is a monster, and if he finds you after your escape, he will kill you, or come close. You have never seen the rest of our country beyond Sliabh Mis.[50] You should escape to the west."

Aogán was about to continue, but Succat interrupted.

"The west!" he exclaimed. "Why west, with ships coming in only thirty kilometers or less away?"

"Because," said Aogán, "you are most likely to be caught close to home. Meelco will have spies looking out for you along the east and north coasts. If you go west, staying away from the coast closest to here, you have a better chance of escape. On the west coast there are the yew forests, and I have heard from the seanchaí that their people are very friendly and receptive. They have a seaboard, and it is likely that ships from An Bhreatain[51] and An Frainc[52] do business over there too. And it is most improbable that Meelco will send seekers in that direction. He will most likely believe that you will be found around Beal Feirsde[53] and farther south."

Succat was quietly thoughtful before he responded, and his reaction showed agreement with Aogán's argument.

"It will be a long trudge," he said.

"Yes, but you have all the time in the world. You will be free, and you won't be a slave any longer. Your chances of being caught will be minimized. And believe me I have heard nothing but good about the people from Máigheo."[54]

"God's will be done," said Succat.

"Say ... in three weeks' time, your back should be healed, and let's

---

[50] Located in County Antrim, Ireland.
[51] England.
[52] France.
[53] Belfast.
[54] County Mayo in Western Ireland, from Máigh Eó, meaning Plain of the Yew Tree.

hope Meelco doesn't come back. I will ready some clothes for you as well as a knapsack to carry over your shoulder. I will also try to find out exactly the directions in which you begin your escape. You know, Succat, I am going to miss you."

"I will miss you, too," replied Succat. "Your friendship has saved my life. I will need to pray to my Lord to keep Meelco away, and I will also pray for you, my great friend."

"You have told me about your Lord," said Aogán. "I am beginning to think perhaps I should pray to Him myself. Nobody has to know. And perhaps He can do wonderful things for me too."

"He can, and He will," said Succat.

"Well," said Aogán, "I will be going home now. I will come again tomorrow when it is dark. The moon is out tonight, and it looks as if you will have a dry night. I hope your sore back allows you some sleep."

"*Slán abhaile*,"[55] replied Succat.

On this quiet night, the rustling sounds of Aogán leaving the woods continued to reach Succat's ears until they gradually faded away, and Succat could hear only the murmur of the fast-flowing stream nearby. The sheep had settled down quietly in the moonlight along the edge of the trees, predicting to Succat it was going to be a calm and dry night. His pain from the whipping was abating, and as he knelt by his makeshift bed to pray, he felt the presence of God within him and a hope of better things to come.

Three weeks had passed. Succat was ready for the next great adventure in his life. He had been in slavery for so long that he wondered what freedom might mean.

His back, though not perfect, was ready for travel. Aogán had supplied clothes and some food for his journey.

---

[55] Safe home.

The young men embraced in tears.

Succat spoke. "May we meet again, and I have a feeling we shall."

They looked into each other's eyes. Then Succat turned, placed his knapsack on his right shoulder, and headed southwest as planned. A hundred metres away or so, he turned and waved to his friend, who was still standing where they had parted. Even the sheep, who had settled down for the night, seemed to be gazing after him. The decision was to depart by nightfall, and it was well into the Celtic twilight by this time. The plan was to go southwest, avoid the coastline until he had crossed the Abhainn na Sionainne[56] as had been directed by Aogán, and then head northwest to the territory of Máigheo. Succat had no idea at all how far away an tSionna[57] might be, and there would be other rivers to ford before he would reach the big one. He would travel as far as possible in darkness, so as not to be seen by either local inhabitants or Meelco's men if they happened to spread that way. He knew the latter was unlikely, but no chances were to be taken. By day he would try to avoid meeting local farmers or anyone who might guess he was an escaping slave.

So he trudged on. Fortunately it was a dry, moonlit night, making his journey that much easier. He must have walked for at least three hours before tiredness began to take over. Then he spotted a cluster of furze plants at the corner of a field. They would provide good shelter for the night, and here he would lay his head upon his knapsack and enjoy the privacy the plants provided. The night had become chilly, but Succat was by now well used to sleeping in the air of a chilly night, and there would be little if any disturbance. Indeed, when he entered he saw a rabbit burrow, and set up his snare in hopes of meat for a morning breakfast. He lay back his head, commended himself to God, and sleep descended in a few minutes.

The sun was beginning to peep from the east when Succat awoke. It was a totally new experience, and he first thought of Meelco and

---

[56] River Shannon.

[57] The Shannon.

wondered if his disappearance had been discovered yet. There had been days when one of Meelco's henchmen had arrived late in the afternoon. These slave masters had grown accustomed to the condescending complaisance of this slave who had caused no problems at all even though his master's not infrequent lashes served as a reminder of punishment to come had he shown any kind of rebellious conduct. Despite his clouded future, Succat felt a freedom he had almost forgotten. Would that it might continue like this, he thought to himself.

It had been a dry night, and the coming of dawn brought him fully awake. He glanced covertly through the furze and saw no signs of life anywhere. A farmhouse stood at a distance. There was no smoke from the chimney so Succat knew its inhabitants had not yet awakened to the new day. Through the stillness of the morning a dog was barking, allowing Succat to know his presence had been recognized. A little stream of water flowed just a stone's throw away. He used it to put some water over his face, then knelt and sipped the water to refresh his system. That done, he checked out the rabbit burrow. Sure enough, breakfast was awaiting.

Then time to renew his journey. It was a desolate area, and he met not a soul until he came to a river that had to be traversed. He stood for a few moments figuring out the best place to cross. Then without warning someone was speaking to him from a few metres behind.

"May the gods be with you! You are out early."

Succat recovered quickly from the surprise given him by the unexpected and unwanted visitor. He turned around and saw an elderly man carrying a knapsack and walking with a stick.

"You seem to be traveling like myself," said the stranger.

"Well, yes," said Succat. "I am heading west for Máigheo."

"Now let us go south along this river, and we will find a place to cross," was the stranger's first comment.

The crossing didn't take long, and obviously the stranger had been this way before.

"That's a long journey you are taking on," said the stranger. "I am going a distance myself too. Sure, I'm going to Cruachán.[58] That is over there in the west, too, not as far as Máigheo, but far enough. I am Eochaidh O'Flaighearta. I was born and raised in the west of Éireann, but I have been a seanchaí for more than twenty years, and I cover a lot of ground. I am returning to my people in the west, and I will stay with them until the gods decide otherwise for me. Yes, I will continue to entertain and help people enjoy life, but I don't think I will come this far north anymore. I am getting old. Now what should I call *you*, and what brings you west? You speak like a man from the north."

Succat had to think quickly. A seanchaí, but not going north again for quite a while and perhaps never. It would be safe to tell him his secret.

"Well," he said, "I am called Succat. I am escaping from a slave master at Sliabh Mis,[59] far away now to the northeast. I spent years tending sheep on that mountain, and my master Meelco always called me Succata. And I can tell you now only God kept me alive."

"I have come across Meelco. He has a bad reputation, and he is a very unfeeling man who treats his workers as if they were animals. Tell me how you got into slavery."

Succat went through the whole story, including the last glance he had of his mother Conchessa being thrown roughly to the ground by a Celtic marauder, and the terrible journey across the Celtic Sea, as well as the unimaginable life he was forced to live in the wilderness under Meelco.

"I would ask you not to reveal details of my life to anyone. I am still afraid of the word getting back to Meelco who might send a search party into the west to find me. He might flog me to death."

"You have my word" said Eochaidh. "It's the word of a traveling seanchaí, and your wish will be honored."

"*Míle buíochas*,"[60] said Succat, using the native Celtic multithanks

---

[58] Nameplace translated Croghan, County Roscommon, Ireland.
[59] Slemish Mountain, County Antrim, Ireland.
[60] A thousand thanks.

offer. He had come to realize the Celts rarely expressed gratitude with a simple "thanks" but rather with a multiplication of their present feelings. In the span of his slave years Succat had become Celticized despite his infrequency of social visiting.

It was time for Eochaidh to speak again.

"I am going to Cruachán, back to my people. Let me tell you about Cruachán. Cruachán is a site for the kings … yes … and queens of Connacht. Queen Maedb was one of the most famous. Funny thing, but she went to war with the king of Ulainn over a bull. He had the bull she wanted, and he refused to allow her to have it, so she sent her army to get it."

Succat was listening intently.

"What would have driven her to do that in the first place?"

"Well …" said Eochaidh, "you see … she was married to King Ailill, and they both were very wealthy. They counted their possessions, and Ailill had a famous white bull. The fact is … the bull had been born into Maedb's herd, but … disdained his owner … because she was a woman. So … that bull made a nuisance of himself and kept leaping fences into Ailill's herd. So that in the end, Ailill got full possession of the white bull.

"Now Maedb heard about a brown bull in the northern kingdom, and she wanted it. Funny thing, the owner had agreed to lease the bull to her for a couple of years, but when the messengers arrived to get the bull, they got drunk with *uisce beatha*[61] in a friendly celebration. In their drunken orgy, they told the owner they would have taken the bull anyway even if he had not agreed. This really angered the owner, and he then and there terminated his agreement.

"When word got to Maedb, she was very angry and sent a huge army into Ulaidh[62] … you were a slave in Ulaidh for all those years. It became a terrible conflict with soldiers killing each other … and mind you … all over a bull. Well … neither side was having much

---

[61] Whiskey.

[62] Province of Ulster.

success until a young fellow in the Ulaidh army … his name was
Cúchullain[63] … demanded single combat at fords in accordance with
the custom of the time. Cúchullain eliminated every hero who came
against him until in the end he was faced with his own stepbrother
Ferdia, who had joined Maedb's army years previously. The two close
relatives faced each other at a ford. They had grown up together, were
great friends—but here duty called upon them that one or the other
should die.

"'My brother,' said Ferdia, 'it's a sad day for both of us.'

"'Yes indeed,' replied Cúchullain. 'Do you wish to sit and chat
before we fight?'

"'No,' replied Ferdia. 'We know we love each other, but we are in
the terrible situation where duty calls on one of us to live or to die.
Talking to each other before that might lessen the determination of
the other. Let's say goodbye and begin our combat.'

"They exchanged a handshake and each warrior returned to his
own safe space.

"'May the gods be with the victor, and may the loser find himself
in Tir na nOg. Some day may we meet again.'

"Both warriors roared from their throats sounds that echoed a
long way off. Each drew his sword, and the battle was on. For a very
long period the encounter endured. Before long both were covered
in sweat, but there was to be no ceasing. Occasionally blood covered
both frames, the cloths that girded their loins were torn to pieces. But
there was to be no respite. Each army believed its hero had the upper
hand, each groaned at times that its champion was failing.

"But there was no surrender by the man from Ulaidh, nor was
his half brother from the Connacht army about to quit. In time both
were lame, and both had arms dripping with blood. Each looked
exhausted. The sun had moved a long distance in the sky before the
duel ended. Cúchullain's sword finally pierced his half brother's heart.

---

[63] A famous warrior, noted for his athletic skills and his ability in hand-to-hand
fighting. The name Cúchulainn, directly translated, means "The Hound of Ulster."

Ferdia fell in a mass of blood. His opponent stood over the bloodied body, sword in hand looking down at the man who had put him to the test for the first time—his own half brother.

Ferdia, the playmate of his younger days, was dead.

"The Connacht army retreated in dismay. But can you believe it? In the midst of the battle, a few men of Maedb's army managed to sneak away and stole the bull. They escaped by a circuitous route and were able to join their defeated troops at another point on their way back home!

"So the bull came to Cruachán, but it was a bad experience for Maedb."

Eochaidh stopped the story to draw his breath.

"Why was it a bad experience?" asked Succat. "Of course, I know the battle about the bull was terrible. Maedb should have minded her own business."

"Well indeed," said Eochaidh. "I'll tell you why. And it didn't work out the way Maedb had planned. Things went very wrong. Maedb's first bull, remember, didn't like her! It was the same story with the second, except he didn't like her husband either. So very soon he tore the ground with his hooves, snorted the snort of battle, and tore through the fence to attack Ailill's bull. He made short work of him! The helpless owners looked on.

"The brown bull of Cooley then went on a rampage. He left the king and queen behind him and headed for the An tSionnan.[64] With his mouth frothing and his nostrils blowing angry air, he killed every other bull that came in his path. He followed An tSionnan to Áthaluain[65] but he had himself worn out! In his last battle at Áthaluain, he encountered a young bull that was as strong as himself. In the battle his body was badly torn. There was no more fight left in him. He limped all the way back to the North and died shortly afterward."

---

[64] The River Shannon.
[65] Athlone, County Westmeath, Ireland.

"And what about Maedb?" inquired the fascinated Succat.

"Maedb and Ailill eventually became the king and queen of Éireann, and lived at Teamhair,[66] seat of the high king. Finally Maedb thought it was best for her to retire and return to Connacht, a place she greatly missed. So … she lived in a grandiose island palace in Loch Cé.[67] Well, she had made an enemy who waited all those years to repay her for destroying his family and friends during the Cattle Raid of Cooley. And he had sworn to get even.

"Well … unknown to her, he came secretly to Loch Cé. He noted that she came frequently to bathe in the lake. You see, Maedb loved that lake, and during the warm days of summer she went to swim every day."

Eochaidh paused for a moment. They walked in silence once more. Succat was becoming impatient to hear the end of the story.

"So what happened?" he asked.

Eochaidh shuffled his body, his chest swaying from side to side.

"He shot Maedb in the neck with an arrow. She bled to death almost on the shore."

"So who was he and what became of him?" asked the intrigued Succat.

"He was a Celt from the north, and his name was Fachtna Faiteach … poor fellow … he met a bad end. Low and behold, he himself went on to be high king living at Teamhair. But he made a mistake. He went back north to see his friends, and while he was away, Teamhair was attacked by a Connacht army. Fachtna rushed back, but it was too late, and he himself lost his life in a battle against the victorious Westerners."

Succat thought for a few seconds and then remarked, "You make it sound as if the Westerners, who I am on my way to join, are a dangerously aggressive people."

Eochaidh reflected for a moment and continued, "You've got it

---

[66] Tara, ancient seat of high kings of Ireland, County Meath.
[67] Lough Key, County Roscommon.

wrong. That story indicates something that relates to all of us. Maedb was greedy. Her greed led to a war. Many people died as a result, and did Maedb ever know that she herself would be one of them? Wars are bad, and they are mostly caused by jealousy and greed, and that's the moral of the story. Let me say the story does not refer to any particular group of Celtic people but to all of them. And, of course, you won't be joining the upper classes. The ordinary people are just like you and me. Many of them were forced to join those armies, people who would have preferred to be home at peace.

"The moral of the story is that it is better to live in peace. Greed is the cause of all wars. The people who cause the wars don't realize what they are doing, and it's easy to get men killed on your behalf. But some day it all comes back to haunt. If Maedb hadn't caused a war in the first place, she would have died in peace."

In time they reached the An tSionnan and a crossing place in the little village of Carraig.[68] When they put their feet on the other side, Eochaidh said, "You are now in the kingdom of Connacht, and another day or two will bring us to Cruachán. But for this evening, I think we will bed down here. I have friends around here who always welcome a seanchaí, and just like the rest of the journey since we met, I am sure they will welcome you, too, with a place to sleep and good food."

"You have spoiled me," said Succat. "When you leave me, I will be sleeping in the open again and trying to stay warm."

"When I get to my family," said Eochaidh, "I will get you a new woolen rug, and that will keep you warm, and of course you stay with us the night we arrive."

Succat felt good about that. Just the same, he still envisioned his lone journey in the coming days, together with his lack of knowledge of the countryside. But he reminded himself that God would be his companion.

---

[68] Carrick-on-Shannon, County Leitrim, Ireland.

Chapter 11

Learning on the Run

The travelers stayed in a good home that night, a home filled with hospitality and friendship. Next morning, Succat felt a little sad as he and Eochaidh departed. This was his first experience of Connacht,[69] and the warmth of the people had already made its mark within his heart. On their departure, Eochaidh was made to promise he would return "for a session" at some future date. Then it was hugs and goodbyes.

They walked in silence for a little while. It was Eochaidh who broke the quiet with a question.

"What do you think of our Connacht people so far?"

"They are a wonderfully friendly people," replied Succat.

Eochaidh then spoke. "Well … I have a couple of more stories to tell you that will shorten the journey. And they are both about famed men from Connacht. The first is about a man called Conn who originated somewhere in the middle of Connacht. He was a huge man. He joined the army of Connacht, and whenever there was a war, Conn led his men to victory after victory. He got the name 'Conn of the Hundred Battles,' but you might add a couple of more battles that he won, perhaps nearly another fifty."

---

[69] Province of Connaught.

"My goodness," said Succat, "was there any peace at all?"

"The problem was," said Eochaidh, "that if you were king of Connacht you had a good likelihood of becoming high king of Éireann. Your men mostly did the fighting; they were well paid, and they, too, had a good chance of living on Teamhair at the palace of the high king and being regarded as the best soldiers in the land.

"Yes … Conn became high king, and he reigned a long time. These were dangerous times, and Conn was eventually assassinated by a man from Ulainn[70] who wanted his throne. I need to tell you that when Conn took over as high king, there was a stone at Teamhair called the Lia Fáil.[71] When a new king was installed, the Lia Fáil would roar aloud, and the longer it roared, the longer the king would reign. Well … during Cúchulainn's lifetime he favored the installation of a high king from Ulainn. But … would you believe it … the stone remained silent. This really angered Cúchulainn, and didn't he split the stone with his spear? That silenced it forever, or so everybody thought. The stone itself got lost, and nobody was sure where it might lie. But after Conn became king, he was walking on the parapets one evening, and the next thing he heard was a voice roaring 'Long live Conn; long live Conn.' The shouting was so repetitious that at first Conn thought an admirer was screaming at him. He looked all around but could not see anybody. Then, as he kept walking, he realized the voice was coming from beneath his feet. It was the stone—the Lia Fáil—and Conn was standing right over it. The roaring meant that Conn was the designated high king, and as the roaring went on, it told Conn he would be there for a long time as king.

"Conn had a lot of opposition from the kings of An Mumha[72] as well as much hostility from Ulaidh. He was called upon to defend his kingship time and again but won all his battles. Mug Nuadat, son of the king of Munster, was his chief enemy. However, his forces were

---

[70] Province of Ulster.
[71] The Stone of Destiny, always used at the coronation of a high king of Ireland.
[72] Province of Munster.

not strong enough to overpower Conn, and in the end Mug Nuadat escaped to Spain. There he married a daughter of the king of Spain, and low and behold, nine years later, didn't he come back to Éireann with reinforcements and took on Conn again? He lost again too! The trouble for poor Conn was that everybody was envious of his success and his bravery in battle. So how do you think he died?"

"Tell me!" said Succat. "This is a very interesting piece of the history of Éireann, and they sure did carry on a lot of wars and fighting." Succat continued smilingly, "I am surprised there is anybody left in this land at all!"

"It was the nature of the times," said Eochaidh. "Power begets thirst for more power, and, of course, there is always jealousy of success."

"You are right," said Succat, "but let's get back to your story."

"Well …" said Eochaidh, holding his hand under his chin as they walked, "Conn eventually lost his life to a trick. The king of Ulaidh sent fifty warriors dressed as women to Teamhair.

"This was something totally unexpected. When they reached the sentries around the palace, they pretended they were friends of Conn.

"'We have come from Ulaidh,' they said, 'as a gesture of good faith from our king. We would like to spend a few days speaking to the high king of Eireann and learning from him. Then we can go back and inform our king of the kind man Conn is.'

"A message was sent to the king. Fifty women wanted to visit with him in order to allow peace between the kingdoms and to assure him of their own king's real desire for peace.

"'Conduct them to my presence,' said Conn.

"And so it was that fifty Ulaidh soldiers dressed in disguise were invited into the king's presence. Conn welcomed them. But keep in mind Conn was a Connacht man, and they say Connacht people are very kind and also very gullible. Indeed they were feasted at the palace with Conn calling on his servants to serve all kinds of delicious dishes. Conn had sleeping quarters allotted to all these 'women' and so everybody went to bed happily, including Conn. After all, to know that there would be no threat from his northern neighbors was assuring.

"Too late when Conn learned it was all a falsehood. He was not long asleep when fifty soldiers entered his quarters. They killed him on the spot. After all his battles, Conn was a victim of a subterfuge.

"Now … quite a while later, a generation or less I would think … a grandson of Conn came to the throne of the high king in Teamhair. I know you will ask me if he was from the West, and the answer is yes. In fact he was born in Céash,[73] not a great distance from Cruachán at all. His name was Cormac Mach Airt. He had a wonderful reputation and was judged as a very fair king. He fought very few wars, and he loved his people.

"In his older years, and after a long reign, he was meandering down the Boyne River at a place called Ross,[74] where he had a supernatural vision.

"The vision told him that the druids were not good people and, more astonishingly, that God's own Son had come into the world at a place called Bethlehem away to the southeast of An Roimh.[75] He came among us as a real man to take us all to His own place. Bad people—especially the Romans who were controlling the area—had crucified Him with the help of a small minority of locals. They buried Him, and He rose from the dead three days later. They say that now He has a big following throughout many parts of the Roman world."

Eochaidh continued, "The vision told Cormac not to allow himself to be buried at Brú na Bóinne[76] where most of the high kings were buried. Rather, in his vision he was told he should be buried

---

[73] Keash, County Sligo, Ireland.

[74] Near Slane, County Meath, about twenty-six miles north of Dublin. Ross Crossroads is a well-known junction on the Navan Dublin Road. Slane, remarkably, will come into this story later.

[75] Rome.

[76] Located on the River Boyne approximately thirty miles north of Dublin. The tourist site of Newgrange is within this area.

right at the spot where he was standing. Cormac instructed his palace guards and his druids that Ross was to be his burial place. But on his death—caused they say by the druids, who choked him on a salmon bone wrapped in food—the druids decided that Brú na Bóinne would be his burial place, where he would lie with his forefathers. The funeral procession wielded its way down along the river and crossed over An Bhóinn[77] at a ford commonly used by the people. But lo and behold, the river rose in flood, and the coffin bearers had to withdraw to dry ground as fast as they could. They tried again for the next two days … at the same place, with the same result. Their fourth effort was also a failure, except that this time the waters swept the bier off their shoulders and took it at fast speed down the river. Next morning, at Ross, shepherds going to work found the bier, and unbeknownst to themselves, entombed it as King Cormac had wanted—with his face to the rising sun as he awaited the arrival of the perpetual light that would never go away. So Cormac lies peacefully there still, awaiting the light whose brilliance is eternal."

Succat was silent for a moment. Then he spoke. "You know, Eochaidh, the Son of God did come among us about four hundred years ago. He *was* crucified by the Romans, and He *did* rise from the dead. I am one of His followers. King Cormac was given a special insight by the One True God."

There was silence for a few moments. Eochaidh's features were showing a certain amount of surprise. Then he spoke again. "You will have to tell me all about that before we reach home … I am very interested. Succat … this makes more sense than the twelve gods of the druids."

"Yes it does," said Succat. "Why don't we talk about it now? Do you believe the Son of God came among us?"

"Now I am confused. It never occurred to me before that Cormac may have had a revelation from God. You say there is only one God. In a way, that makes a lot of sense," said Eochaidh, "and that is what

---

[77] River Boyne.

I am thinking about. I am wondering if I should become a follower of your Jesus Christ."

"You believe," said Succat. "That is the most important thing. Let me explain the teachings of Jesus to you as we go along."

They had walked several kilometers when Eochaidh asked, "Could I become a follower of Jesus now?"

"Yes, you can!" replied Succat. "First I will baptize you. We need to find a stream. After that I will teach you the prayer of the Lord and give you some further information about the Christian Church."

And so it was done. They found a little stream nearby where Eochaidh became a Christian. They sat by the stream, had something to eat, and Eochaidh learned about Jesus.

Following a good resting period, the two travelers continued on their journey. Eochaidh was very happy and kept repeating the prayer of the Lord with Succat until he was able to recite it perfectly. As a seanchaí his memory was very sharp, and he had little problem recalling what Succat was saying.

Eventually Succat changed the subject. His thoughts had spread further afield.

"Tell me, where is Teamhair? What do you know about it? Is it a mighty fortification?"

"Well," replied Eochaidh, "not much fortification. You see, Teamhair is one huge hill, and the entire top is taken up with living quarters—for the king, his servants, his soldiers—and, of course, the druids, who are never far away from where things are good. But they have an influence on the king, and he normally tends to follow their wishes. Except, of course, Cormac, and they quietly murdered him."

"Where is Teamhair?" asked Succat.

"A good way from here, and close enough to Dubhlinn,[78] where lies Éireann's biggest population. You see there is great land surrounding the area. The king owns a lot of that land, and he can find plenty of workers to help farm it. Now, the view from Teamhair, depending

---

[78] Dublin.

on how far up you are allowed to go, is a sight to behold, and from the top they say you can see almost all of Éireann, including the eastern seaboard. Indeed, there's a high hill, Cnoc Shláine,[79] across the way from the Hill of Teamhair—only about ten kilometers. I have never been there, but I have met seanchaí who were."

Succat responded, "Interesting, but I guess I will never get to Teamhair or Cnoc Shláine."

"And then again, you might," responded Eochaidh. "There is no way of predicting the twists and turns of one's life."

In his heart Succat knew that he would be leaving Éireann as soon as possible to find his parents and relatives in Breatain Bheag, but he remained silent on his future plans.

There was a little banter for a while, with Succat admiring the scenery, and wondering when he would get to Máigheo.

Then Eochaidh announced, "We are just a short distance from my home, and don't be surprised if there is a lot of celebration and joy at my return."

And, sure enough, there was great excitement when all of the inhabitants found an opportunity to hug and welcome Eochaidh home. It was now Eochaidh's opportunity to introduce his friend to his own family. They were full of welcome and were quick to invite Succat to spend the night.

"Where are you headed to?" asked one young man.

"I am going to An tAonach Beag,[80] and I intend to leave early tomorrow morning."

Eochaidh was quick in his response.

"No, you can't leave then. I have to take you to see the royal palace of the kings and queens of Connacht. We won't get all that close to it, as it is so well guarded, but at least you will see it from a distance.

---

[79] Anglicized "The Hill of Slane." The Village of Slane lies at the bottom of this hill, along the left bank of the River Boyne at a crossroads forty miles from Dublin. The population is still small, but Slane stands in an area of historic sites.

[80] Now Killala, County Mayo, named for Ala (Alan?), a companion of Saint Patrick.

And you will have a notion where some of the people we talked about, like Queen Maedb, lived, who went on to become high kings or high queens of Éireann."

So Succat agreed with Eochaidh's plan. In the morning, they took off to see the regal buildings at Cruachán. After about sixty minutes of walking, they arrived and saw a set of buildings on top of a hill. The place was indeed surrounded by soldiers of the king of Connacht, Brían Echach Muigmedóin.[81] For a thousand years, kings of Connacht had gone on to be high kings living in Teamhair.

There would be no hope of getting any closer than a quarter of a mile from the state buildings. Although he did not reveal his sentiments, the living quarters looked far below Roman standards, and, indeed, in Succat's mind, they did not even approach the level of Roman officers' quarters. They spent quite a length of time just walking around, viewing them from different angles, and then Eochaidh chose a place beside a stream where they could have a little meal. Thereafter they traced their steps to Eochaidh's home, taking time to enjoy the countryside. Dinner was served that evening with generous portions of duck and wild turkey. Later on, Succat reflected on the blessing Eochaidh had been to him, and thanked God for having sent him such a wonderful friend.

But all good things come to an end! In the morning they hugged and expressed blessings to each other. It was hard parting, and Eochaidh's generosity still maintained itself as he handed Succat a bag of food that would keep him going for probably two days. He was to go toward the setting sun in order to reach the town of An tAonach Beag. They parted in tears, with Succat again advising Eochaidh to remember that he was now a follower of Christ and to offer the prayers that he had taught him.

His travels took him to a wooded area where he thought he could rest throughout the night. Then he heard a rustling in the trees and a voice that said to him, "May the gods be with you."

---

[81] Very famous king who most likely became high king of Ireland.

The voice was that of an older man, probably just past his middle-age years. Thrown across his back were a brace of rabbits and a couple of snares, as well as a pouch he wore in front that seemed to be a carrier for arrows.

The young Succat returned his greeting and remarked about the rabbits.

"I have got a snare too," he said, "and I wonder if rabbits are plentiful around here."

"Plentiful as the water in the ocean," replied the stranger. "But tell me, where are you going? And what kind of job are you looking for?"

"I am a shepherd," said Succat, "and I heard that near the village of An tAonach Beag there are farmers who employ people like me, and I wanted to try out for myself the generosity that I heard attributed to some of these people."

"Come with me," said the stranger. "My name is Brian, Brian O'Dubpthain.[82] What is your name?"

"My name is Succat."

"Very good. If you'd like to come with me, I have a place to put you up for the night. You see, my wife died a year after we married, and the druids forbade me to marry again. You don't cross up the druids. They are a dangerous people who have no problem in having what they call transgressors put to death. So here I am, for all those years, living on my own. But you will like my little home. It is comfortable and cozy. Sometimes I trap a wild duck or two, but tonight it is going to be rabbit stew. I have a little garden of vegetables, and thankfully the druids never come near me. Nor do I have anything to do with them. They are a dangerous lot."

Brian turned out to be a good cook, and together they had a very nice dinner in Brian's warm cottage. They talked some more about the druids, and Brian warned Succat to be very careful to stay out of their way. Next morning, Succat left for the rest of his journey, and Brian directed him to follow the setting sun that would eventually

---

[82] In modern terms, Brian Duffy.

bring him to the river Muaidh,[83] which emptied into the bay of An tAonach Beag. Succat did not have to worry about food as he still had all the food given him by Eochaidh. He journeyed through wooded areas filled with yew trees and knew he was in Máigheo.

That night, he reached the Muaidh.

It was a wide river, and he decided to rest for the night. Plans for tomorrow could wait.

---

[83] Today the River Moy, which empties into Killala Bay.

The Burial of King Cormac

By Sir Samuel Ferguson (1864)

"Crom Cruach and his sub-gods twelve,'
Said Cormac, "are but craven treene;
The axe that made them, haft or helve,
Hath worthier of our worship been.

"But He who made the tree to grow,
And his in earth the iron-stone,
And made the man with mind to know
The axe's use, is God alone."

Anon to priests of Crom was brought—
Where, girded in their service dread,
They minister'd on red Moy Slaught—
Word of the words King Cormac said.

They loosed their curse against the king;
They cursed him in his flesh and bones;
And daily in their mystic ring
They turn'd the maledictive stones.

Till, where at meat the monarch sate,
Amid the revel and the wine,
He choked upon the food he ate,
At Sletty, southward of the Boyne.

High vaunted then the priestly throng,
And far and wide they noised abroad
With trump and loud liturgic song
The praise of their avenging God.

But ere the voice was wholly spent
That priest and prince should still obey,
To awed attendants o'er him bent
Great Cormac gathered breath to say,—

"Spread not the beds of Brugh for me
When restless death-bed's use is done:
But bury me at Rossnaree
And face me to the rising sun.

"For all the kings who lie in Brugh
Put trust in gods of wood and stone;
And 'twas at Ross that first I knew
One, Unseen, who is God alone.

"His glory lightens from the east;
His message soon shall reach our shore;
And idol-god, and cursing priest
Shall plague us from Moy Slaught no more."

Dead Cormac on his bier they laid:
"He reign'd a king for forty years,
And shame it were," his captains said,
"He lay not with his royal peers.

"His grandsire, Hundred-Battle, sleeps
Serene in Brugh: and, all around,
Dead kings in stone sepulchral keeps
Protect the sacred burial ground.

"What though a dying man should rave
Of changes o'er the eastern sea?
In Brugh of Boyne shall be his grave,
And not in noteless Rossnaree."

Then northward forth they bore the bier,
And down from Sletty side they drew,
With horsemen and with charioteer,
To cross the fords of Boyne to Brugh.

There came a breath of finer air
That touched the Boyne with ruffling wings,
It stirr'd him in his sedgy lair
And in his mossy moorland springs.

And as the burial train came down
With dirge and savage dolorous shows,
Across their pathway, broad and brown
The deep, full-hearted river rose;

From bank to bank through all his fords,
'Neath blackening squalls he swell'd and boil'd;
And thrice the wondering gentile lords
Essay'd to cross, and thrice recoil'd.

Then forth stepp'd grey-haired warriors four:
They said, "Through angrier floods than these,
On link'd shields once our king we bore
From Dread-Spear and the hosts of Deece.

"And long as loyal will holds good,
And limbs respond with helpful thews,
Nor flood, not fiend within the flood,
Shall bar him of his burial dues."

With slanted necks they stoop'd to lift;
They heaved him up to neck and chin:
And, pair and pair, with footsteps swift,
Lock'd arm and shoulder, bore him in.

'Twas brave to see them leave the shore;
To mark the deep'ning surges rise,
And fall subdued in foam before
The tension of their striding thighs.

'Twas brave, when now a spear-cast out,
Breast-high the battling surges ran;
For weight was great, and limbs were stout,
And loyal man put trust in man.

But ere they reach'd the middle deep,
Nor steadying weight of clay they bore,
Nor strain of sinewy limbs could keep
Their feet beneath the swerving four.

And now they slide, and now they swim,
and now, amid the blackening squall,
Grey locks afloat, with clutching grim,
They plunge around the floating pall.

While, as a youth with practised spear
Through justling crowds bears off the ring,
Boyne from their shoulders caught the bier
And proudly bore away the king.

At morning, on the grassy marge
Of Rossnaree, the corpse was found,
And shepherds at their early charge
Entomb'd it in the peaceful ground.

A tranquil spot: a hopeful sound
Comes from the ever youthful stream,
And still on daisied mead and mound
The dawn delays with tender beam.

Round Cormac Spring renews her buds:
In march perpetual by her side,
Down come the earth-fresh April floods,
And up the sea-fresh salmon glide;

And life and time rejoicing run
From age to age their wonted way;
But still he waits the risen Sun,
For still 'tis only dawning Day.

Chapter 12

At Home in Máigh Eó

Succat picked out a yew tree under which he would shelter for the night and began to prepare his sleeping materials. Suddenly he saw a snake creep from the river and then another. There seemed to be snakes everywhere, so Succat decided he had better move away from the river and try to bed in a safer place. It was the first time he had seen snakes in Éireann, and he wondered if this was a regular feature and promised himself to inquire later on.

His sleep was fitful, and his dreams were filled with crawling creatures swimming on the waters and then inching close beside him. In the morning Succat enjoyed the food Eochaidh had given him and felt refreshed and ready to follow the Muaidh as far as he could to An tAonach Beag. Much farther down, where the river became shallower, he was able to tread his way on the rocks to the western side, as directed by Brian. Now he knew all he had to do was to remain on that side until he reached his destination.

Surprisingly, the journey seemed shorter than he thought it would be, and in no length of time he had reached the village of Béal an Átha.[84] But now that he was getting so close, he determined he would not stop there but would keep going until he got to journey's end.

---

[84] Ballina, County Mayo, Ireland.

An tAonach Beag was a very small village. There he found a wide harbor and a nice quay where incoming ships could tie up. He visited the harbor, walking along the quay just to enjoy the lapping of the water. Quite a number of people were on the quay, and Succat decided to see if he could become friendly with one of them. So he gave the usual Celtic blessing … "the gods be with you" … and the young man to whom he spoke responded in a friendly fashion.

"Where are you going, sir?" he asked. "You look like you have come a journey, and you have traces of the north of Éireann in your speech. So what brings you to Máigheo?"

"I heard that the people in Máigheo were a very generous and nice people. I am a shepherd, and I will look for a job around An tAonach Beag."

"Very good," said the stranger. "Most of the sheep farmers are toward the northwest of here. There is a place called Foghill[85] where there are quite a number of sheep farmers. One or two of them are quite wealthy, and sometimes they have druids living on their estate. So my advice to you is to stay away from where there are druids. Choose a smaller sheep farmer and just make sure that he is honest and will pay you your wages."

"Thank you," said Succat. "Now how do I get to Foghill?"

"Well, said the stranger, "you follow another little river that flows into the ocean. It is called the Abhainn Mór.[86] You will need to get across that river after about three kilometers. In fact, you will come upon a narrow neck of the river where you will be able to cross. Then keep going directly north close to the sea inlet, where it meets the river, and you will come to Foghill. There are some nice people there who I am sure will take care of you."

"Thank you," said Succat. "You have been very kind, and I will be on my way."

He followed the directions, found the narrow crossing place, and headed straight on to Foghill. That part of the area was hilly, and having

---

[85] Now Fohill near Killala in County Mayo, Ireland.

[86] Today in the Killala area this waterway is known as the Palmerstown River.

climbed a hill or two, he saw the farms with lots of sheep, some of the farms seemingly huge. He spotted a small cottage close to the river and decided he would make inquiries there. The family were most welcoming and didn't seem at all concerned about the stranger in their home.

Palmerstown Bridge on the Abhainn Mór, the place where Patrick may have crossed to go to Foghill

"I am Succat," he said, "and I would like to be employed herding sheep, but I was told to be careful who I worked for."

"Well," said the homeowners smilingly, "come in, sit down, and let us give you a meal. You look like you have traveled a long way."

The master of the house extended his hand and said, "I am Caolán MacMulruaidh.[87] I own a small farm, but I am not a sheep owner,

---

[87] Caolán is a name that has mostly fallen into disuse; MacMulruaidh means Mulroy.

and I can see why you may have been advised to stay away from the large landowners. But I know a family about a kilometer from here who may need somebody like you. And you will be safe with them" … whisperingly, "the druids don't bother them."

"Thank you," said Succat. "I will wander down that way to visit that family."

"Not until you have had a meal with us first, and it won't take long to get ready. You will find yourself eating a lot of lamb in Máigheo. Just stay away from druids. My wife is stirring up some food for all of us, and you must join us."

"Thank you," said Succat. "I will be glad to, and I appreciate your kindness and advice."

With that, through the opening to the living place, a beautiful teenage girl walked in. She had not known their family had a visitor, but when she saw Succat she went straight toward him, bowed her head, and said, "I am Oona. I am a member of the household. In fact, I am the only member apart from my parents. I do a little work here and there to help the local farmers who send for me frequently. Today I was helping to do some shepherding. It was a long day, and I am glad to get the odor of food. You are staying for a meal, are you not?"

"Yes," said Succat, "your parents are most gracious people, and have become my friends already."

Then he reiterated to her his search for a job with the smaller sheep farmer, and told her he was going to visit the family her father had recommended.

"Oh, good," she said. "They are a lovely family, and I was helping them today. It may well be they have a job for you. I can accompany you there."

Succat was not familiar with such hospitality, and he responded, "Thank you. That will be most kind of you."

Then they sat and enjoyed a most delicious meal during which Succat gave some details about his life, being very careful not to reveal anything about his origins or his years of slavery.

Shortly thereafter he left, having expressed his deep gratitude, took his shoulder bundle, and headed to visit the recommended family, with Oona at his side as she had promised.

Once again he received another wonderful welcome. The prospective employer, bearded and apparently kind, expressed his gladness that Succat wanted some work, telling him that even though his farm was small and he raised sheep, he was shorthanded and would be glad to hire him. There was no difficulty in arriving at an acceptable wage. The landowner told Succat his home was very small (as Succat could see) but invited him to sleep in the loft of the barn, which was very clean and cozy, and was already set up for previous employees. He then led Succat to the loft, which indeed had a very comfortable bed, and the owner told Succat there was a stream very close by where he could wash himself when he wanted to. Succat was grateful and was glad that he was settled for the time being in Máigheo.

In the morning his new employer came to invite Succat to view his farm and took him to a field that contained about seventy sheep. That field appeared to Succat to include almost the entire holding of this particularly friendly farmer. His job was to keep count of the sheep, prevent any wayward animals from escaping over the barriers, and make sure that the sheep were fed when necessary, and he could finish his work at sundown. And so Succat began his first day's work, still among strangers but entirely pleased with their hospitality and unusual friendship.

He was at work less than a week when Oona, whom he had met on his first arrival, came to visit.

"Come," she said, "let us sit and talk a little while. Do you have any time off?"

Succat informed her he had not discussed that with the owner of the farm.

"I think the farmer will give you a day here and there for yourself, and when he does I will take you along the coast and through the neighborhood so that you will learn a little bit about where you are.

This man is far too poor to be bothered by the druids, so you are in a safe place."

They sat and chatted for another hour; then Oona told him she had to return home, but she would be back again soon. As she walked through the field on her way, Succat watched her stride and the way she graciously carried her body, her head held high in an air of confidence. She was the first and only female that had ever been a friend, and Succat began to wonder about his own feelings toward her. It was evident to him he had the affections of this young girl, and he began to think about an entirely new life as a married man here on the shores of An tAigéan atlantach,[88] far away from where he was born.

"I must pray a lot," he promised himself, "because I have no notion where this relationship may lead me."

Oona came many more times, on one of which Succat was released for the day by his employer. Oona showed him the neighborhood, told him about the large landowners and the druids, and in general familiarized him with the locality.

Succat did pray … and prayed a lot … about his relationship with this girl. And God answered him, as he always answers prayer. Succat knew what he was going to do. One day when Oona kissed him gently on the cheek, and told him how she loved him so much, he replied that he loved her, too, but it was not in God's will that they should be a married couple.

Oona seemed stunned by his reply and remarked, "You say it is not in the will of your God, but what about all the other gods?"

Succat then signaled her to sit beside him, and he explained to her his belief in one God and told her the story of the coming of that God among us and that His name was Jesus Christ.

"Now," said Succat, "I am going to tell you a secret because I trust you, and I know you love me."

Whereupon he told her the entire story of his life from his childhood to his kidnapping and his slavery on Sliabh Mis, to his exposure

---

[88] The Atlantic Ocean.

to the snows there in wintertime and, finally, his escape after six years of unimaginable cruelty.

Then he went on, "Oona, the real reason that brought me to An tAonach Beag and Foghill, was the hope that I might be able to catch a ship that would take me to An Frainc or An Bhreatain,[89] where I could seek out my relatives and try to make contact with my mother and father. Ships come in here frequently, I am told, and I am hoping to be able to get on one and go back to my native place. You see, my father is a Roman officer, and was in charge of a battalion in Bhreatain Bheag when I was enslaved, and if I get to Bhreatain Bheag or An Frainc, I will be able to discover where my father and mother may be, and try to make contact with the rest of my family. Oona, I told you about Jesus Christ and how He lives with me and how He lives with you, too, should you like to be a follower. There are thousands of Christians, as we are called, all over Europa, and possibly some even in southern Éireann. And if you come to Christ, you will find peace and contentment. When I go, Oona, I have a feeling I may be back some day in Foghill, as I would like to become a priest of the Lord Jesus, and bring His news to the wonderful people of Éireann."

Oona, through tears in her eyes, replied that she would indeed like to know the true God and asked Succat to give her some more instructions. Sitting on a sunny hill that day as the sheep grazed around, Succat gave Oona his introduction to Christianity, whereupon she asked, "How can I become a Christian?"

"We can baptize you," replied Succat, "but you must tell absolutely nobody, for fear of the druids who could have you offered up as a human sacrifice. I will teach you the prayer of the Lord, who came among us, and I want you to say it every day, and when you are praying, be sure to focus your mind on Jesus the Lord."

"I will," replied Oona.

"So perhaps one of these days we may be able to baptize you in

---

[89] Britain.

the stream just down the hill and bring you into the family of God. We will then be closer than ever in spirit."

"That will be wonderful," replied Oona, "but I still don't want you to go back to An Frainc, or to leave me here on my own."

"Oona, I must go. I have no choice. I must find my relatives wherever they may be. Whether in An Frainc or An Bhreatain or An Róimh."

"No, no," replied Oona, "I can't let you go."

She threw her arms around him.

"Oona," said Succat gently, "I have to go, and I am asking you to pray to my God, who is now yours, too, for direction and solace."

They parted silently, Oona saying that she would be back to see him in a day or two, and again Succat watched her gracefulness as she walked down the hill.

Two days later, Oona did return.

"I am ready for baptism," she told Succat. "Let us go to the stream. I want to tell you that I prayed to our God for direction, and in a dream last night I got a message from an angel not to interfere with your plans and that everything will work out well in the end."

Succat replied, "Oh, thank God; you know I would never leave you on your own if I could avoid it, and I have a great feeling that I will be seeing Foghill again in the years to come. Who knows? We may meet and be able to help each other."

Oona was tearful but she said, "Let's go to the stream. I want your God to be my God."

And so it was that Succat had made another Christian in Éireann.

"Oona, I want to ask you a favor. Keep a lookout for galleys that may be coming into the bay and let me know so I can try to hurry there and find a way to get back to An Frainc."

"I will do that," said Oona, "and I will most certainly watch the bay every day for you. When I see a galley coming in, I will come quickly and tell you."

More than six months went by. Oona visited Succat on a frequent basis. The news was always the same. No galley in sight! ... until one day Oona came excitedly with the news there was an incoming galley in the bay heading for An tAonach Beag!

"How long do you think they will stay?" asked Succat.

"Probably not for long," said Oona. "If they have a cargo, they will deliver it, and most likely they will be gone before too long."

"Well," said Succat, "I need to go immediately and tell my employer that I will be leaving today. I must try to get aboard that galley."

Oona's tears came flowing rapidly.

"My heart is breaking," she said through her tears, "but I know it is God's will you must go."

"I believe God is answering my prayers," replied Succat. "I am going to really miss you."

They hugged for the last time and went their separate ways, each glancing back at the other as distance separated them. Succat had no problem settling accounts with his employer, who wished him well, also telling him to return if he did not get on the galley.

Late that evening the one-time slave found himself down by the quay in An tAonach Beag.

Chapter 13

The French are in
An tAonach Beag

Succat dallied along the quay, all the while watching the crew of the galley emptying its cargo. Eventually he decided to find somebody from the vessel to whom he could speak. He knew already by listening to the men that they were from La France,[90] and so, in their native language, in which he was fluent, he asked a crew member when they expected to move out again.

"Oh, we won't be long here," replied the worker, "but tell me— how did a Frenchman get to An tAonach Beag?"

Succat did not want to reveal too much confidential material, at least until he knew that he would be accepted by the crew.

"When do you think you will be sailing out?"

"As soon as we can," replied the worker, "but first we have to load a pack of wolfhounds destined for La France. You know they say that the Celtic wolfhound is very pleasing to the upper class and very easy to handle. Indeed, having a wolfhound is a sign of regality."

"I am going to ask you a favor," said Succat. "I want to get back

---

[90] France. Succat has set aside his knowledge of the Celtic language and reverts to the native French in which he was brought up.

to La France. I don't have a lot of money, but I could help the crew in whatever way they would wish."

"I can't make that decision," replied the worker, "but I will pass your message on to the captain."

A few hours later there was nothing but disappointment for Succat. The worker returned to tell him there would be no welcome for a roving French man and the captain did not want him on his boat. Succat was disheartened but still offered a prayer of thanksgiving to God for at least giving him an opportunity. Later in the day he watched them load the wolfhounds, put up their sails, and row out to sea on their way home.

As he saw the galley depart he was a lonely figure on the quay, hopes dashed, and disappointment penetrating his very soul.

"Well," said Succat to himself, "I will sleep here on the quay and perhaps the Lord may send another ship tomorrow. There has to be a good reason why God brought me here."

The weather had been very pleasant that day, but suddenly an unexpected thunderstorm broke. He watched as the ship ran into difficulties through the storm and wondered how they would manage to cross the bar,[91] whose waters were now more turbulent than ever.

Killala Bay as it appears today

---

[91] The meeting of the River Moy and the Owenmore with the Atlantic Ocean, Killala Bay, County Mayo, Ireland.

The vessel appeared as if it were trying to turn back. He saw the sails come down and watched as the oarsmen worked hard to keep their galley from being overpowered by the waves. He knew that something serious was afoot.

"Yes! Yes!"

They were returning to An tAonach Beag and had surrendered to the dangerous challenge of the waters of the bar. He watched as the oarsmen brought the ship back to anchor at the dock.

The thunderstorm and the elements had calmed somewhat, and it was apparent to him the crew were getting ready to tie up for the night. This storm and the bar had changed their plans. By this time Succat had moved off the quay to a sheltered area where he could see what was going on. Several of the crew left the ship to find sleeping quarters with two or three remaining to guard the wolfhounds.

The night passed quickly, and very early in the morning Succat was aware that there was action on the quay. The crew were returning.

Perhaps the Lord wants me to try to get on board again, thought Succat.

In a flurry of excitement Succat picked up his shoulder pack and was quickly at the galley. The captain was still standing on the quay watching his men get on board. He appeared agitated, with a grouchy disposition and not at all friendly to any of his crew. Despite this situation, Succat decided to be valiant.

He spoke courageously to the captain, saying, "I will do any kind of work if you will take me on board. I need to get back to La France as soon as I can, and it looks like this is my only hope."

The captain glared.

"You must pay me if you want to get on board."

"I cannot," spoke Succat. "I do not have the wherewithal, but I can work as part of your crew, and I will be able to help you to get through those rough seas."

The captain was obviously thinking about what Succat had said.

It took him at least half a minute before he replied, "All right, get on board … you can help us."

Succat hoped that the galley would row out before the captain might change his mind. But within a short space of time he was assigned as a rower at the back of the galley.

This had echoes for Succat of his first sea journey when taken by the Celtic marauders.

The captain eventually gave the order to pull out to sea. This time the crossing of the bar was easier, and they managed to get clear into the open waters of the Atlantique.[92] The captain gave the order to pull to port. This meant the ship would work its way through the Atlantique, down along the west coast of Éireann, and through the Baie de Biscayne.[93]

As they rowed south, Succat watched the land of his captivity and for some reason felt a great affection in his heart for its people. He remembered Aogán, the friendship between them, and how Aogán had helped him escape from his cruel captor. He recalled also the very friendly seanchaís he had been blessed to meet during his slave days as well as on his way toward Máigheo, and how he had learned from them about the Celtic culture … even their search for God. Flashing into his mind also were memories of the welcome he had received in An tAonach Beag and, of course, thoughts of Oona frequently invaded his mind.

But all of that was over now. He had a new life ahead … though he had an inner feeling that someday he would be back again in Éireann.

He was taken from his home as a young boy, and now here he was, praise God, returning to the land of his ancestry as a matured young man. He would immediately begin his search for his parents and relatives. His heart ached to meet his parents once more.

Suddenly, in the distance, he caught a glimpse of the land of La

---

[92] Atlantic.

[93] Bay of Biscayne.

France. He was filled with happiness. And he praised God for the gifts he had been receiving. Home to La France. He could hardly wait until the ship pulled into the port of Le Havre. Good things lay ahead!

Or did they?

The traditional turbulent waters of the Baie de Biscayne might have something to say! And they did.

It had been a hard enough crossing. Now squalls were breaking out, and the tempestuous waters of the bay became more furious, so much so that the oarsmen found it impossible to keep on course. Despite their sweat-filled exertions, even after the sails were lowered, the forces of nature took charge. They finally made land, but nowhere near their original destination, a long way from their intended port. The sands were welcoming, and they were able to tie up on a large rock that jutted into the ocean.

The cranky captain spoke, "We are going to leave the galley here. It is late in the day. We are out of food. We need to go ashore to see what we can find."

The tired and hungry crew, who were now irritated not only with the captain but with each other, hiked inland only to find that their landing place had no inhabitants. As mariners, it did not take them long to realize that they were on an island, and there was no sign of human life. As the evening began to succumb to darkness, they cursed and complained at the fate that had befallen them.

"We are going to die in this place," complained an oarsman, "and Succat, why is it that your One God does not help us?"

The question brought scowls at Succat as if he had been the cause of all their troubles.

"Yes, Succat, why doesn't your God save us?"

Succat remained silent. He was quietly praying, fearing that the turn of events might lead to violence, and his own life might be endangered. His prayers were heard!

Suddenly Succat retorted, "Look! There is a herd of swine only a short distance away. God has provided food aplenty."

The herd began to scatter at the sight of the onrushing attackers. Not fast enough, however, before three of them had fallen victim to the knives of their hungry assailers. Succat uttered a prayer of thanksgiving. He knew that God was always on his side![94]

The crew returned to their galley with full stomachs, as well as enough food to satisfy the starving wolfhounds. They slept on the boat that night. By morning the bay was extraordinarily calm. The captain gave the order, and the galley glided over the waters of the bay, northward to the port of La Havre. Here and there they rowed into angry waves, but this time they landed safely at their destination.

It was early next morning.

As the rowers brought their barque dockside in Le Havre, Succat was filled with an inner joy and an inner peace that here he was … home … and would eventually find his own family members.

The petulant captain ordered the crew to empty the boat of the cargo of wolfhounds, which took quite a while because the hounds were caged and the crew had to await the arrival of the new owners. Finally the last cage was cleared of the ship. The owners all paid their levies on the transportation, and the crew began to gather their own equipment.

Succat gathered his small shoulder pack and went toward the exit from the ship. Unexpectedly the captain barked at him, "My friend, you have not paid your way. All you did was a little rowing, and I order you to stand ready to be taken to the slave market."

Succat was shocked beyond belief. He could not make sense of what was happening to him. He was going into slavery again. Although the ship was not a slave ship, the captain roughly announced that he knew where there were buyers for Succat.

His mind took him back to An tAonach Beag where he had gotten on board. The realization that he was the victim of the captain's prevarication overtook him.

---

[94] See *The Wisdom of St. Patrick*—Faith, Greg Tobin, Fall River Press, 122 Fifth Avenue, New York, NY 10011.

With tears running down his face, Succat turned to the Lord, saying, "Thy will be done."

The captain ordered two of the crew to accompany him to the slave market where he took Succat and announced to the prospective purchasers that he had a hard-working fellow who had not paid his way and who could be acquired for his fare from Irlande[95] to La France. Most of the buyers tested Succat with prodding and some humiliating investigations, and all of them rejected him—all of them, that is, but one. He was a French farmer who looked at Succat and said, "You come with me."

Thereupon, he paid Succat's fare to the captain, and together Succat and his new owner left the area.

Succat's heart was broken, but he soon found out that perhaps the future might not be equivalent to the cruelty he suffered on Sliabh Mis. Indeed, his new owner seemed quite friendly and said to Succat, "You are a Frenchman like myself. I just paid your fare from Irlande to Le Havre, and I am asking you to work for me just for one year. I will treat you well, and then I will release you. My name is Pierre. What is yours?"

"I am Succat," replied the newly purchased slave. "My father is an officer in the Roman army. I am his only child, and the emperor posted my father and my mother to Caledonia,[96] where I was born. One day another order came, directing my father, with some of his legionnaires, to take up office in Leucarum in Pays de Galles.[97] It was from there that Celtic pirates captured me and sold me into slavery in the north of Irlande."

"And how long," asked Pierre, "were you in slavery?"

"For about six years," said Succat, "possibly a little less, possibly a little more. You lose track of months and years when you are in the kind of slavery that I had to endure."

---

[95] Ireland.

[96] Scotland.

[97] Wales.

Succat continued, giving him a true narrative of his time in Irlande, the cruelty of his first slave master, Meelco, how he had escaped to An tAonach Beag, and how he was taken on board this merchant ship. He knew the galley was heading for La France, and he understood from the captain that being a part of the crew would be his payment for the journey. He told his new master of his total shock when he was taken to the slave market.

"Well," said Pierre, "I am not like Meelco. It appears to me you have come from a noble family. You belong to our own land, and there will be no herding sheep in the snow, and you will have a place to live in one of my barns. And I promise you, too, my wife and I will maintain you with plenty of food. So hopefully you will stay with me. I already promised you what I would do for you, and now I ask you to pledge to me that you will not try to escape. When the year is completed, you will then be released."

Succat had a thousand thoughts run through his mind. But as he looked back on his former life, he decided it would be best for him to remain with this man rather than be chased down for a long time to come in regions unknown to him. He had never been to La France before.

"I promise to stay with you until the year is up," he said, "and I will work for you to the best of my ability."

"Very good," said Pierre. "Let us go to my farm. You will meet my wife Gabrielle … now tell me what your plans are for the future."

"I was looking forward to seeking my family," said Succat, "and I especially need to try to make contact with my parents. When I finish my time with you, I will be off to the south of La France to begin my search among my relatives and family friends."

The journey "home" was by horse and buggy and was much less punitive than sitting in the back of a horse cart as was used when he was first taken as a slave. They reached their destination, and he was introduced to Gabrielle, the wife of his new slave master.

Gabrielle appeared to be a kind and caring person, and Succat began to realize that God had blessed him after all, as he might well have been taken as slave by an uncaring family, as happened in Irlande. His quarters in the barn were spacious and comfortable, with a bed and hand basin and good lighting from outside. It was now late in the evening and Succat reflected that the tasty food served hopefully was an omen of things to come.

"We will see you in the morning," said Pierre, "and I will show you how I expect you to tend my sheep. Meantime I hope you sleep well, and I am sure Gabrielle will have a good breakfast for you before you leave for work."

Succat retired to his quarters and threw himself in a posture of prayer against his bed.

"Oh, Lord, I thank you for taking me through this awful crisis, even though I had hoped to start the search for my parents and friends, I know that you will be with me in the year to come, and I am sure if I work hard it will pass quickly."

He then recited innumerable prayers before climbing into his surprisingly soporific bed.

In the morning he heard Pierre's voice shouting up to him, saying, "It is time for breakfast. I hope you are ready for a good day's work."

"All right," replied Succat, "I will be there very shortly."

And so the day began. Pierre took him to his sheep and pointed out how he was to guard and feed them.

"Don't worry about losing any sheep. They will all get to know you and to rely on you for your friendship. There is no need to worry about any of the sheep knocking down a wall. As you can see, the walls are high, and the sheep are quite content to stay together, and they won't make any great effort to escape to another grazing ground. When the sun is disappearing from the sky, you can come back to your lodgings. Gabrielle will have a good meal for you. You can count the sheep every morning just to make sure they are all there. If a sheep is missing, it will likely come back unless it has been stolen."

And so it was for a year and a day. Unlike his previous captivity,

Succat was well taken care of and spent most of his time in the field with the sheep, making sure they were fed and watered. Indeed, the sheep recognized him and came toward him whenever he showed up in the morning. He missed the companionship of Aogan and Oona and remembered them frequently in prayer. But he thanked his God that he would not have to sleep in the open on a wet or snowy night as formerly. For a rainy day, his master, Pierre, had given him a little waterproof tent where he could sit and look out at the rain. All in all he settled in well, and before he realized it, the year was gone.

Pierre came to him and said, "You have kept your promise very well, and I am going to keep mine. You are released, as from tomorrow. Do you know where you are going to travel? It will be a long journey on foot, but you may be able to make contact with the Roman legionnaires who might well help you in your journey south."

Succat thanked his master profusely and said that he had been happy in his service. Next day, he took his departure, but not before Pierre had bestowed on him quite a number of valuable Roman coins. His new life was beginning at last.

The question for him now was in which direction he should travel. If he went to Pays de Galles, back to his old home, where he was captured, he might catch up with his parents.

Then again, thought Succat, *Roman officers are normally assigned by the emperor until he decides they are needed elsewhere, and it is now seven years since I last saw my parents.*

His mother, Conchessa, was the niece of Martin of Tours,[98] but Bishop Martin had died even before Succat was a teenager. However, there would be relatives of Succat's family around Tours, the area which gave birth to his ancestors.

It could be easier to get back to the home from which he was

---

[98] Bishop of Tours, 371–97.

captured in Pays de Galles. He thought to himself that Pays de Galles seemed a shorter journey, should he be able to catch a galley that would take him. There was a port in Calais that was frequently used by the Roman legionnaires. Succat decided to head for Calais. It would be a long trek, so he inquired where the nearest Roman fort might be.

As it turned out, there was a Roman stronghold not too far from Le Havre, so he decided to go there first. The legionnaires accepted him graciously, especially when they heard he was the son of a Roman officer. Succat asked if there might be any possibility that a Roman galley would be going to Angleterre[99] anytime soon. The news was good. Foot soldiers would be leaving for Londres[100] in about ten days. The legionnaires would be glad to carry the son of a Roman officer across the channel, and no pay was required. Succat was delighted with the news and decided to wait the ten days. During that time he remained a guest at the outpost and enjoyed his time visiting its occupants. The time passed quickly.

The galley left for Londres on the appointed day with Succat on board. It was an easy crossing, and their destination was reached without any problems. Succat knew he had to make his way west to Leucarum, where he had high hopes of finding his parents.

It took about ten days to reach Leucarum even though he had been transported for short distances by the legionnaires. His heart began to race as he reached the borders of the city, and memories flooded back of his early teenage years, the fun with his friends on the beach, one of whom, Blasius, was now gone to the Lord. He made his way directly to his old home, but when he reached the house, there was a big disappointment in store. Somebody else greeted him there, a lady who was a complete stranger.

He informed the lady that he was searching for his parents and how he had been captured by Celtic invaders more than seven years

---

[99] England.
[100] London.

ago. He was immediately invited in and welcomed back to his old home that was now in the possession of another Roman legionnaire. She quietly and sympathetically informed him that both of his parents had died.

In fact, his mother died from harsh treatment by the Celts on the day he was captured, as she tried to defend him. His father was bro- kenhearted. He had lost his wife and his son on the same day. He was filled with remorse that this tragedy had happened under his watch. Thereupon he pledged that never again would pirates be successful in any place under his domain.

Just a year or so later, more Celtic pirates had arrived. This time the Roman troops were ready for them. But Succat's father, remem- bering how he lost his family, was ready for the attackers and took more risks than necessary. Calpurnius met them on the beach. A battle ensued, and Calpurnius died from his wounds leading his men.

"You are sure that this is true?" he asked.

The lady nodded her head and told him she had known his father and mother, and she was certain that both had died. So now he had no relatives that she knew of living in that area. This was news that Succat did not expect. He was overcome by emotion as he recalled his mother's efforts to protect him and his father's loving care.

It was an overwhelming situation—he had no parent alive. He asked where they might have been buried and was told that as far as she knew, the Romans took both bodies back to their native place in Tours and buried them there.

Brokenheartedly he decided to stay around for a while and roamed through the neighborhood anyway, looking up old friends who had been playmates in his boyhood. Some had grown into hardy men who were preparing to join the Roman legionnaires, while others were farming, some happily married with families. The Celtic piracy, he learned, had stopped because of his father's leadership and the preparedness of the Roman army for such attacks, but, unfortunately, Calpurnius had given his life for the cause.

His visit to Leucarum nevertheless helped his emotions, recalling sentimental memories of happier times and a childhood filled with love. After several weeks, he decided to go back to La France and go to Tours, where he would meet close relatives and friends. In time he found himself back among his parental ancestry in a city that had a very Christian population already and was soon to be established as the first Christian Diocese in La France.[101]

Martin of Tours had accomplished wonderful progress among the Christian population, and the edict of Constantine[102] had made it less dangerous to be a Christian. Succat first sought information on who might have known his family. After long inquiries he found a priest, Lucien, who appeared knowledgeable and friendly, and ready to help him in his quest. The priest inquired what his plans were now and got the response that he had been seriously thinking of becoming a priest and returning someday to Irlande. He told his priest friend that Irlande was ready for evangelization.

Lucien replied, "I am so glad to hear of your plans for the future. I will do everything I can to help you out. But first I will need to talk to Archbishop Bricius[103] to see if he may be able to help you in your quest. And in the meantime, I will guide you to your relatives."

That meeting was a happy one. Succat found he had more relatives living around Tours than he ever believed. When he had completed his visitations and had been the focal point of the welcome and joy expressed by all, a good many months had passed.

In his own mind it was time for him to endeavor to begin his studies for the priesthood. He found himself once more journeying

---

[101] The Diocese of Tours, later to become an archdiocese, was one of the first dioceses of the Catholic Church named in France, circa 249, and before the edict of Constantine.

[102] Edict of Milan allowing Christians the freedom to practice their religion, issued in 313 by Constantine I, who, in 325, declared Christianity to be the religion of the Roman Empire.

[103] Fourth bishop of Tours, from 397 until 443.

to Lucien to have his support and assistance in beginning his priestly studies.

"Well," said Lucien, "I am happy for you. Now I will need to find a scholarly prêtre[104] for you who will accept the task of teaching you the theology of the Church. Before your ordination as a priest, you will be well known to the Bishop of Tours, who may be able to get Pope Celestine to make you a bishop and send you forth on your missionary dream. But keep in mind it looks to me like a dangerous mission if the druids are that powerful."

"Ah, yes, it will be dangerous, but nothing is impossible with God, and on Him I will rely."

"Very good," said Lucien. "I shall investigate who might educate you, and it is possible I may go to the bishop and tell him your plans. But keep in mind there is no guarantee yet the bishop will accept you, and less guarantee that he will allow you to go to Irlande as a missionary."

"All right. I am very grateful for your help; I will commit my plans to God and leave the rest to His Divine Will."

"You are a good man," said Lucien, "and I will do my best to help fulfill your dream."

---

[104] The modern seminary for the education of future priests had not yet been established, and students aspiring to the priesthood were trained by a qualified priest who both taught and measured their ability for their future ministry.

Chapter 14

Priesthood and a
New Mission

Lucien was true to his word and in short time had found, with
the permission of the bishop, a very informed priest who had
previous experience in educating aspirants in the theology
and laws of the Church. Succat began his apprenticeship enthusiasti-
cally with a distinguished clergyman, Father Marcel, near Tours, and
took up residence in the priest's home. Four years further on, he was
given the news that he would soon be ordained to the priesthood, the
great desire within his heart.

Father Marcel and he developed a close friendship.

Throughout his student period, he became aware of the monks at
the recently founded monastery at Lérins.[105] He wanted to experience
the disciplines and learning of the monks prior to his ordination.

He first mentioned his idea to Father Marcel, who was somewhat
bemused at the desire and seeming determination of his young student to learn about monastic life and his very apparent piety.

"I am not the person to speak to the bishop about this. Our friend

---

[105] Lérins Abbey is a Cistercian monastery on the island of Saint-Honorat, one of
the Lérins Islands, on the French Riviera, with an active monastic community. It
was founded c. 410 by Saint Honoratus.

Lucien is a friend of the bishop; let's mention it to him and see if he can do anything for you."

As if by Divine Providence, Lucien came to visit the student the next day.

"I have been thinking of seeing what life is like in the monastery at Lérins. Do you think it would be possible for me to spend time there before I am ordained priest?"

Lucien thought for a moment.

"That is a long way from here. Do you think you can learn more than we taught you here? It is a long distance to travel, and do you really think you would benefit from it?" he asked smilingly.

"Oh, no, it is not that at all, but I would like to look into monastic life and see what is to be learned."

"Yes," replied his friend, "monastic life, as it is being introduced, appears to have many advantages, but on the other hand I am not sure how it would blend in with pastoral care. And how long would you intend to spend in that monastery?"

"Probably about a year, and then, with God's help, I will be ready for ordination."

"You are indeed a man of God, and I see no reason why our bishop would wish to prevent you from going. I will inform him, and I am sure there will be no problem."

There *was* no problem. Shortly thereafter, Succat found himself on the island of Saint-Honorat in the monastery and living with about thirty monks who had dedicated themselves entirely to a life of prayer. This was truly a very different life. For one thing, his daily routine had been completely altered. The monastery bell summoned all monks to night prayer at six forty-five in the evening, and it rang out again at two thirty in the morning, announcing the beginning of a new day. Members of the community then gathered in the monastery chapel to sing and praise God in psalms and hymns. For Succat this was a wonderful way to be in communion with God.

Memories of his slave days in Irlande came floating back. It was much easier to pray here under the warmth of a roof and surrounded by the love of a community rather than under the branches of a tree on the side of a mountain in midwinter. The day passed quickly between spiritual talks, study, and personal and community prayer times. The monks observed a strict silence at mealtime and indeed mostly throughout the day. They did not eat meat, something that, at the beginning, reminded Succat of his rabbit-hunting days. He was very happy.

He became a new man—in every sense. Every monk had accepted a new name when he entered the monastery, a reminder that he was leaving his old life behind. The abbot had decided on a new name for Succat too. The name with which he began his journey through life would no longer be used. From now on he would be known as Pátraic,[106] a man of God committing himself entirely to the will of the Most Holy Trinity.

Time marches on! The year sped by, and the day came for Pátraic to say farewell.

"You have been a worthy aspirant while with us. We will miss you, but I wish God's blessings on the work you plan in your future. And we will remember you and your intentions in all our prayers. Go in peace and in the love of the Lord."

With that farewell, the abbot handed him a letter addressed to Bricius, the Bishop of Tours.

"Please take this letter to your bishop. Have no fear; I am heartily recommending that you be ordained as a priest. You are more than ready for that office."

On the evening of his departure from the monastery, something extraordinary happened. He had a dream! It was a vivid dream during which Pátraic saw and heard the children of Foghill in Máigheo calling him back to bring them the Good News of the Savior of the world.

The children were pleading, "Come back to us, O holy man, and teach us all about your God."

---

[106] In French, Patrick, as also in English. The name Pátraic was evidently adapted into the Celtic language. We shall continue to use Pátraic.

The shores around An tAonach Beag were very visible to him, and he saw himself reentering the village. When he awoke, he felt as if he had received a message from the supernatural. He always felt an inclination to spread the Good News of the gospel in Irlande, and now he felt sure that missionary work was in his future and destined for him by Divine Providence.

On his return to Tours, there was bad news. He would not be going to Irlande. Pope Celestine had instead nominated Bishop Palladius to that ministry. The news was broken to him by Lucien.

"I am sorry for what has happened. I was trying to encourage you, but in my heart I always felt you were too young to be sent back among the unruly Celts."

Pátraic was dismayed.

"But you told me you would do everything you could, and now you have shattered my dreams. Why did you not tell me before this?"

Lucien was becoming upset at Pátraic's demeanor.

"You wanted to go to Irlande. I told Bishop Bricius of your desires. And this is the thanks I am getting."

Pátraic showed his irritation.

"How long have you known that Palladius has been chosen? Was my desire not communicated to Pope Celestine?"

"I presume it was communicated by Bishop Bricius, and my part ended there. Keep in mind young man that you are not even ordained priest yet."

"So your undertaking on my account was merely on the surface. It seems to me you did little to impress my bishop, and you are telling me that you felt released from your promise when you left the bishop's presence. Very obviously your befriending me was pretense."

Pátraic was angry.

"You allowed me to really believe that after my ordination I would be destined for Irlande. I relied too much on you and your friendship."

He went immediately to see his former tutor, Father Marcel, to talk about the possibility of his ordination. Pátraic handed him the letter from the abbot.

"I will take this letter to Bishop Bricius, and I have a great feeling he will be very pleased. I will recommend that you be ordained at the bishop's pleasure."

Marcel was correct. Bishop Bricius read the letter intently and then looked up at the priest.

"This is a wonderful recommendation, and I am not surprised. From what you told me, this young man is worthy of our endorsement. Let us give him a period in which to notify his friends, and then we can set a suitable date for the ceremony of ordination."

Marcel took the news back to Pátraic.

"The bishop is delighted that you are so ready to be ordained. He would like you to inform your friends and choose a time within the next five or six weeks when Bishop Bricius will proclaim your priesthood in a happy ceremony at the cathedral."

That celebration took place on a Sunday in June.[107] At that same ceremony Bricius announced that Pátraic was appointed as curé in Tours.

The appointment was no surprise to Pátraic. He was aware that, despite his desires to return to Irlande, he would still be expected to improve his talents in pastoral care, and the various other attributes required for the priesthood. Marcel remained his friend and mentor, and they visited frequently.

The people of Irlande were never far from Pátraic's heart.

In Rome, Pope Celestine was engaged in his own problems. He had already sent Bishop Palladius to Irlande, and all seemed to be going well. A bishop named Novatian had previously become an antipope in Rome. Even though almost two hundred years had passed since then, the contradictions of Novatianists were still in existence,

---

[107] The ordaining bishop is in dispute. Sometimes attributed to Saint Germanus of Auxerre, but there appears to be little to validate this tradition.

and now the present Pope was dealing with a continuance of the misleading creed of Novatian and his followers. This sect held beliefs contrary to the Church of Rome.[108] Among them were various theories, especially one that was extraordinarily extreme. It stated that anyone who had left Christianity or who had pretended to leave Christianity under persecution could not be forgiven and would not be accepted back into the faith of the Church. Pope Celestine had declared the Novatianists as schismatic and refused to allow them to minister in any church in Rome or elsewhere.

Novatianists had also spread their teachings and beliefs to almost all parts of Christian La France. Celestine decided to condemn them in a public letter, written especially to the priests of La France. In the letter he was most likely the first to make the statement that "to remain silent about evil is to consent to the evil."

Celestine wrote a little differently.

"We are deservedly to blame if we encourage error by silence ..."

Every priest in La France read the letter. Pátraic discussed it with his friend Marcel.

"It is something like that in Irlande too. The druids are pernicious. They send forth teachings that nobody challenges ... mostly because they are afraid. But doesn't this letter cover Irlande though in a somewhat different way? Here it is the Novatianists. In Irlande it is the druids who have their own gods and frighten their communities into at least pretending they accept this teaching.

"So you can't get the place of your captivity and the people who captured you out of your mind! Are you still determined to go back there and give opposition openly to the druids?"

"Indeed I am determined, and I want to go. I think I have enough experience now to be able to deal with the situation over there, and I

---

[108] Novatianism was an early heresy in the church that lasted down to the papacy of Pope Celestine I. It had been condemned previously in another council but still existed in various disguises, possibly up to the present day. It denied Mary's motherhood of the Divine. The matter was decided at the Council of Ephesus in 431.

believe I shall immediately apply for permission to go from my Bishop Brecius and from Pope Celestine. After all, Celestine tells us we should not be silent in the face of evil. You are a friend of the bishop and perhaps you might be able to set up an appointment for me so I can discuss my desires with him personally."

Marcel replied, "I admire your tenacity. I will most certainly try to help you out, and we will see where this takes us."

A short time later, Pátraic had a meeting with Brecius.

"So you still want to take on the dangerous mission to Irlande? Those people did not treat you very well before. Why do you feel you would like this mission in the first place? Bishop Palladius is already there. I suppose we could ask you to take care of one half of the country and allow Palladius to be in charge of the other half ... possibly you to the north and he to the south."

"That would be fine with me," said Pátraic, "but I can't go without your blessings as well as a directive from Pope Celestine."

Bishop Brecius nodded.

"You will have my blessing. I will send an emissary to the Pope, and he will make the final decision."

A few months later, the Pope's reply came back to Brecius and to Pátraic. He extended his blessings to both of them and decreed that Pátraic would be his second missionary bishop to Irlande. He should depart whenever it would be feasible for him.

Before then, however, Brecius would ordain him bishop.

Chapter 15

A Slave Returns

As a new bishop, Pátraic remained in his present appointment as curé. His people responded with love and delight. They were highly motivated to help him when they heard he would be going to Irlande to help Christianize that country.

Within a few months, Pátraic had accumulated enough funds to hire a galley that would take him to the shores of Irlande, and since he knew not where the landing would be, he gave the sailors more than would normally be expected to cover whatever length of extra time it might take for him to find a friendly landing place. Bishop Bricius inquired from his priests to find out if any might like to accompany Pátraic on his mission. The response was overwhelming. More than twenty priests offered to make themselves available. That, of course, was more than enough, and Pátraic and the bishop decided on seven. These were regarded as not only priests of deep faith but also as energetic and vigorous individuals for the task that lay ahead.

When all was ready, Pátraic and his companions made their way to the port of Saint-Nazaire where a galley was awaiting them, and in no time they were all on board.

This would be a different kind of journey to Éireann than when he was first captured. He knew the land. He knew the people. He knew their culture. He had high hopes of developing Christianity along with

Bishop Palladius. In his mind, Pátraic had a sure and certain plan. His chief plan was to convert the princes and those who held power. That would lead to the people following suit. Then, of course, there were the druids. He remembered them and the horrendous power they had over the people, a power that went back for centuries, so much so that the druids domineered even the kings and princes, as well as the ordinary people. The druids were capable of offering human sacrifice, and even though this practice was mostly in the past, the odd occurrence still frightened the citizens they pretended to serve.

By this time the galley had been rowed out to sea, and the power of the surging waves against their boat brought Pátraic back to reality. The Bay of Biscayne was continuously stormy, and Pátraic asked the captain to go as far out to sea as possible in order to avoid the chaotic turbulence these waves might cause. The captain agreed, and in a few days the shores of the south of Éireann came into sight. It was now a question of where to land. An tAonach Beag would be a friendly place, but the distance around the coast would demand a mighty effort from the oarsmen. At Pátraic's instruction, the captain turned north by northeast, and several hours later in the dusk the vessel arrived at Bré.[109] It was too late to land, and the passengers and crew decided the galley would be their sleeping quarters until daybreak. Next morning, they pulled into the Bré River, and Pátraic and his fellow missionaries disembarked to determine if they might be accepted here. A group of curious natives had gathered. Pátraic and his seven companions greeted them, and Pátraic spoke to them in their native language.

"We have come," he said, "to bring the Good News of Jesus Christ to all of you."

There wasn't much friendship in the response.

"Who is Jesus Christ? Why should He interest us?"

"Because He is the God of heaven and earth. He is also the Son of God, and He came among us to show us how to live our lives and find a happy home in eternity."

---

[109] Bray, County Wicklow, Ireland.

The crowd listened intently. A voice was heard saying, "We have twelve gods. Now you are telling us there is an extra god. Be gone before we call in our druids. We do not want you here."

Pátraic realized he could make a better start than this and would find a friendlier region for the beginning of his efforts at conversion to Christianity.

"Let's leave this place," Pátraic said to his companions, "and travel north. I began my stay in Éireann in the north. It might be best for us to begin my second coming to Éireann by going northward where I know better the culture of the people."

His companions all nodded their heads, and with that, Pátraic replied, "Let us gather our belongings and head back to the galley."

They embarked and rowed north past Dubhlinn and eventually saw an inlet. He consulted with the captain if this might be a safe waterway to enter.

"It looks safe enough to me, and we will direct our oarsmen to take a slower pace just in case we might run into shallow waters."

The oarsmen received their instructions, and the galley slowed to a much more relaxed pace. All eyes were on the surrounding countryside. Slowly they advanced quite a distance.

"Look," said an oarsman, "there is a little village over there."

He was pointing to the north side of the inlet. Pátraic followed the oarsman's gaze and saw the hamlet too.

Pátraic addressed his galley workers.

"I don't know how long we will remain here, but I ask you to stay for a little while until I find whether we are welcome or not."

The oarsmen, all of them Christian, readily agreed and one said, "We will follow you, Pátraic, and if you need our help on land, we will be glad to give it to you."

Pátraic replied, "I am very grateful for your help, and I thank you for your dedication. Once I find a place where we are welcomed— and it might be here—you can then return to La France with God's blessings."

Pátraic and his followers trekked well inland until they reached the little hamlet they had seen from the galley. The inhabitants were curious but welcoming. One of them asked the usual question.

"Where are you from? Why did you come here?"

"I am Pátraic, and I come to you from An Frainc to bring the Good News of our God to Éireann, and if you will allow me, I would like to stay here for a while and meet the people, tell them the Good News, and possibly build a place of worship."

Pátraic's reply brought no hostility and the listeners invited him to tell them more about the Good News and the difference it might make in their lives.

Then another asked, "What about the druids? Have you heard of them? They say they are priests of the twelve gods. These gods also have subgods, so we don't know how many gods there are. And they have taught us to worship all of those gods. The trouble is they are hostile when confronted about their teachings, and they can be vicious and vengeful."

Pátraic then explained that he had been a slave at Sliabh Mis for many years, that he knew about the druids, and that he felt he could handle them. The listeners were sympathetic to his cause and invited him to stay. They told him, too, that they would help him in any way they could. With that, Pátraic blessed his oarsmen and wished them a safe journey home.

Within a short time, Pátraic had established a Christian community that was strong and that regarded him as their leader. Druids did not come near them, and so the new foundation began to flourish day by day along the shores of Loch Cúan.[110].

---

[110] Strangford Lough.

Chapter 16

Joy and Sadness

After four months or so, news was brought to Pátraic that a prince whose name was Dícho was angry about Pátraic's arrival, and the prince believed that Pátraic's efforts were dishonest. He had ordered that Pátraic and his companions be banished. When Pátraic received this news he was, of course, greatly concerned and decided to go see Dícho himself.

When he arrived at Dícho's castle, he told the attendant his name and asked to see the prince.

"He is home," said the attendant, "but I am not sure if he will agree to see you. He has been talking for several months now about ridding the area of you, but now I will go and see if he wishes to speak to you."

The attendant left, and in a few minutes Dícho arrived on the scene. He was a tall man with reddish hair and indeed looked regal. When he saw Pátraic, he seemed hostile and perhaps a little angry.

"Why are you here?" he inquired with haughtiness.

"I have come," said Pátraic, "to bring you the good news of the Christian faith."

"And what is faith?" inquired Dícho.

"Faith is belief in the One True God."

"We have many gods," was the reply.

They were still standing at the door of Dícho's domain. No invitation was extended to the visitor to enter the home!

"I know that well," said Pátraic. "That is what your druids have taught you. But they are wrong."

"Please come within," Dícho finally uttered. "I have a couple of druids advising me, and are you telling me they are misleading me?"

They had entered a well-furnished room that had wooden chairs and a large dining table. A fire was blazing, throwing its heat throughout the chamber.

"They are indeed misleading you. Have any of your subjects been offered in human sacrifice to the so-called gods? Your druids are xenophobes. They consider themselves above everybody and show total intolerance to anyone who may oppose them. They pretend to predict the future, but they have absolutely no power except that which they have bestowed on themselves."

Pátraic knew he had touched a nerve. He could see Dicho's expression softening.

Now his native culture came through.

"May I offer you a meal and the hospitality of my dwelling?" he asked.

Pátraic knew it would be foolish to refuse the prince's invitation. Besides it would be time well spent, a time to educate his host on the teachings of the faith. Not only did Dícho dine with Pátraic, but his wife Fiona joined them as well. The discussion went on until evening shadows were announcing the end of another day.

"It is time for me to go back to my monastery," said Pátraic.

Dícho and Fiona were smiling. The attitude of the host had completely changed. His wife and he looked at each other inquiringly. Then Dícho spoke.

"Truthfully I must tell you I was beginning to have doubts about my druids. I will see what we will do with them. We offer you our apologies for the reception you received. My own fear was that you, too, were some kind of conjurer who had come to deceive the people, possibly in a different way. How soon can we become members of your faith?"

Pátraic's heart leaped. This had been exactly his plan. To convert the leaders! A prince would become a Christian … he probably would dismiss his druids. His subjects would now become interested.

"I will send one of my priests to instruct you and bring you into our faith. He will arrive very soon, probably in a few days. Meantime you might like to tell your people that you will be baptized, and possibly host a celebration on the occasion."

As Pátraic walked the pathways back to his monastery, he spent his time in prayer, thanking the Most Holy Trinity for the miracle that had taken place. A prince of the people would become a Christian. Pátraic prayed the Lord's Prayer over and over again with frequent invocations of *thy kingdom come.*

On his return home, Pátraic announced the joyful news to his monastic companions. A prince of the people would become Christian! There were shouts of "Alleluia," and the room was filled with elation. First success had come in a very short time indeed.

Pátraic was overjoyed. Thoughts of Blawse and Aogán and the seanchaí flowed through his mind. God's providence was at work!

Blawse had been called to God. He had been a wonderful companion in the early days of slavery. Pátraic remembered him in affectionate prayer. He was not very far away from Sliabh Mis and decided he would make an effort to visit Aogán. After all those years it would be a happy meeting.

When he knocked on Aogán's door he was greeted by Aogán himself.

Aogán wasn't sure to whom he was speaking, as Pátraic's beard had mostly disappeared and now he looked much more stately.

"Aogán," said Pátraic, "don't you remember me? Do you recall trekking up to where I was on Sliabh Mis Mountain, and how you introduced me to the seanchaí visitations and celebrations? And you also taught me the Celtic language. You helped me escape. I eventually got to An Frainc, and I will tell you the rest later. But now, I am a Christian bishop and I have come back to bring Christianity to all of Éireann and hopefully get rid of the druids."

He didn't need to say anymore. Aogán threw himself at Pátraic in a blissful embrace. His voice was hoarse.

"I can't believe it. You are back, and after all those years we meet again."

"You kept me strong for those awful years. You are my friend and my companion, especially after the death of Blawse. And how could I ever forget you?"

"Come in, come in," said Aogán, "My parents are still here. Of course they have gotten older, but they will be delighted to see you."

With that he took Pátraic by his arm and led him into their little home. It hadn't changed much since his years of slavery.

The welcome from Aogán's parents equaled that of Aogán himself, and they, too, were ecstatic at seeing their past slave friend returned in such a triumphant way. A great meal was prepared for Pátraic and his companions. Pátraic was allotted a comfortable bed, while his companions slept on the kitchen floor.

At morning breakfast there was discussion about many things. After all, there was indeed much to talk about. Pátraic inquired about Meelco.

"He is the same as ever, possibly even worse. His wife died a short time after your escape."

"What did he do after I escaped?" asked Pátraic.

Aogán spoke, "After you went missing, Meelco came to our door in a rage and accused my parents and me for helping you to escape. In actual fact, he drew his whip and lashed me on the back. I am not sure whether he had spies looking out for you at Beal Feirste, but I would guess he had. Following the death of his wife, he has become a loner and rarely goes among his tenants."

"I would like to visit him," said Pátraic.

"You are a brave man, but I would urge you to be careful."

"Then," said Pátraic, "I would like to send him a message that I am coming, to find out if he will receive me."

"My best suggestion," replied Aogán, "would be to send one of your companions to Meelco's door. Meelco will never have met him before, and so he may listen to what your emissary tells him."

With that, Pátraic nodded his head, turned to one of his companions, and asked him to go to Meelco and let him know that his one-time slave Succat had returned to Éireann, and he wanted to see his old master. It was done. It took the selected courier about an hour to get to Meelco. Everything was quiet outside, and there didn't seem to be any sign of life. To the visitor it looked like a deteriorated home.

He stood at the opening to the home and called out several times, "Meelco, are you here?"

It took Meelco several minutes to appear. The messenger saw an old, stooped, and unkempt man with a long beard and a kitchen in disarray at his back. No woman was around.

"May the gods be with you," said the messenger, using the old Celtic manner of greeting.

"What is your business?" inquired Meelco, his voice lacking welcome or hospitality.

"I am here to let you know that your former slave Succat has returned to Éireann with the Good News of Christianity, and he would like to visit with his old master."

"Succat is back?" inquired Meelco with an air of surprise and suspicion. "If he comes close to me, I will kill him with my own hands."

"No, you won't; he is now a very respected man who is spreading good news through Éireann, and he would very much like to see you."

By this time Meelco seemed to have a bellicose attitude that went from his first quiet question to an inexplicable rage.

"You are a stupid man," said Meelco, "if you think I am going to allow an escaped slave to visit my home."

"He will give you good advice," replied Pátraic's representative, "and I feel certain that a very prudent man like you would enjoy meeting him, and seeing how much he has changed."

"He will never enter my house," exclaimed Meelco, who appeared to be getting more and more agitated at the conversation.

"He is only a short distance away," replied the representative, "and he can be here within the afternoon."

"I said," bellowed Meelco, "that he will never enter this house."

He was now talking like a mentally deranged person. He turned around and quickly took coals from the fire and scattered them around the kitchen.

"I will burn this house down," said Meelco, "before I allow that miserable Succat to enter this dwelling."

The furnishings in the kitchen caught fire immediately, and the emissary ran to safety. In seconds the house was in flames. Meelco never came out, and the remains of his body were found among the ashes by neighbors who ran to the home when they saw the conflagration. Because of the flames, they could do nothing, as Meelco was trapped by the inferno all around him.

Pátraic's emissary sadly headed back to relate the incident to Pátraic, who was awaiting his return at Aogán's home.

When he heard the bad news, Pátraic shook his head.

"It is tragic that Meelco had become so mentally deranged. Let us pray for his soul."

He remained silent for a moment as if in prayer. Then he spoke.

"We need to return to our monastery for a little rest. There we can make plans to visit Teamhair and the high king."

"It is not likely he will see you," said Aogán, "and I wish I could join your companions, but I am the only one here to take care of my aging parents. However, let me say, your visit brought joy. I would like to be baptized before you leave and become a member of your Christian faith."

The baptism was done within a short time, as Pátraic's companions explained the truths of Christianity to Aogán.

"How will I practice my faith?" Aogán asked.

"By their deeds you shall know them, said Christ, so I urge you to be kind and loving and caring for all of those around you. Indeed, you had that quality when you came to me first, and we were setting the traps to catch the rabbits. And don't forget to pray to the One True God every day. Keep in mind our little monastery that is surrounded by a very good Christian community is not very far away from you, and perhaps at one time or another you may be able to come join us in our worship."

Aogán nodded. He reflected how Pátraic had changed since their first meeting so many years ago. And now, so had he.

Pátraic and his companions left to return toward Loch Cúan.

Chapter 17

Flames at Twilight

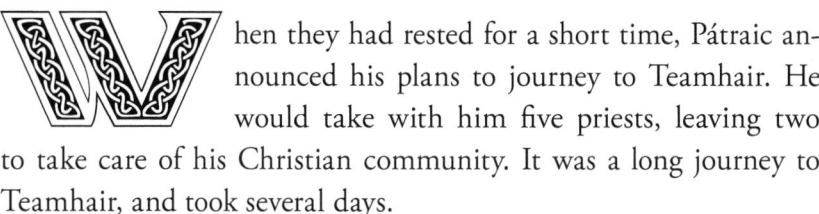hen they had rested for a short time, Pátraic announced his plans to journey to Teamhair. He would take with him five priests, leaving two to take care of his Christian community. It was a long journey to Teamhair, and took several days.

Along the way, Pátraic received some bad news. Bishop Palladius was no longer in Éireann. Some months ago he had been banished from the country by the king of Laigheann,[111] Bréssal Bélach.[112] The news was deflating. It meant Pátraic was now the only bishop in Éireann. He was on his own, but in his mind he decided he would change all that. He would consecrate new bishops as necessary.

Pátraic's passion to spread the faith was unquenchable. Eventually they reached the outskirts of the Hill of Teamhair and from a distance viewed the palace of Laoghaire,[113] high king of Éireann.

Pátraic saw, too, the Cnoc Shláine. He remembered Eochaidh's story that Cnoc Shláine was a little bit lower than Teamhair but that, on the other hand, most of Teamhair could be easily seen from the top of the Cnoc Shláine. It was the month of March 433. It was I July

---

[111] Province of Leinster.

[112] wikipedia.org/List_of_kings_of_Leinster.

[113] Spelling now shortened to Laoire, pronounced Lee-ra.

Week, when Christians celebrate the death and resurrection of Jesus the Lord.

That year, it turned out, the spring celebration of the druidic gods coincided with the Christian Holy Saturday evening. By order of the king, farmers throughout the land were directed to light large bonfires immediately after King Laoghaire had lit his own fire on Teamhair. This custom was to alleviate the gods as spring took over. Following the ceremonious torching on the Hill of Teamhair, the country would be spectacularly ablaze as far as the eye could behold. Surely the gods had to take notice!

This news came to Pátraic as a surprise. The high king's fire! On Holy Saturday evening! He already knew the religious ceremonies he would lead somewhere or other on that very same evening would begin with the Paschal Fire that announced the Light of Christ in the world. How interesting! Pátraic was no coward! He would go ahead with his own ceremonies, and the flames announcing the "Light of Christ" would light the sky in advance of the king's fire. It was a daunting task! But he would make it happen!

He turned to his companions and told them they were all going to climb the Cnoc Shláine on Holy Saturday evening and celebrate the Paschal Liturgy at twilight.

"But you will wait until the king's fire has been lit? That would be a very dangerous thing to do," remarked one of his companions. "We will all be arrested, possibly executed for such a grievous offense. The druids will surely be offended, probably even more than the king, and our lives will be in peril."

"Yes, I understand," exclaimed Pátraic. "It is a way of bringing the king's people to us irrespective of what they do when they get here. We have to put our trust in God. Remember the words of the psalm, used by Jesus, too: 'For he shall send his angels to guard you, and on their hands they shall bear you up.'"[114]

"But," said one of his companion priests, "how can this be a

---

[114] Psalm 91, New American Bible.

successful mission? It will anger the high king and possibly turn him against Christians in a way that our Christian communities may be eliminated. Remember Palladius? A short time ago we heard he was expelled by the king of Laighainn for almost nothing other than the king's hatred for his teaching."

Pátraic replied, "We must have confidence in God. Our battle is not against the high king, but against his druids who are all over the land, a greedy, jealous, mendacious horde who are looking after their own interests. For our mission to succeed, we must combat the druids."

"But how will we get to meet the druids if we are all killed here on this Cnoc Shláine?"

"We all have heard that King Laoghaire is a peaceful and generous king, so we really have to hope that instead of killing us we will be put on trial at the king's palace. Now let's gather materials for the fire and carry them to the top of the hill so that when it comes to twilight we will be ready to begin our sacred ceremonies and light our Paschal Fire before the king lights his fire. In that way we will be announcing the dawning of the Light of Christ to all the people. Now if any of you would prefer to leave and be safe, you may do so."

It was obvious to all that Pátraic was adamant. His courage was contagious. Nobody left. On top of Cnoc Shláine they made preparations for their liturgical Easter fire in celebration of the Resurrection of the Lord. It would be large enough to be seen not only on Teamhair, but throughout a large span of countryside. The missionaries waited nervously as the sun began to set. Pátraic encouraged them not to be afraid.

Finally the light of day was beginning to fade and Pátraic announced, "Lumen Christi."[115]

The Easter ceremony had begun. The fire was lighted. There was still no sign of a fire from Teamhair. The flame that had been put to the kindling had erupted into a massive furnace that lit up the sky as far as the eye could see.

---

[115] Light of Christ. begins the Paschal Liturgy of the Catholic Church to this day.

In the palace at Teamhair arch-druid Cuan Toirneach[116] was busy with his subordinates preparing the fire to mollify the god of spring and all the gods and subgods. There was an abrupt commotion among his fellows. They were all looking toward the northeast.

"Look at the huge fire on Cnoc Shláine! The king's law has been violated. This has never happened before! What kind of madman has done this?"

Anger spewed from the mouth of Cuan Toirneach, displaying a fury that frightened all around him.

"That fire is an insult to the god of spring. Now we are obligated to placate the god who has received such contempt."

His voice was getting louder.

"I am going to inform the king now, and I will advise him to send his troops and destroy whoever is guilty of this treacherous act."

He raced to the king and reported there was a huge fire on Cnoc Shláine.

"This is a great offense against the gods and against your majesty. We were just about to come and escort you to the place of our own fire. You are the one, O King, who lights the first fire."

King Laoghaire appeared very upset, but his expression of anger came nowhere near that of Cuan Toirneach. He did not immediately make any response, but still sitting in his seat he looked at the floor in a posture of thought.

Cuan Toirneach was impatient.

"O King, we need to lose no time in tracking down the rebel who has done this. We can have him put to death immediately. Allow our soldiers to do this right now."

The king finally looked at Cuan Toirneach.

"Send my troops to Cnoc Shláine, and bring the guilty here to me. He is not to be touched until I have seen him. He has violated the law, but we do not know why. If he is insane, why should we kill him?"

Cuan Toirneach replied, "I believe we should kill him in either

---

[116] The Hound of Thunder.

case. This fire that has been started sets an unacceptable example for your subjects. We must extinguish this fire immediately, otherwise it may lead to something—another fire—that will be impossible to quench."

King Laoghaire responded impatiently, "What you are saying may indeed be correct. But I am sure our reign will not collapse because some foolish or insane person has lit a fire ahead of us."

Toirneach was now frustrated, and this frustration, joined with his state of mind, compelled him to respond.

"O King, we are losing time. Something *has to be* done. We need to do it now. It will be essential to have this person or persons arrested and brought here."

"Very good, I will immediately get word to my soldiers to go in pursuit of the enemy. However, there is to be no killing or maiming until the guilty comes before me," responded the king.

Thereupon Laoghaire sent for his commanding officer and ordered him to send a battalion of troops to find the culprit. Then he gave him an order that nobody was to be interfered with physically until they had appeared before him.

On Cnoc Shláine, Pátraic and his companions were nervously carrying out their own religious ceremony. They had almost come to the end when a troop of soldiers came into view down in the valley.

Pátraic then announced, "This is according to our plan. Let us all trust the Lord."

In no time the soldiers were upon them, but Pátraic and his companions remained still.

The leader of the battalion shouted loudly, "You have violated the king's order and the law of the land."

With that, one of the soldiers leaned forward, pointing a spear at Pátraic, but the head of the battalion yelled, "Do not touch him. The king has ordered that he wants to speak to these people and then put them on trial at the palace."

Meanwhile, the battalion head arrested the accused, bound their hands behind their backs, and told them they were all going to be taken to the palace.

"But," added the commander, "not for long. You will all be tried and put to death. Our king and our druids will not put up with this."

Pátraic's little group was led down the hill toward Teamhair. They were able to speak with each other in the French language, which was entirely unknown to their Celtic captors.

"What do you think will happen?" asked one of Pátraic's priests.

"We can't be sure of that," answered Pátraic, "but I suspect there will be a confrontation with the druids. Most likely in front of the king. Try to leave the answers to me."

By the time they traveled through the valley and climbed the Hill of Teamhair, they could see the country around them alight with bonfires, with the king's fire, of course, a mighty incendiary colossus. They were taken into the presence of the king, who was sitting at an oak table.

"Who among you lit that fire? Who is your leader?"

"I am," replied Pátraic.

Laoghaire gestured with an air of aggravation.

"Sit here," he said to Pátraic, pointing to a seat to his left at the top of the table. "The rest of you villains may take your seats beside your leader."

At the same time a large number of druids seated themselves to the right hand of the king. Pátraic noticed immediately his group was facing a multitude of adversaries.

The king spoke first. He looked at Pátraic and said, "Well, my friend, how do you defend yourself? You and your companions have violated my orders. This is the first time a happening of this kind has taken place."

Before Pátraic could reply, a druid spoke up.

"This man," he said, "with his companions, dared you, O King, and I suggest we dispatch them immediately."

The king replied with a scowl to the druid, "Let him speak for himself."

Then he looked at Pátraic as if expecting him to defend himself. Pátraic knew the king was waiting for an answer.

"O King," he said, "our intention when we lit the fire was to join in unity with Christian peoples all over the world in worshipping the One True God."

Again a druid interrupted with a sarcastic question.

"And tell us, who is the One True God? We have twelve gods here in Éireann, and we mollify them all."

"Tell me," replied Pátraic, "how you explain the existence of twelve gods? How do they communicate with each other? And has there ever been a war between your gods? The fact is if there are many gods, there is no god at all. We Christians believe in a loving God. He is a God of three persons: Father, Son, and Holy Spirit."

There was another interruption by a druid.

"Then you have three gods."

Pátraic signaled to his companion saying, "Please go out and bring in a shamrock."

The companion was back in a few minutes.

Pátraic held up the shamrock.

"What have I got here in my hand?"

"A shamrock," replied the druid. "What's that got to do with this discussion?"

Pátraic replied, "Can you see the stem? How many leaves are on it?"

"Three," replied the druid.

"Three," replied Pátraic, "and how many stems?"

"I am not blind," replied the druid, who at this time was increasing his hostility.

"Well," said Pátraic quietly, not looking at the druid but at the king, "there are three leaves in this one little stem, so there are three Divine Persons in the one God."

The king was impressed. The druids were looking more and more anxious.

Pátraic continued, "You, O King, and the majority of the people of Éireann, are being misled and tricked by these druids you have around you. They are interested only in themselves, and you won't find a druid who lives with a poor farmer. You will find them in the rich homes of the princes and making pretense that somehow or other they have a special connection with the gods. And let me say, these are the gods who don't exist. Our God is a loving God who sent His Divine Son down here to earth to show us how to love and forgive, and how to live our lives close to Him."

Then he addressed the most hostile of the druids, who turned out to be Cuan Toirneach, and said to him, "Tell me, oh druid, do you offer sacrifice to your gods?"

"Well, indeed we do. And we do it frequently."

"You offer human sacrifice, where you tie up a young man or a young woman and slay them. What makes you think this pleases your gods? And if you believe it so much, I am curious to find out why you don't take one of your druids who you claim is so pleasing to your gods—why not take such a pleasing person and offer him in human sacrifice?"

Cuan Toirneach replied, "If we were to do that, there would be fewer druids, and that would not be pleasing to the gods either."

Pátraic replied, "So you think that killing someone is an act of reparation, but you never sentence any of yourselves to such a death. Now, let me tell you about the Son of God—and I am talking about the One True God—He would never want His people to be murdered in reparation, but taught us to love each other."

Pátraic turned to the king.

"O King, when the Son of God came among us He allowed Himself to be put to death and crucified by His enemies. His Father in Heaven allowed this one act of reparation by His Divine Son to cover for all eternity the sins and weaknesses of His people. Keep in mind this was the Son of God, and His offering of Himself was approved and accepted by the Father who sent Him. O King, the Son of God died for us, and

His was the only human sacrifice ever pleasing to God. So much so that His death, the death of a man who had taken on our own nature, ended all human sacrifice because what could be more pleasing to the Father than the offering made by His own Divine Son? And because He had taken on human nature, His offering represented all of us, and we are all saved and look forward to Heaven, thanks to the Blood of Christ, shed on our behalf. I am sure you know about King Cormac and how he had a vision telling him that this Son of God would come again and accept the souls of the people who followed Him, or who wanted to be good people—and you know that Cormac wanted to be buried at Ross, where he had the vision. His druids wanted to bury him at Bru Na Ri. Most of the kings of Ireland were buried there, but Cormac wanted to be buried facing the rising sun and expecting that when the Son of God comes again he would be able to see Him immediately. The druids disagreed, and wanted to bury him in the cemetery of all the previous kings. But you will recall when they tried to cross the Boine the waters rose and took the body away and deposited it at the place nearby where Cormac wanted to be buried in the first place. That was a sign of God helping His people and that Cormac's vision was indeed a true vision, a revelation by God Himself, that He has more power than all of the druids together and that what He says must be followed."

By this time the druids were all looking anxious.

"But, O King," said Toirneach, "that was a freak of nature."

Pátraic interjected, "A freak of nature? Tell us how this freak of nature happened four times in a row."

"It was just a freak of nature that has never happened since."

"Let me ask you," said Pátraic, "how many times the River Boine has interfered by capturing the bodies of the dead who were being transported across the river."

There was a murmur among the druids, and one blurted out, "First it was a shamrock, and now it has to do with the burial of King Cormac. I appeal to you, O King, to sentence these men to death immediately."

Pátraic turned to the king.

"O, King," he said, "your druids are so desperate for power. They do not want any discussion on the One True God. At this very time millions of people throughout An Euróip[117] are gathering to celebrate the death of the Son of God. There is more I want to tell you. This Divine Son, who was scourged, tortured, and finally crucified, rose again three days afterward. In fact, He was crucified on a Friday morning, and many people came to understand how much God loves us. And we have been promised that we, too, are able to understand the Love of God for us. And His yearning that we be with Him in Heaven."

Toirneach finally could take no more. He replied, "Pátraic, you are a scoundrel who came in here lying to us and trying to change our beliefs."

There was silence for a while, and finally the king spoke.

"I am going to consider this matter, and I will order my attendants to prepare quarters for this man and his friends so that he can fully inform me on his beliefs. I am impressed by his courage and his commitment to come to a strange country, where he might be in danger of death. Take Pátraic and give him the best room in the palace, and settle his companions comfortably so that they can rest peacefully during the night. And I assure you there will be no executions, no more offerings of human beings—and tomorrow I will sit with Pátraic and try to learn more about his beliefs and the Christian way of living."

The druids looked at each other. They would not dare argue with the king.

Pátraic's dream of ruining the druids was beginning to take effect.

---

[117] Europe.

Chapter 18

A Royal Decree

Next morning was bright and breezy. King Laoghaire was up early. He inquired from his servants if Pátraic and his companions might have begun their day too. Said Laoghaire, "Go and tell Pátraic and the others that the king wishes to meet with them over breakfast."

The servant bowed and left the room. He found them still sleeping. The uncertainties of the day before had taken their toll. However, the servant did manage to get the word across that King Laoghaire would have breakfast with them. This pleased Pátraic because it indicated that King Laoghaire was seriously considering his faith beliefs.

When they got to the breakfast room, the king was already seated with his wife, Angias,[118] at his side, awaiting their arrival. On the table was a large bowl of quail eggs and other delicacies. The king signaled them to be seated, inviting Pátraic to sit by him.

Pátraic greeted the king in a friendly fashion.

"How are you this morning, O, King?"

The king replied with a smile that it was a lovely day outside, and he liked the crisp March weather.

---

[118] Angias appears to have belonged to a royal Munster family. Tradition says she asked Pátraic to pray that she would have a son who would become high king of Ireland. It so happened. His name was Lugaid Mac Lóegairi.

Pátraic was bold in his reply.

"And which of the gods do you think is in charge of weather?"

The king did not answer immediately, and there was silence at the table for several seconds. Then the king replied, "Your God is in charge of the weather, and if I understand correctly, He is the governor of all things. There is only one God. Now, I have been thinking all night about your message yesterday, and I have decided to learn more. I invite you all to stay here in my palace for three or four more days so that I can learn and try to understand the Christianity you talk about."

"We will be glad," said Pátraic, "to stay here. We can take turns at instruction, and I am sure that when you hear the good news, you will be impressed and happy. So when, O, King, would you like us to begin? When you are ready, I will go first, and then an hour or so afterward, one of my companions will come and continue the lesson."

The king replied, "That would be several hours, and we must eat sometime again, and perhaps take a walk outside in the spring air."

"Well," said Pátraic, "that would be very good, and since you invited us to stay, we can remain here for whatever length of time is necessary. And, O King, I would be glad to walk with you outside and get some breath of the good March air myself."

"I will be happy to have you with me," replied Laoghaire, "and perhaps even then we can discuss some of my uncertainties about your Christianity."

"Be assured, O King, you will be fully educated, with your uncertainties gone, by the time we leave here."

The king smiled.

"You seem very sure of yourself," he replied, "but I will cooperate with everything you tell me, and ask questions when I am unsure."

"Excellent," said Pátraic. "We will be happy to begin at any time that pleases you."

Laoghaire replied, "I would like to meet you in my comfortable living quarters, just down the corridor, in about an hour or so. And your companions may entertain themselves any way they wish by looking around the palace, speaking with my soldiers, or just resting. I would guess you are all very tired. It is a long way from Loch Cúan to Teamhair on foot."

"It is indeed," replied Pátraic. "I am sure my friends will wish to spend time in prayer, communicating with our God of Love, and whatever time they have left over can be used as you say. I will come to your living quarters in an hour's time, and we can begin our discussions."

Again, the king smiled and said, "Be prepared for a lot of questions. You have made me very curious about your Christian religion, and I can hardly wait to begin our conversations. Now let us take a breather, and I will meet you in an hour's time. I hope you all enjoyed your breakfast. I am so glad you have come to visit me, even though it put your life at stake. Whether I become a Christian or not, you are good men, and I will send word to the druids they are not to interfere with you. In fact, I may invite some of my favorite druids to listen to the discussions with me."

The hour's break gave Pátraic time to go to his room and pray. He spent all that time kneeling and sitting with the Lord. By the time the hour was up, his passion for the gospel had been increased, and he continued to pray that Laoghaire would become Christian. This, of course, would be bad for the druids as it would signal the end of their authority over the people and their self-indulgence with wealthy landowners.

In due time, Pátraic went to meet the king in his living quarters. The quarters were not as stately as he might have expected. His youthful association with Roman leaders was never far from his mind. The room was nicely furnished with oak chairs, and some of the chairs were equipped with cushions, and were basically the equivalent of an armchair. It was the very first time that Pátraic had been introduced to Éireann nobility of this kind. He had thoughts of his visit to Prince Dicho, who was his first upper-class convert. But Dicho's home was much less opulent than that of the high king. Pátraic was sitting in the room praying when King Laoghaire entered. Pátraic stood and bowed.

Laoghaire immediately invited him to be seated on a comfortable chair. Then he himself sat across from Pátraic, just a few feet away.

"First of all," said Laoghaire, "tell me about Christianity and how it got that name."

Pátraic replied, "A Christian is a follower of Christ, who is the Son of God. As I mentioned previously, when I showed you the shamrock, He is Divine. You must always keep in mind the meaning of the Trinity and that Christ is the second person of the Blessed Trinity. There are three Divine Persons in one God."

The king became very involved in learning the new religion. And so, throughout that day, Pátraic's companions, and Pátraic himself, took turns continuing the story and the teachings of the Christian Church. Toward late afternoon, while being instructed, the king asked to see Pátraic again. The king seemed to be impressed, but he had a problem when it came to the resurrection of Christ.

"How could that be?" he asked. "And how can you be sure the body wasn't stolen and hidden by his followers?"

"Well," said Pátraic, "the Resurrection is the solid proof that Christ is Divine. Many people saw Him after His Resurrection and every one of His disciples faced death because of their belief. Now, if the story of the Resurrection was a lie, and the followers of Christ were not sure about it, why would they give their lives defending a story that might be false? The fact is, they had seen the Christ after His Resurrection, and they knew that He was God and that when they died they would be a part of His heavenly kingdom."

"So they saw Him after His Resurrection," said the king, "but how do you know that?"

Pátraic replied, "It is a historical fact that the body of Christ was never found, and four of His followers wrote histories of His life. It is a beautiful story. It makes a lot of sense, and it tells us that Christ remained with His followers for forty days thereafter. And then He ascended into Heaven to be with God His Father. His twelve disciples faced death for Him.[119] Who would allow themselves to die on a mere possibility? They saw the Risen Lord and therefore knew that He would take them to Himself in His heavenly kingdom."

"Pátraic, what you have told me about the life of your Christ is impressive. You have answered all of my questions with so much certainty in your voice that I believe everything you told me, and I wish to become a Christian. We did talk about the special ceremony of baptism, and I would like to be baptized in a few days' time. I need to get the word out to my subjects, my friends, and my relatives that I have found the One True God and that He is all powerful. So that is why I want to join you, but I would also like my people to watch the ceremony and to know that I really am a Christian."

"Good," said Pátraic. "You can be baptized on any day you choose, and you can be assured you will never regret it."

"I am not sure how I will handle the druids," said the king. "I know they will object. They are my counselors, and if I am a Christian they can't give me Christian advice. I will notify them tomorrow morning. I will gather them in this very room. I hope you can be present with your own companions."

"Very good," said Pátraic, "and I know you will be blessed all the days of your life. Your announcement may shock your subjects, but that may make them inquire into the One True God, and many of them may become Christian themselves."

"That would be good for Éireann," replied the king. "Our subjects may imitate me when they find the truth. It will all take time."

"All right," said Pátraic, "my companions and I will gather here in the morning and be present to support you in your arguments with them. You know, O, King, that it will be a confrontational meeting, and you will need help. So have a good rest until we meet again."

Pátraic left the room and assembled his companions.

---

[119] Eleven were martyred; one, John, was saved miraculously from a cistern of boiling oil.

Morning came, and all were assembled at the king's table. The druids were scowling in anticipation of what the message of the king might be.

"I called you all here," said the king, "to talk to you about the one God, whom I have discovered through my friend Pátraic."

The king reached out while saying this and put his hand on Pátraic's shoulder in a gesture of high respect.

"I have to tell you now that I am going to become a Christian, and I will allow you all to do what you please. However, at this moment, none of you is qualified to advise me in a way that follows Christian pursuits."

"But we have been advising you for many years," said Cuan Toirneach (many druids were present).

"I am afraid," said the king, "you won't be able to counsel me anymore, and I will have to let you go. However, if you care to inquire with Pátraic and his companions, as did I, about the veracity of the Christian faith, I have no doubt these visitors who brought the Good News will be glad to inform you and to teach you. For example, from now on there will be no human sacrifices, no torture of suspects, and each person will receive the same justice. Do you understand what I am saying?"

There was total silence in the room. None would dare to question the king in public. The druids feared that their power was being destroyed. Pátraic encouragingly invited each of them to learn the faith and use their Christianity when rendering their opinions to the king. Only one druid came forward to seek instruction.

Cuan Toirneach—the chief druid—spoke up.

"I am resigning now, O, King. It is my fear that these flames at twilight will continue to glow. I still believe this man and his accomplices should be put to death."

Laoghaire glared at the druid who dared to speak to him this way and said, "You will no longer tell me what to do. Nor will I allow you to stay on and poison me. Unless you wish to follow me into Christianity, you are dismissed from this meeting as of now."

Cuan stood up, bowed to the king, and with a look of dejection that was evident to all, left the room.

Those who did not resign lost their positions of power and were eventually forced to leave the palace of King Laoghaire. Meanwhile, Laoghaire invited Pátraic to remain on for further time so that he and his companions could answer any questions or doubts the king might have. The one druid did indeed follow up on his promise that he wanted to learn about the Christian faith, and before the weekend he was well educated in the truth of Christianity.

Pátraic spoke to the king about leaving, but the king said, "No. You must remain for a few days more. I am going to summon my subjects and tell them about my newfound beliefs, and when they gather, you will baptize me as the people are gathered around. I want the message made known that there is a new regime here and that the druids will no longer have power to interfere with people's lives."

"*Sár mhaith,*"[120] replied Pátraic. But before he could say anymore, Loaghaire spoke again.

"At my baptism, another fire will be lit that will be seen all around. When my subjects inquire, they will be told there is a new light in Éireann, and the king is a Christian."

For Pátraic this was a major victory. The high king of Éireann was going to announce his Christianity. He felt there was a major likelihood that those who would be present at the king's baptism might ask a lot of questions, and some might even want to be baptized themselves. Pátraic had remained longer than he had intended at Teamhair, so he asked the king if he would choose a day coming up soon to celebrate the occasion. The king readily agreed, noting that he wanted to let his people know and he would send the word out that anyone who wanted to come to his baptism would be welcome.

On the following Saturday evening the crowds, including princes and nobles, did indeed gather outside the palace of the king, in a show of respect. Pátraic and his companions accompanied the king to the

---

[120] Excellent.

raised platform that had been placed there for the occasion. At the beginning of the service, Pátraic bowed humbly toward His Majesty. Then he spoke. He explained what baptism meant, how hospitable King Laoghaire was, and told the group hospitality was one of the tenets of Christianity. Having made his explanation, Pátraic baptized the king, saying, while pouring water over his head, "Laoghaire, I baptize you in the name of the Father, and of the Son, and of the Holy Spirit."

At that moment, flames ascended once more from the Hill of Teamhair. The light of day was fading as the flames of Laoghaire's bonfire ascended heavenward, diminishing the shadows created by the setting sun.

Following Laoghaire's baptism, Pátraic continued with the two other baptisms—Angias and the one nondissenting druid.

Those in attendance were cheering. They were especially happy that the reign of the druids had been well-indented, to be replaced by a belief that encompassed compassion and forgiveness. The king waved to his people, all of whom bowed to him as he spoke.

"Listen to Pátraic and his companions," said the king. "You will be happier and wiser if you do."[121]

The ceremonies came to an end as all were singing the anthem of the king. The day was dying; its light was fading fast. But in Pátraic's heart he felt the glow of the perpetual light, of which King Cormac had dreamed—that was now enveloping a land that he loved.

---

[121] Although converted, this king became somewhat disinterested in practicing his religion. It is the opinion of scholars that while he supported Pátraic, his deeds did not manifest his beliefs.

Chapter 19

A Saintly Meeting

The weekend had passed with celebrations at Teamhair in honor of King Laoghaire, who had minimized the power of the druids and whose popularity rose to a larger degree than it had ever been before. The king was happy to be a Christian, and Pátraic and his companions delighted in his conversion.

"I would like to visit with Deaglán,[122] one of the converts of Bishop Palladius, who was banished, you may recall, by Bréssal Bélach, the king of Leinster. Word has come to me that Deaglán is doing wonderful work in the south, and I would like to visit him both for encouragement and even advice."

"But you have no transport," replied the king. "Are you planning to walk all that distance?"

---

[122] Deaglán, known in English as Saint Declan, was the son of a Déisi chief. He appears to have been approximately the same age as Patrick and also died around the same time. He is credited with founding a major monastery at Ardmore, County Waterford, Ireland, and is known for his outstanding zeal in helping Christianize Ireland. His monastery, in later years to be known itself as the Déisi, became very famous. The ruins of his church are still to be seen in Ardmore. The nickname for all of County Waterford is now The Déisi. The Déisi was originally a family living near Tara, the seat of the high king of Ireland. They had a dispute with King Cormac MacAirt and were banished from Leinster and appropriated lands in the region of Ardmore, County Waterford.

"Those are my plans," replied Pátraic. "It will take us quite a while, and perhaps we can give the Word of Christ to people along the way."

"You may do that," said the king, "but I am going to give all of you horses so you can get to your destination much faster. Do you know exactly where you are going?"

"First," replied Pátraic, "I thank your Majesty for your gift that will surely help us. I don't know exactly where Deaglán lives, but I will inquire along the way, and certainly someone will know the exact location of his church."

"Very good," said the king. "I wish you the blessings of the One True God, and please be assured we will welcome you back to Teamhair at any time. Let me call my servants, who will find the horses for you. They have plenty to choose from, horses already trained, and I want you and your companions to be comfortable on your journey. If you stay at an inn, they will take care of your horses."

Then unexpectedly and without formality the king handed Pátraic a bag of precious nuggets.

"These will help you on your way and hopefully for a good while beyond."

Pátraic blessed the king. His companions and he rode away on young horses that would certainly be capable of serving them for a long time to come. They galloped out of Teamhair around noon, and Pátraic used the sun to direct him to the south. The journey was not in keeping with their expectations. Up to this time they had not found themselves in jeopardy as they traveled along. This journey was going to be different!

They had traveled for a day when they stopped to inquire about lodgings. The man to whom they spoke appeared friendly as they asked for directions. They thanked him and journeyed according to his instructions. Suddenly from a clump of trees they were accosted by four dangerous-looking characters. The first one signaled them to stop. There was a hostile vibe in their voices.

The leader shouted, "Who are you?"

Pátraic replied, "I am Pátraic, and these men riding with me are my companions. We are bringing the news of the One True God to Éireann. We mean no harm to anyone, and we are on our way to find lodgings for the night."

"So you are, are you? And why are you traveling at all in this area?"

"As I said, we are spreading the Good News, and we want it to be heard by all the people."

"We have heard that! You were visiting King Laoghaire recently, and because of you a number of druids were displaced. Are you trying to get rid of our druids?"

"No, we mean no harm to the druids, but the truth may hurt them. They believe in many gods. My companions and I know there is only one God."

"We don't believe that, and we are sure you are simply enriching yourselves by spreading lies about your one God. Get down off your horses. You are coming with us."

Pátraic's companions were looking toward him for a response.

Pátraic calmly replied, "You have no reason to hold us up. Are you looking for ransom?"

The leader shouted once more, "Get down off your horses or be killed!"

Pátraic slowly lowered himself to the ground, with his companions following suit.

"Now each one of you walk with your horse in the direction you are led. Do not try to escape, or you will be pierced with our arrows. You will know we mean it when the first arrow goes straight through your body."

The little band realized they were captives. They were dealing with dangerous men—men who more than likely were highway robbers and who would have no compassion on their victims. As they bid the doing of the rogue leader, Pátraic was praying for safety and so were his other priests. They walked through a little wood for a short time and then came into the open again. A home appeared not very far away. Someone was standing at the door. As they got closer, they realized it was the man who had given them directions. Now they knew he had callously directed them into this situation. Their horses were tied to a couple of trees out front, and the captives were led into the home.

The individual who appeared to be the leader of the ruffians spoke.

"Take a look outside," he said, "and see it for the last time. You have misled our king with untruths. You are deceitfully profiting for yourselves, and you are enemies of the people."

Pátraic spoke up.

"We spent a week at the palace on Teamhair with King Laoghaire. How does that make us enemies of the people? The king became a Christian; he is now one of us, and I am sure he will punish severely anyone who may interfere with his sovereignty."

Pátraic's voice rose.

"The king is our friend, a great friend. Anyone who tries to harm us will suffer the consequences."

"We don't care about the king. He will be gone in a short time. He has enemies who would like to see him dead.[123] The druids have been honored for hundreds of years. They are our priests. They communicate with the gods."

"So you wish to dispute about the druids?"

"The druids are not thieves like all of you. Where did you find those horses?"

"They are the horses of King Laoghaire."

The leader fell suddenly silent as if stopped in his tracks! After a long pause he spoke again.

"Did you steal them from the palace?"

---

[123] Traditions of King Laoghaire's death are varied. He was not killed, and there are references that he died somewhere in the Liffey Valley. (The River Liffey flows through Dublin, Ireland.) Other myths report he was cursed by the druids and died as a result of the curse. cf History of St. Patrick, google.com.

Pátraic's voice had great strength in the reply he made.

"Are you saying we are thieves? You well know it would be impossible to steal from the abode of the king."

The man who had directed them into ambush along the way now spoke for the first time.

"They are valuable horses, and they are ours now."

One of Pátraic's companions spoke defiantly. "You would steal the king's horses would you? I can tell you now that if you do that you will suffer the loss of your head at Teamhair!"

"If we take your heads first, how will the king find out?"

"For two reasons. First, we are representing the Son of God, who came among us only five centuries ago. He has sent His angels to watch over us. And second, it won't take very long until the news reaches Teamhair that we have been killed and the king's horses stolen."

"What are angels?" asked the leader of the ruffians.

"Angels are Spirits," retorted Pátraic. "They are God's servants sent specially to watch over us and care for us. They are not spirits of the dead as you are accustomed to hearing. Their purpose is to be messengers of God and guardians of God's people. Right now, here in this room, we are surrounded by God's angels. That is why we are not afraid."

"You are telling us we are surrounded by spirits at all times? Our druids tell us the spirits come only at special times, such as at Samhain."[124]

"Your druids mislead you. The spirits of the dead do not wander around. The angels who are assigned to each of us by God stay with us. They protect us at all times."

The captors were thinking, almost out loud! They had been so accustomed to the teaching of the druids that the word *spirit* frightened them. This was all new.

---

[124] Gaelic festival marking the end of the harvest season and the beginning of winter. See wikipedia.org.

Pátraic took advantage of the situation. He had quickly noted the reflective attitude of their captors.

"And there is more to it. The God of heaven and earth is here with us, too. He is not like your sun god away out there in the sky. He lives within us. He is supreme. The angels are attending on Him right now here in this room."

The leader of the group asked, "So you are saying your one God is everywhere? How can that be?"

"Because He is an almighty God. He created heaven and earth, the sun and the moon and the stars. He is in charge of all things. And that is why we are not afraid. Even if you kill us, we are still with God. Oh! You may be able to bury our bodies, as you will have to, but you see all you have killed will be our bodies. Our spirits will be very happy with God."

Light of day was fading fast. The ruffians looked at each other, and the leader signaled them to come outside with him. They held a discussion as to what to do. The band of scoundrels with him, having heard the previous arguments, now appeared to be unsure of their situation. If Pátraic was correct, there would be a certain danger in interfering with him or his companions.

"Perhaps," suggested the leader having heard their various opinions, "we should postpone our decision until after we have slept, and in the morning we can meet to make a final judgment."

The hands of the captives were still tied, leaving them powerless. They had not eaten for many hours, and everything they had with them had been confiscated.

Their captors once again entered the room, and the leader announced his decision.

"We have decided to let you live until morning, and when daylight comes, we will have action."

The threat in his voice increased as he told them they could lie on the floor and wait until morning to learn their fate.

"And you should pray to your God to keep away the daylight

because when it comes, your time may have come too. You have reason to fear there will be blood."

The captives followed orders and painfully lay on the floor. At the same time their accosters retired to the only other room in the home. Immediately after they had left, Pátraic led his companions in community prayer until one by one the fatigue of the day with the distress it had brought saw each of them drift into restless slumber.

The gray arrival of dawn found them all awake and wondering about their fate. Pátraic as usual called for prayer, and they offered themselves in acceptance of God's will. Dawn had barely broken when their ruffian captors arrived on the scene from their own sleeping quarters.

The leader spoke.

"We are going out to have another conference, and when we come back be ready for whatever may happen."

Pátraic expressed no fear in his voice.

"God is a God of justice. He sent His Son to die for us, and in return we offer Him our lives if that be your decision."

They then disappeared through the entranceway, and the prisoners once more agonizingly raised themselves to standing positions and were one in prayer.

Pátraic reminded them of their mission and the depth of their commitment.

"If today signals the end of our mission through the loss of our lives, the seed we have planted will grow, and our blood will fertilize that seed."

Within a very short time, the bandits were back in the room. Once again their leader spoke.

"Is your God watching us? Can He stop us?"

"Yes, our God, who is also your God, is watching over all of us. You may kill us, but in the end you will not have achieved anything other than proving you are a murderous horde. God can stop you if that be His will. But on the other hand, if we are bloody victims of your loathing, He will allow our deaths to promote the very idea you are trying to destroy. God is a God of justice. He sent His Son to die for us, and in return we offer Him our lives if that be your decision."

There was a reply from the leader.

"As a matter of fact we want to hear more about the God you announced to us. He is so different to the gods of the druids. We want you to stay here with us for a few days. We will release you from bondage, and all we ask is that you tell us more about this God of yours. We admit we are surprised at your readiness to die for Him. So please ... stay with us."

Within the week, Pátraic had added five more converts to his already growing numbers. Despite the hardship he endured, he and his little company were very happy as they journeyed on to meet with Deaglán.

Deaglán's church was not very large, but Pátraic understood that the scarcity of priests would not allow him to build any further churches. He and his companions were welcomed profusely by Deaglán, who told him he knew of the conversion of the high king.

Deaglán invited Pátraic and his company to stay with him in his cramped quarters for the night and, indeed, as long as they wished to remain. Next morning, over a delicious helping of soup and bread, they were able to discuss together Deaglán's relationship with Bishop Palladius, who was the person who first introduced him to Christianity.

Deaglán told Pátraic of his burning desire to spread the new religion, and he had done so with considerable success. In the course of their time with Deaglán, Pátraic inquired whether Deaglán would be pleased if Pátraic ordained some priests to help him in his work. They discussed their way of life, and Pátraic said that he hoped that someday Deaglán would be able to build a monastery where his priests could live together and go out from there to spread the gospel.

"It won't be easy," said Deaglán. "I will try to do it, but I will first have to look for the masons who might help me."

"Nothing is impossible with God," replied Pátraic, "and I am sure that if you try, you will be very successful."

It was time for Pátraic and his fellow priests to leave Deáglan.

"Do you intend to go home to Samhail?" inquired Deáglan.

Pátraic replied, "No indeed. We will travel through An Muaimh. Possibly we might call to see the king at Caishil na Ri. Do you think he might see us?"

"His name is Aongus,"[125] said Deáglan, "and he has a very good reputation. I have never traveled there, but you may be able to make a contact in one way or another. Most likely he is aware of your interaction with King Laoghaire. You may meet up with several opportunities to bring the Good News to other little hamlets on your way. The people of An Muaimh are very hospitable. Just be aware of those who may give you directions!"

Deáglan was smiling.

"I think we have learned our lesson," said Pátraic. Turning to his companions he said, "We all walk with God. He is all around us, and within us. God is closer to us than we are to ourselves. His angels are with us, too, and they are designated as our guardians. We live our lives in the hands of a wonderful God."

There were friendly farewells, and Deáglan himself showed a little tear. He was keenly aware he had met a saintly man. That man had given him new strength for future endeavors. As Pátraic and his companions rode away, Deáglan could hear them pray together. The words were distinguishable until they faded from his hearing.

"I arise today through a mighty strength, the invocation of the Trinity. Through belief in the threeness, through confession of the Oneness of the Creator of Creation …"[126]

---

[125] King Aongus (King of Munster from 453 to 489) and his wife Eithne (known as "the hated") were killed in battle c. 489 in an attack on his kingdom. He has a reputation as a devout king who brought clerics to the palace and eventually built a monastery on the grounds. The remains of the palace—known as the Rock of Cashil—(probably destroyed by Cromwell c. 1643) still stand to this day and attract many visitors.

[126] From the prayer *St. Patrick's Breastplate*.

Chapter 20

Baptism in Blood

The journey went well, and they reached several villages that were not at all unfriendly. Pátraic had the opportunity to gather many of the inhabitants around him, all of them coming with characteristic Celtic curiosity and even extending their native hospitality. In many of the villages the little company took time to teach and baptize—and even to listen. The farther they went, the more good news they heard about Aongus. He was a good ruler and a kindly and compassionate king. His palace was atop a height that overlooked the surrounding countryside. Finally they could see the royal residence in the distance. And in a nearby village they were in for a surprise!

The king had heard they were in the area. He wanted to see the man who had faced down Laoghaire, escaped death by royal command, and had somehow or other brought grievous hurt to the druidic system in Éireann. A messenger arrived telling Pátraic the king wished to see him at his palace.

"You may tell His Royal Highness," said Pátraic, "we will gladly acccpt his invitation."

Aongus was delighted on hearing the response. He called his charioteer.

"Go down and bring Pátraic and his men to the palace."

The charioteer quickly obeyed, and in less than an hour had reached his destination.

"King Aongus has sent me to bring you to his palace as soon as you are ready. I am not to return without you."

Pátraic looked at his companions. It was a look that assured them God was at work through them. There were more of them than could fit into the king's chariot.

"May my companions ride on their horses behind your chariot?" he inquired.

"Yes, of course. His Majesty will be happy to visit with them too. He has heard a lot about you and is very anxious to meet with you all."

Soon Pátraic was sitting beside the king's charioteer in the adorned carriage, with his missionaries riding behind. Pátraic and his driver were engaged in a lively conversation. The palace seemed but a short distance away. Then suddenly there was a scream from the surrounding trees along the path. There was no mistake the message did not bode well for Pátraic.

"You are not from the gods. You have come to destroy them and our beliefs. But they will conquer you, and you will die for your evil teachings. Die now."

The words were hardly finished when an arrow shot into the neck of Pátraic's driver. With the expectation of another arrow coming, Pátraic jumped from the carriage to find cover. Then he saw the driver bleeding profusely and mounted the carriage again in an effort to tend to the victim. At that moment another arrow flew over his head. Pátraic was praying, "Christ to shield me today against poison, against burning, against drowning, against wounding, so that there may come to me abundance of reward …"[127]

His valiant companions, like their leader, had no fears. Their adrenalin began to flow. They galloped toward the trees, without any weapon except their faith and the courage Pátraic had exhibited to them. A horseman was galloping away at full tilt. They followed for

---

[127] From *Breastplate of St. Patrick.*

a while until it was clear to them it would be foolish and dangerous to follow him any farther. Within the carriage, despite Pátraic's best efforts, the charioteer had died.

"We will take him with us," said Pátraic. "The death of his charioteer may rile King Aongus and possibly compromise our mission to him. The forces of evil are working powerfully to destroy us."

With sadness in their hearts, they rode quietly up the hill to the royal domain.

At the gates they were challenged by one of the royal guards. He immediately saw the dead body of the driver. The guard looked apprehensive.

"Who are you? What has happened? Are you Pátraic and are these men your protectors?"

"Yes, I am Pátraic, and a terrible thing has happened. Surely you realize this is the chariot of the monarch. It was sent to bring us to meet King Aongus. On our way here we were accosted by a scoundrel who was trying to kill us, but mistakenly shot an arrow through the neck of the driver, an arrow that was meant for me. My companions are not armed; they followed him, but he got away. I have no idea who he was, but he did shout deprecating remarks and screamed to me that he was about to kill me."

The guard looked suspiciously over the group, making sure they were not armed. The arrow that killed him was still in the neck of the driver, and a pool of blood encircled his body. The sentinel appeared confused. Then he turned and called out to his fellow patrols, "Go and inform the palace that the king's charioteer is dead. Pátraic and his priests have returned his body to us. The driver was killed by a fanatic whose arrow was meant for Pátraic. Does His Majesty still wish to receive his visitor?"

The message was delivered, and within minutes the response came that the visiting band should be welcomed, and the king awaited them. The visitors were allowed through while at the same time the body of the dead charioteer and his chariot were being removed to other quarters.

It was a somber meeting at first. King Aongus was seated in his ornamented guest room. He arose from his chair to welcome Pátraic and his group, but his greeting was numbed by the news of the killing. He signaled the visitors to be seated at a large oak table, which Pátraic assumed was a dining place for his guests.

Aongus spoke.

"I extend to you *céad míle fáilte*.[128] This is a tragic day for me. My charioteer was a good and gracious man. It breaks my heart to know that he is no longer with us."

Then angrily he added, "I am going to make sure that the perpetrator will be brought to justice."

The newcomers expressed their sympathy to the king and were trying to comfort him when a messenger came in to tell him that the arrow taken from the neck of the dead man was identifiable, and it would lead to the capture of the assailant. Aongus was pleased.

"I must immediately send out a squadron of my soldiers to arrest this fellow and take him here for trial. Whoever carried out this awful tragedy must face the consequences. Please excuse me for a few minutes while I help develop a search party to go after this man here and now."

While the king was absent, the visitors were not left long on their own. A striking lady entered.

"I am Eithne," she said, "wife of King Aongus."

There was a pause that spoke louder than words, a sort of silence that conveyed to the visitors a sense of uncertainty. There was really no welcome in her voice or in her demeanor.

The silence ended when Pátraic spoke.

"It is a privilege to be here. We are honored to meet the king and you."

"Well ... the king wanted to meet you. He has heard about you. He is interested in hearing about your meeting with King Laoghaire.

---

[128] One hundred thousand welcomes.

It is almost impossible for the king and me to understand how you got away with breaking the law. You know, you should be dead. King Aongus is anxious to talk to you, but both of us believe you are an imposter."

"You really think Pátraic should have been killed by that arrow?" remarked one of the companions.

Eithne replied rudely, "I am referring to King Laoghaire. You broke his laws, and you all got away with it. That is something I cannot understand at all—the high king of Éireann falling for your questionable teachings. I am amazed you got around him so easily."

Pátraic spoke again.

"We brought good news to the high king, and we have no apology to offer for that. He accepted our teachings and adopted them for himself. As high king, he must surely be a man of great intelligence. I believe in the One True God. His Divine Son has saved all of us from damnation. He simply asks us to believe and love. I will be glad to speak about it to the king."

Eithne had a look of unreserved disbelief.

"I expect my husband to return very shortly, and then I am sure he will see through your preposterous charade. We are told that you speak of One God who then becomes three gods. The king is a very intelligent man, and I have no doubt he will not be impressed."

Following this initial and somewhat inimical beginning, Eithne became calmer. Her voice was softer, and she became more gracious.

Finally she appeared more hospitable. The king was slow in arriving, and this gave the visitors time to discuss the local culture. They talked about many things, about Teamhair, the jurisdiction of kings and princes in relation to each other—and the relationship of both to the high king. Eithne informed them that she abhorred the wars that were occasionally taking place, and expressed her opinion that seeking the high kingship by force of armies was repulsive to her husband and herself.

Eventually King Aongus returned. He once again acknowledged the presence of Pátraic and his company.

"I am sorry I have kept you waiting," said Aongus. "The arrow was taken from the neck of my charioteer, and I think we have established the identity of the miscreant. I have sent my soldiers to arrest him and bring him here for trial. But I do hope that my Eithne has been hospitable to you and made you feel at home."

"Yes. Eithne has been most gracious, and we have enjoyed being in her company."

"Now," said the king, "before any further conversation, I would like to invite you to share a meal."

"You are most gracious," replied Pátraic, "and we accept your invitation."

Eithne left the room to issue instructions to the servants on the forthcoming meal.

"Tell me," said the king, "of your dangerous adventure with King Laoghaire."

The visitors told him the whole story, with one interjecting a piece of information the other had forgotten.

"You are a brave man," said Aongus, "but my wife says you are an imposter."

"My strength is in the Lord who created all things. It is He who gives me inspiration to bring His message to the people of Éireann," said Pátraic.

"Tell me about your One God," asked Aongus.

That was the opportunity Pátraic was awaiting. As always, he gave the teaching on the Blessed Trinity, the coming of Jesus, and His death and resurrection.

The king nodded his head.

"I wish the queen were present to hear what you are telling me. She is stubborn in her own beliefs and holds that all of you are imposters. I think, however, we will have to go over all these teachings with her, so that she, too, may come to be a follower of this Jesus you speak about."

In due course the banquet was served. The king's druids—with their leader Amhlac—sat at the table, from time-to-time throwing hostile glances at Pátraic. They already knew his reputation. They knew, too, that their tenure was being put to the test, and they weren't sure whether or not they should speak up in defense of their twelve gods. But they decided it was better be sure than sorry.

Amhlac spoke up.

"How could anyone believe this nonsense? The Son of God dies! If He is the Son of God, He is Divine, and how could He die?" The question was directed at Pátraic.

Pátraic's explanation was readily forthcoming. The discussion lasted right through the banquet, and continued afterward. Eithne was listening but did not reveal her thoughts. In time she joined the debate, and despite her earlier silence, appeared very involved in the deliberation. Unexpectedly she made a statement that was not good news for the druids. Looking directly at the king she said, "Now I understand your interest in this new teaching. I admit I was skeptical, but now I am assured."

"I am glad we are of the same opinion on this," responded Aongus, "and we should be baptized at the same time. Why don't we move outside; it is not yet twilight, and I will ask a servant to find utensils for the water. That way we can invite our soldiers and all of our servants to witness our new beliefs. There is only one God."

It took an hour or so to have everything ready and everyone present. Due to the popularity of the king, great numbers of his subjects showed up. They were intrigued by what was taking place and wanted to find out for themselves the meaning of this new religion that worshipped only one God.

As twilight was approaching, the king and his queen were ready to be baptized. They were surrounded by their soldiers and their servants, all of whom were curiously interested in the ceremony and showed surprise at the new turn of events in the life of the palace. The king and his queen would now be Christian. Should they themselves follow? Or will the king expect all of his subjects to take on the new religion?

It was time for the baptism. Significantly the king decided to allow Pátraic to baptize him first. This would be an indication of the importance of what was taking place.

The monarch was always first in leading his people. And so it would be with his baptism as well. An air of excitement mingled with curiosity was growing by the minute.

Everything was ready. Pátraic, with his crozier[129] in hand, moved into the middle of the circle. The crozier was specially made, with a pointed end, to allow it to stand on its own in the ground so that an outside ceremony, of which there were many, could be held.

Pátraic took the water that he would pour on the head of the king. He planted his crozier in the ground, and immediately the king winced but said nothing. The baptism took place. Bishop Pátraic was congratulating Aongus when he noticed the king's right foot gushing blood. He had put his crozier through that foot. Pátraic was shocked. Speaking to the king he asked, "Why did you not inform me?"

"Because I thought it was part of the ceremony," came the reply.

Meanwhile, after Pátraic and his companions had taken their leave, Deaglán began to think a lot about the building of the new monastery, and through prayer, he resolved that he would make every effort to find the masons and the finances to erect such a building. As Pátraic had assured him, it took no time at all to get the good will

---

[129] The long staff carried by a bishop at religious ceremonies. It symbolizes the shepherd's staff.. The bishop is shepherd of his people. The present-day crozier is much more ornate than the long piece of stick carried by the original shepherds.

of the people for the monastery, which blossomed three years later. It was known as "Na Déisi."[130] Within a couple of years it had attracted pilgrims from long distances and eventually became a pilgrimage site for thousands of people. Deaglán's monastery had been blessed, and Pátraic's assertion that God would bless the work certainly came true.

Having completed his visit with King Aongus, Pátraic had a decision to make. Would he go back home and check on his community at Loch Cúan, or should he head for the west of Éireann where the people in Máigheo always welcomed him with open arms? He consulted with his companions, and it was decided it would be best to go back for a little while to his thriving community near Loch Cúan. So they headed in that direction and would be home within a few days. King Laoghaire had given Pátraic a large sum in the precious nuggets he had bestowed on him, and there was still plenty left. Within a few days they were back among their first little Christian community, which they regarded as really home for them.

They were welcomed profusely by the priest companions who had remained on to watch over the community while Pátraic had gone to see Deaglán. Pátraic and his men felt the warmth of their greeting and inquired how everything had gone among the Christians. They informed him that all was very well and that there was a young group ready for the sacrament of confirmation who were awaiting his return. It being early in the week, Pátraic told them that he would do the confirmations on the following Sunday.

It would turn out to be a confirmation Pátraic would never forget.

---

[130] The story of na Déisi is probably historical. They were a tribe residing under King Cormac Mac Airt, as was previously noted, who were expelled by Cormac himself because of a treacherous attempt on his life. The story of their wanderings is convoluted, although one tradition has Cormac restoring them with a large property in present northwest County Waterford, Ireland. It would appear the Déisi name was preserved in history by the success of Saint Declan's Monastery. It drew pilgrims from many parts and eventually took over the name Déisi for itself. "I am going to the Déisi" would mean "I am on a pilgrimage to Saint Declan's Monastery and Church."

Chapter 21

Coroticus

I t was a beautiful Sunday toward the end of March. The confirmation ceremony was set for midafternoon. The new Christians and their children to be confirmed started to gather into the *cill*[131] for a couple of hours beforehand. There were flowers on the altar to express the beauty of the occasion in the lives of the young people who would be confirmed. There were fourteen in all, some of the girls wearing beautiful white dresses, and the boys had on their best apparel.

Eventually it became time to begin the ceremony. Pátraic addressed the gathering, welcoming them and praising them for accepting their newfound faith. He went on to explain to all, one more time, the beauty of confirmation and how it affects their spiritual lives.

"This ceremony of confirmation," he said, "is a gift from God, who first sent His Son to die for our salvation, and now is bestowing upon our new aspirants the gift of the fullness of the Holy Spirit."

He went on to talk about the apostles, who were frightened after the death and resurrection of Jesus, but God the Father sent the Holy Spirit to descend on them, and they immediately found the courage to go out on the streets and proclaim the resurrection of Christ.

---

[131] Small church.

185

"And you," he said, addressing the young candidates, "will find the Holy Spirit in this sacrament and, hopefully, He will bestow on you the courage of faith. Keep in mind we are a small community, surrounded by people who do not believe in one God and who follow as many as twelve gods. Today may you be strengthened to resist the challenges of those non-Christians and deal with them with the love Jesus has shown us."

Pátraic administered the sacrament, and happy young people returned to their seats to be congratulated by grateful parents who had raised them in love, then he proceeded to the altar to continue with the Mass. He was blessing himself in the name of the Father, and of the Son, and of the Holy Spirit when he heard roaring and screaming from outside. Wondering silently what was happening, he kept on with the Mass.

Then suddenly the doors burst open, and about one hundred men came in with swords and clubs. Pátraic immediately recognized them as Roman legionnaires and wondered why on earth they were here in Éireann! The intruders killed quite a number of the adults and, as they left the place, took all of the young girls with them.

Pátraic left his place at the altar and confronted a brutish individual who was ready to club him, suddenly finding the strength to defend himself. He caught the intruder by the arm that held the club while it was in the air and knocked him backward to the floor. In the meantime, the little congregation were fighting to protect their own lives, as well as to protect their leader.

Shouting at one of the leaders, Pátraic demanded, "Why are you here? Are you not Roman legionnaires serving the emperor of Rome? Does a legionnaire act in this loutish way?"

As he looked around, the soldier told him he had been sent by King Coroticus[132] to try to wipe out Pátraic's little community and to gather slaves to bring back home.

---

[132] The area governed by Coroticus is not entirely certain. He was a minor king somewhere in southern Scotland or northern England. His behavior was surprising, as he was thought to be Christian and possibly acquainted with Patrick and his mission. See also *Patrick—The Pilgrim Apostle of Ireland*, Máire B. de Paor, chapter 5, Regan Books. Also, *The Wisdom of St. Patrick*, Greg Tobin, appendix B, Fall River Press.

"Are you talking about Coroticus who is a minor king in An Bhreatain? I know him, and I thought he was my friend."

"I am speaking about the same Coroticus," said the soldier, "and we have been ordered to capture as many of the girls as we can and take them back to Coroticus, who will sell them as slaves."

"Get out of here," shouted Pátraic. "Take any loot you want with you, but leave our community alone. Are you not all Christians? Then why are you killing and looting? Get out!"

"We must follow the orders of King Coroticus," retorted the soldier.

"And I thought all along that Coroticus had joined the Christian faith!"

"He has. But for some reason he wants revenge on you. He told us not to kill you but rather to kill your congregation and take away all the young girls."

Within minutes the carnage was over; the soldiers of Coroticus left a lot of bodies, some holding hands, and all the dead slumped over their benches or hunched together in a protective posture, showing they had died trying to defend themselves. As Pátraic looked around, his heart was breaking, and tears began to run down his cheeks. His companion priests had come rushing in but could do nothing to stop the bloodshed. They had heard the screams of the assembly and the crying of the girls who were snatched in their confirmation garb against their will. What was left of the congregation was sobbing at the massacre, weeping over the dead bodies of their family members and friends who had given their lives for the faith under the swords and clubs of the soldiers of Coroticus.

After several days, Pátraic's anguish had turned to anger, and he decided to write a letter to Coroticus and his soldiers. It was a bold and angry letter, in which he addressed the soldiers and the king by announcing to them that he as bishop was excommunicating them, including King Coroticus.

He said to them, "You are soldiers whom I no longer call my

fellow citizens, or citizens of the Roman saints, but fellow citizens of the devils as a result of your evil deeds … You live only to plunder."[133]

He then called on the king and his soldiers to return the girls immediately.

After this letter had been sent out, it wasn't long until the combined bishops of An Bhreatain and Alba sent their own letter to Pátraic, asking him to explain the excommunication and the harsh language used against the king. Pátraic discussed the letter with his companions, and some were in agreement that he should go and defend himself, while others thought it would simply create more problems to attend the meeting of foreign bishops, who knew nothing about Éireann. Despite some heavy protests from his priests, Pátraic decided to go to An Bhreatain and defend himself with the ecclesiastical authorities in that region.

On his arrival, he found the bishops to be extremely supercilious toward him, as if he himself had been responsible for the killings.

"And who gave you permission to excommunicate members of a Roman legion in An Bhreatain? You have no authority here," exclaimed the bishop, "and how then could you excommunicate members who come under our jurisdiction?"

Pátraic's temper began to rise, and he decided to answer the question as sharply as it had been put to him.

"Yes, I do have authority," he said. "These brutes were within my jurisdiction when they committed their crimes, and I would not expect bishops of An Bhreatain to hold an inquiry into what went on. Come to Éireann and see the graves of the martyred dead."

There was silence in the room. Then Pátraic spoke again.

"They took some beautiful girls to be sold as slaves here in your country. I want those girls back, and if you have any control over Coroticus, who is supposed to be a Christian, I would ask you to challenge him instead of me. Let me tell you, Coroticus and his brutes are still under excommunication. Now that they are back home, you

---

[133] See *The Wisdom of St. Patrick*, Greg Tobin, Fall River Press, "Letter to Coroticus."

have an obligation to look into the problem. You have no jurisdiction whatever in Éireann."

An adversarial bishop intervened.

"You appear to believe that you are not subject to the autonomy of the bishops of these islands. But we believe you are."

Pátraic was well able to defend his position.

"What makes you think that the island of Éireann should be subject to your domain? Tell me what you know about Éireann. I am giving my life to the conversion of these good Celts. At the same time it appears to me that you are encouraging these instruments of the devil by your silence. And you fault me by your invalid accusations. Do you want to enslave my Christian people? I was a slave myself once, and I know all about slavery. Is it your wish that children be taken as slaves to be sold to the deplorable and unbelieving Picts who ride nude into battle? I have dedicated myself to the conversion of the people of Éireann. Unlike Palladius, I have no intention of abandoning my mission when a problem arises, and I ask you here and now to start exercising your authority where it should be exercised ... and let me tell you, you have no authority over me. These men and King Coroticus will remain excommunicated until they return the girls and show remorse for their actions."

One bishop responded, "Pátraic, you are a good man. From our information you have consecrated other bishops to help you in your work. Whether you are subject to the bishops of An Bhreatain will have to be decided by the Pope, and that will take time."

The leader of the bishops immediately spoke.

"Pátraic, this is not the first time we have had problems with you. Perhaps you may be right in this instance, but we are asking you now to lift the excommunication."

The reply came quickly.

"I will not lift the excommunication until the young girls are returned, and Coroticus has made amends for his misdeeds."

The leader of the bishops again replied, "Then let us vote on where you stand with us."

He had barely finished his sentence, before Pátraic replied, "Under whose authority do you judge me? I have left my native land for the love of God … I dedicated myself to the conversion of Éireann. I have traveled and prayed almost everywhere throughout the country. I have stayed close to God, and you are intruding in my ministry."

There was silence in the room. The bishops of An Bhreatain were obviously confused and were whispering to each other. The leading bishop then called for a time for conference among themselves and asked Pátraic to leave the room. About thirty minutes later, they called him back in. This time they appeared to Pátraic to be less confrontational.

"Very well," said the leader of the bishops, "you have explained yourself, and in view of what you have told us, Coroticus appears to be the guilty one, and we will do our best to track him down and demand an explanation. But keep in mind the Pope will have to decide where the sovereignty of the Bishops of An Bhreatain begins and ends."

Pátraic's strength showed itself once more. He had no intention of surrendering on any of his arguments.

"I will return to my people. But please allow me to make one more statement. Éireann is not part of An Bhreatain. To say that it is would be disadvantageous to the development of our ministry. The kings, queens, and princes of Éireann would be hostile to that idea. They want their hierarchy to be totally Celtic."

"We commend you to go back to Éireann and continue your ministry.[134] Time for us bishops to see how Coroticus will defend himself.

---

[134] There is a great likelihood that this was not the only confrontation between Patrick and the bishops of Britain. History seems to suggest that Patrick suffered much tribulation through false accusations, on which occasions he would again have to defend himself outside his own land of mission.

We thank you, Pátraic, for coming to explain to us what happened. May God bless you in your ministry to the people of Éireann."

Pátraic returned to Éireann with a heavy heart, wondering how he could have been put at the center of this tragedy in the first place, but he told himself he was determined to continue as passionately as he could with his ministry, which was still being blessed by the Lord.

Chapter 22

Áró Mhacha

Pádraic rested on his return from his visit to Deaglán.[135] Throughout that time he was reflecting on a new endeavor. It was time for him to establish the first diocese for all of Éireann. He was encouraged with the number of conversions he was making and had already been proclaimed Archbishop by Pope Sixtus III. He would shepherd his people from this first diocese.

His little monastery near Loch Cuan was close to a famed center of Celtic worship. He was aware of the druidic teachings on the goddess Macha. She had twin sons and a famous mountain height not all that far away was dedicated to them. It was called Emhain Mhacha.[136] Patraic was aware that this mound was a site for worship for all of the gods, but especially the goddess Macha. He truly believed the site of this first cathedral, built in a pagan pilgrimage region, would more than offset the worship being paid to pagan gods. The idea was entrenched in his mind and he promised himself that somehow or other it would have to be brought about.

But how to get the land as well as the permission to build?

While he had journeyed south to visit Deaglán a young man had come inquiringly to the monastery.

---

[135] Declan.
[136] Twins of Mhacha.

"I am Benín,"[137] he said to the priest left in charge. "I have come to inquire about all of your teachings. I have heard much about them and I would like to know more. Can you help me?"

"Of course. Come with me and I will set forth for you all the fundamentals of our Christian beliefs."

Benín was a good listener. He asked questions here and there and was particularly interested in the Trinity. After it was explained to him he was satisfied.

"You must understand," said his counselor, "that faith would not be necessary if everything you believe were totally clear. Then you would not need faith. Faith is really belief in things unseen. It leads to hope and love. Take a look at the druids who have commandeered the faith of our Celtic people for centuries upon centuries. But they have no love. They have no problem sentencing someone to death to placate their gods. They take a life without compassion or feeling. They are butchers by another name. The God of the Trinity loves life, he creates it and bestows it lovingly. And it is His will that we live our lives to the full, trying to help those around us, and so bringing happiness and contentment to all."

Benín replied, "Yes, I understand. I want to be baptized. Even more, I wish to become involved in bringing this faith to all. Would it be possible for me to join your group and work directly with you?"

"Pátraic is away at this time, but he should soon be home. Upon his return we shall send for you and I am sure there won't be a problem. Pátraic might like to ask you a few questions, but have no fear; should you wish, I can baptize you now, and then you will be able to walk with the One True God."

It was done. Benin was exhilarated.

On his return, Pátraic was informed about the baptism of Benín. He wanted to meet him and learn for himself the zeal of this young newcomer to his ranks.

---

[137] In English, Benignus.

"Benin, I am glad you are here. I have heard all about you. Where exactly are you from?"

"Not far from Teamhair Na Ri. Probably an hour and a half on my horse. My father is a Prince and I have learned how you brought King Laoghaire to the Christian faith."

"So you became a Christian when you heard of the king's baptism?"

"Yes, but I also heard many things about you. You are a priest and you are so different to the priests of Éireann. I have heard you are a kind and gentle man, but you can be firm too at times."

Pátraic replied, "Jesus was loving and gentle too and I try to be like Him. But there are times in our lives when we are called upon to be firm. Let me tell you the story of Jesus clearing the money changers from the Temple."

Benín listened until Pátraic had finished the tale.

"I am already baptized as you know. I would like to join you. I have a great wish to be counted among your priests and to help bring all the people of Éireann to Christianity."

"Yes, I have heard of your desire. I now offer you the hospitality of our monastery. We will begin to educate you more fully in our beliefs, and when you are ready we can ordain you into the priesthood of Jesus."

"I will carry out your wishes at all times, I will try to imitate you, and I will be a true follower. I wish to be a priest more than I can say."

"And I am sure you will be a good one. You are the son of a prince. I would like to make a connection with Dara who is a prince close to Árd Mhacha, where the druidic pilgrimages and sacrifices take place."

"My father knows him and has visited him. He tells me Dara is a good and kind man. He treats his subjects very well."

"It is time for me to visit the area and meet with Dara. Would you be able to bring him a message than I am coming to see him? You see, I would like to found a monastery and later Cathedral in that area. But I have no ability to purchase the required property."

"I will gladly assist you. Indeed I suggest that perhaps we all travel together as soon as you are ready. I will introduce you to Dara. I have heard you are also a friend of Dicho, and perhaps we may be able to visit him on the way. He may even shelter us on our journey. We can get to Árd Mhacha in about two days."

Pátraic replied, "Dicho is but a day's journey from us. But it would indeed be good to visit with him and perhaps he may have some influence with Dara. I will take five monks with me as well as you. This way you will learn more about our work. We will leave as soon as we can, possibly tomorrow."

Dicho very graciously received his visitors and true to custom entertained them with a hearty meal. He knew Dara very well he said.

"I am sure he will welcome you. Last time we met he was inquiring why I became a Christian. I was glad to tell him all about you and how my clan had come to believe too. He also told me he would like to meet you. He is becoming disillusioned with the druids."

"Do you know why?" inquired Pátraic.

"Well, every prince throughout the land seems to be turning from their teachings, especially about placating their gods. Quite recently a young child was born to a less than wealthy family. One day afterwards two druids accompanied with attendants came knocking at the door. They wanted to offer the child in sacrifice to the gods. They took the child by force, and within a couple of hours they had slaughtered the victim as an offering."

"Did Dara do anything to stop them?"

"No, he didn't hear about it until a day later and then it was too late. But he sent for the druids involved and banished them from his lands. He was very angry."

"What a heartbreaking story," said Benín. "The druids are a heartless lot."

Next morning Pátraic and his little group of companions departed to meet Dara. That evening they arrived at Dara's domain. A servant came to greet them.

"We wish to speak to your master Dara." Benín was speaking.

"Do you have a reason for your visit? What shall I tell him?"

"Tell him that the bishop Pátraic would like to visit with him."

The awestruck servant looked over the group.

"Which one is Pátraic?"

"I am."

The servant had heard much about this man. Now here he was at his gateway! Despite his surprise he had the presence of mind to bow ceremoniously to his famed visitor. He quickly opened the gate.

"Come in, come in. I will inform my chieftan Dara of your wishes."

Two minutes later he was back out, accompanied by a young man with long red hair neatly combed, and dressed in princely clothing, handsome and well groomed. He showed no sign of superiority and appeared to have the humility that matched that of the peasant farmers who were his tenants.

"I am Dara," he said. "I wish you *céad míle fáilte*.[138]"

By this time, Pátraic was approaching the prince.

"I am Pátraic, and I have come to get to know you. I have heard that you are a very fair man, so it will be my hope that you will take time to listen to what my companions and I will have to say."

Dara replied, "My servant will take care of your horses and I hope you will all be able to remain with me for the night. It is getting quite late."

With that, Dara opened wide the door of his home, inviting all to enter.

"I am sure you have not eaten, and we must prepare a meal for all of you. I will introduce you to my wife."

The visitors entered a luxuriously furnished home that appeared to lack no comforts. While they sat back on purple decorated chairs, Dara inquired of their well being expressing again his gladness that they were here. Drinks were brought in by the servants and Dara

---

[138] a hundred thousand welcomes.

toasted his visitors. Before dinner Dara introduced his wife Aoibhann to the party.

Like her husband, she too was most gracious and welcoming. Dinner was served with elegance, and the hosts led amiable discussions, mostly relating to recent happenings, including the joys and sorrows of the tenants.

Pátraic judged that the time was ripe to introduce religious concerns. To Dara he asked a direct question.

"How many druids live freely in your region?"

"Too many," responded Dara. "There must be ten or so to whom I have gifted free land, and until yesterday there were three druids living with me on this estate. I am not sure if I want to continue with the teachings and practices they thrust upon us. They appear to me to have no heart and I am not sure if they have a soul either."

Benín spoke. He was familiar with this kind of banqueting and felt very much at home.

"And what brings you to this conclusion?"

"Well, it is like this. The druids on my estate and even the druids who counsel me appear selfish and uncaring. They show no interest or compassion for the people, yet they say they represent the gods. Are those gods so demanding and why do they want to interfere in such a horrible way with our lives? Druids tell me we must placate the gods. But why? I never see a druid subjecting his family or himself to misery and mortification. They claim to be superior to all of us and look down upon the people in general. Yesterday I dismissed two of them from my territory."

"Will they be allowed to come back?" inquired Pátraic.

Dara bristled, and showed anger for the first time.

"No, I will never allow them back. As far as I am concerned their sacrifice to placate the gods was a heinous and most odious act. They took a newborn baby and killed him upon an altar as their offering. It is hard to believe that any human being could do this. These so-called holy men did not inform me and I heard about it after the fact. They are nothing but ruffians and brutes. I promise you they will never stand on any of my lands again. Indeed I felt like putting them to the sword myself."

Pátraic spoke. "Dara, they are not holy men. They are indeed selfish and uncompromising, and you are right in your question why do they have to continually placate the gods. There is but one God. He is the God of all things. He created all things. Through Him we live and move and have our being. He sent His only Son among us to die for us ... "

Dara interrupted.

"I must hear more about your God."

"It's getting late," said Pátraic, "but we can come back tomorrow and instruct you and Aobhinn and anyone else who might like to hear us. Benín has friends not far from here and we may be able to stay with them."

"I would prefer if you would all stay here with us overnight," suggested Dara, "and we can meet early in the morning after our first meal and learn more of your teachings."

"That is very hospitable of you," replied Pátraic, "and we are very grateful for your offer. We will stay."

They met in the morning. Dara had gathered his two sons and four daughters. Pátraic was struck by the openness and friendliness of this man who also appeared to be gifted with humility. There was no sign of egotism or haughtiness. Friendship prevailed.

By noon Dara, his wife Aoibhinn, their entire family, and a number of the servants asked for baptism.

Pátraic responded graciously. "Might we stay through the afternoon to give you more instruction?"

Dara cheerfully agreed. "I can house you and your companions as long as you wish to stay. Let us first enjoy a meal, then we can learn more."

In the afternoon all who were interested in baptism met again, only this time two more of the servants had joined them. The unassuming Dara decided for baptism there and then.

"Would you not like to hold the ceremony with a gathering of some of your friends?" asked Patraic. "That way they might wish to join you."

"No, we would prefer to become members of your Christian faith immediately. Aoibhinn and I prefer to have the ceremony today, rather than wait. Hopefully we can have one of your priests come now and again to lead us in worship of the one true God. My subjects will soon realize I am no longer under the influence of our druidic priests when they learn that all my druids have been banished."

Pátraic announced that he and his companions would prepare for a late afternoon ceremony. Dara expressed his delight with this arrangement and immediately requested that his kitchen servants prepare a banquet in honor of the occasion.

During the banquet Pátraic sat next to Dara and his wife. The rest of his family and friends and even those servants who had been baptized joined in the festivity. Benín, sitting across from Pátraic, knew exactly what was on Pátraic's mind. He decided to introduce the subject while such contentment permeated the room. "Bishop Pátraic has dreams of promoting Árd Mhacha as the chief location for the governance of the Christian Church in Ireland. He has already appointed bishops in other areas throughout the country."

Dara was all ears. "Árd Mhacha to be at the center of Éireann's Christianity?"

Pátraic replied, "Christianity is growing in Éireann. I have ordained several bishops throughout the land. Our Christian faith calls for central places of worship. These are erected in such a way as to stand as symbols for the area around them, reminding the believers of the presence of the Infinite God of Love."

Dara replied thoughtfully, "I see. But why do we require symbols at all if we are aware of the God in Whom we believe?"

Benín remarked, "The druids used symbols, too, did they not? Take the springtime fire, first lit by the king and then replicated everywhere! Is that not a symbol? In our Christianity we pay great attention to the symbol of the Cross. We try to have it in sight at our worship meetings. It reminds people how good God is."

Aoibhinn was listening with great intent. "I understand what you are saying, but we could place a cross opposite the druidic pilgrim site at Árd Mhacha. Would not that be a great symbol?"

Pátraic spoke. All were listening.

"Aoibhinn, you are right in one aspect ... the Cross is the perpetual symbol, but when it stands on its own all the time it loses its meaning. Ceremonies must be held within its vicinity to demonstrate the beliefs of our people. The building I am thinking about would be as beautiful as the souls of the people who worship within it. In a way it symbolizes itself as the body protecting the soul within. The soul of Christianity is constituted by the faithful people of God."

Dara replied, "So you wish to build a beautiful space that will tell a story about all of us who believe in the One True God?"

"Exactly," said Pátraic. "That structure would represent the beauty of the faith of all our Christian people on this island."

"So you are asking for property on which to build on my land."

Pátraic smiled at his host and hostess. "Yes, I am entreating you to benefit our faith by donating the land on which we can build."

"Well ..." said Dara, "let us think about it. But I have an idea, too. We need a priest to be with us all the time and I will donate the land for a new monastery that would be the home of a couple of priests. Then we could offer our worship on a regular basis."

Dara's offer was much less than they had hoped for. There was silence around the table for a moment or two. All eyes were on Pátraic. What response would he make?

Pátraic calmly spoke, "I certainly accept that offer. Our monastery at Sabhall is a good distance from here and if you can build a new monastery for us I will be glad to place a couple of priests there to take care of your spiritual needs. But I am still hopeful that we can bring fame to Árd Mhacha by establishing our first cathedral here. It will be the primary diocese for all of Éireann."

"Very good," said Dara, "but first let us see how far we can get with our new monastery. I will order that construction begin immediately."

As construction neared completion, Aoibhinn and Dara visited most every week and eagerly awaited the arrival of the new priests. The monastery was a humble building that could easily house three people. Pátraic himself came a few times too, always visiting Dara.

Pátraic expressed his gratitude time and time again. Aoibhinn and Dara seemed to have caught a fever of Christianity. They left no doubt of their belief in the one true God, and when the task was finished both were exhilarated. Now they knew they would soon have a couple of priests to enable them to grow in their Christian faith. Pátraic was true to his word. He sent two of his priest companions to occupy the new home and serve the needs of the people most of whom were tenants of Dara.

In the meantime, Pátraic and Dara had developed a great friendship. Pátraic became Dara's chief counselor to the extent that even before the new monastery was completed Dara would journey to Pátraic in Sabhall to seek his advice on many matters.

The opening of the new monastery led to a higher regard for Dara in the surrounding area. There were less and less problems with the paying of rent from the many who had followed him into Christianity.

Whenever time allowed Pátraic came to visit the new monastery. He and his priests were very happy that at least part of Pátraic's dream to establish a significant Christian presence at Árd Mhacha was being realized.

Pátraic continued to advise his missionary companions. "Dara is a very good man. He is truly dedicated to Christianity. We must continue to pray that he will allow us to construct our new cathedral close to this spot. Let us also persist in our prayers for Dara and his family that the Most Holy Trinity may continue to bless them."

Time passed. In two years Pátraic ordained Benín as a priest. A great friendship had developed between them. Benín was bright and enthusiastic. He had the gift of being able to attract people to the faith. Even more so it appeared to Pátraic that he was extraordinarily tactful and discreet in his conversations.

Pátraic wanted him at Árd Mhacha.

Dara was impressed with Benín's piety and open prayerfulness. Within the year Benín and Dara became allies in the promotion of the Trinitarian beliefs. Benín was determined to try to have Pátraic's wishes regarding the building of the first cathedral fulfilled. Subtly he continued to keep the topic alive with Dara, frequently reminding Dara in one way or another that there was still need of a striking structure that would stand as testimony to the flourishing religion that was developing all around.

Dara and Aoibhinn understood well what Benín had been inferring. They discussed the situation time and again. "Benín's reminders of the need for a special church are beginning to weigh heavily on my mind," Dara said to Aoibhinn.

"As well they should," responded Aoibhinn. "I am surprised that you were not ready to help build the cathedral two years ago when Pátraic first broached with subject with us. Now you have the completed monastery and two priests who are always available to us. Your tenants seem to be much happier and we have no problem gathering rent. In my opinion, we should donate the land that Pátraic needs. We won't miss it. Indeed I believe we will be blessed for helping him."

Dara replied, *"Aoibhinn, mo grádh,*[139] I wish you had given me this advise sooner. I know exactly what I will do. I will meet with Pátraic

---

[139] my love.

and Benín to find out how much property they may need to build this outstanding house of worship."

"And you will employ the workers needed?" asked Aoibhinn.

"Indeed I will."

Aoibhinn threw her arms around Dara in a spontaneous gesture of gratitude. "You are a wonderful man and your generosity and love will touch the lives of many Christians and bring them closer to the one true God. Your name will be forever remembered in the annals of our Christian faith in Éireann. Let's send a message to the monastery inviting the priests and Pátraic to dine with us in the very near future, and then we can give them the good news."

When the invitation was delivered to the monastery it was accepted graciously. Benín told the messenger he would send word to Pátraic and that he would then inform Dara as to when Pátraic would arrive.

Dara's behest nevertheless created questions in the minds of the recipients. Benín wondered what might be the purpose of this sudden invitation. He was very friendly with Dara, and the latter had never expressed any concerns to him regarding the activities of either priest at the monastery. Then again why would Dara not have consulted with Pátraic himself if this were the case? The same thoughts arose in Pátraic's mind on receipt of the message. "No, Benín is most conscientious in how he expresses himself and I have never known him to be abrasive. Then again, I wonder, could it be possible Dara might let us have the land for the Catháoirchill[140]."

This flight of fancy filled his mind with emotions, ideas and thoughts that seemed to emerge from the deepest chasms of his brain. It was a marvelous mind-set that created a temporary ecstasy. But only for seconds. Each time the thought arose he dismissed it, not allowing another brainwave.

"Then again it is 'Deiradh Fomhair'[141] and on the last day of this

---

[140] Gaelic for Cathedral.

[141] October.

month the druids will be celebrating the eve of a new year and holding their annual festivities in honor of their gods. They always have a large number of the local people who take part in their tine chnámh,[142] bring their offerings and help in placating the gods for another year. Our little monastery is just a short distance away from there and it may be possible that Dara has some fears for our safety. Last year the druids used threatening language and he may be expecting more inflammatory remarks this time around."

When Pátraic and his priests arrived, they were welcomed warmly.

"I am so glad to see you," said Dara, "and thank you for the great priests you gave us. Come, let us celebrate!"

Many guests were at the table. Pátraic knew some of them, but Benín and his companion knew them all. It was obvious to Pátraic that his men had been working hard. There were toasts of welcome all around, good conversation throughout the meal and it was clear that no problems would be introduced. Dara seemed exceptionally happy.

The banquet was well nigh over when Pátraic carefully introduced the topic that was bothering him. He addressed Dara directly "The Oiche Shamhna[143] festival will soon be here. Have you any fears of the druids and their followers? Will our little monastery be safe?"

"Don't worry," said Dara. "I will make certain of the safety of your monastery. There will be guards. So your men can sleep in peace! I can't prevent the noise of course, but understand you will be protected."

"I suppose the druids will lead their followers in moanings and creative screaming and beseeching. At least that is what I am told," replied Pátraic.

"They will do that. Some of their people will bring oxen to be offered in holocaust. They will be thrown into a roaring fire. Pieces of their bones will be taken home by each follower and maintained as a sign of attrition to the gods. That's why they call it *tine chnámh*

---

[142] Bonfire; literally bone fire.
[143] Halloween.

na Shamhna.[144] It is really a festival to the dead, and the spirits of the dead are believed to come back and visit the world on this night. They appear to the druids too, or so they tell us. They give them a message about the fruition of the spring crops and of course you can be sure it is nearly always a good message! The god of spring has been appeased!"

"And the people believe that?"

"Yes they do. And anyway it is in their best interests to at least pretend to believe. But many of them have made a long journey to Árd Mhaca to participate and they would be the true believers."

"But you have banished the druids from your territories. Why do you allow them to come back for this occasion?"

"Because I can't stop them. That place of worship has existed for centuries and is known to thousands far and wide. I would need an army -- that I don't have -- to protect the area. And besides, the king of Ulaidh might well be angry with me and that would lead to more and more problems. Pátraic, you are the man who will stop them! It will take time but in the end you shall prevail. Our God has given you to us to be our leader and help us to overcome paganism."

"I am indeed grateful for your wonderful support," replied Pátraic. "Aobhinn and you are great friends, not just to me but to the God who created us and died for us ..."

Dara interrupted. Everybody around the table was listening intently. Silence pervaded the room, except for the voice of Dara. "Thank you. We are all indebted to you."

There was a burst of applause among the guests. Dara nodded, and then continued, "There is only one God in three persons. He is the God of all seasons. Some day He will rule in Árd Mhacha and all over Éireann. You want Him to rule in Éireann with Árd Mhacha as His chief governing place and you will be first bishop of all the land. Well ... you can't build that Cathaoirchill without our help. I want you to know that the land you need is yours. Choose what you want.

---

[144] Halloween bone fire.

We will try to build it of stone and we will look for stone masons far and wide so that it can be the kind of building you seek."

Another burst of applause filled the room. All around the table were on their feet.

At last, Pátraic knew his dream was coming to fulfillment. By the time he and his companions left for home their hearts were filled with gratitude at the goodness of God.

There would be a cathedral in Armagh that would stand for years and years to come as a symbol of the Christianity of Ireland and a reminder of the defeat of the druids.

Chapter 23

Into the West

Following his acrimonious visit to An Bhreatain, Pátraic rested for a considerable time in his monastery with his priests. His dream of the children of Foghill kept recurring, even at this time, causing him to wonder if God wanted him to spend much more time on the western shores. He had not spent enough time there since arriving in Ireland, he decided. He was overwhelmed with memories of his early days and how he was received in An tAonach Beag, and the kindness of the people there after his escape from slavery. He decided to head west to Máigheo once more.

Pátraic invited four of his companion priests to come with him to An Cruach,[145] a mountain in southern Máigheo. He told his priest companions he wished to climb the mountain, as Jesus had climbed to high areas where He and His apostles spent time in prayer.

"I would like," said Pátraic, "to imitate the Lord. Let us try to get up there to pray, fast, and bring ourselves closer to God. Besides, the Druids climb that mountain to honor their gods. We will transform their practice into a Christian pilgrimage.

One of his companions remarked, "I recall seeing that mountain

---

[145] Known today as Cruagh Pátraic or Saint Patrick's Mountain, or The Reek, in southern County Mayo, Ireland.

on one of our visits to Máigheo. It looks very similar to Sliabh Mis. I wonder if you are trying to bring back memories of your slave days!"

"Possibly," said Pátraic, "but it was on Sliabh Mis that I first came to recognize the real presence of God in my life. While in my own home I had no cares. Life was good, and I practiced my religion messily. I had the love of my parents and friends, and I didn't feel any need of God. My life on Sliabh Mis changed all that. I was on my own without care or love. It was then I really turned to God, and I could feel His presence with me. I tell you I must have prayed forty times by day and forty times by night. Now here I am, bringing the truth to the Celtic people. Yes, certainly it will be good for me to be on a mountain again, only this time surrounded by the love of good priest companions, and there may we all grow closer to the God of the Trinity. I would like to spend our time asking God to always care for the people of Éireann and to never allow them to become separated from Him."

All heads nodded.

"We are with you, Pátraic, wherever you go. Let us take with us a couple of tents to shelter ourselves."

This equipment and food for the journey was quickly prepared, and Pátraic and his men set out for the West.

This time his route would take him by the north shores of Éireann. He had been in those areas several times. There were little Christian communities that had been formed during his earlier ministry. He wanted to visit with them once more.

As in every place he traveled, he received a warm welcome. But there was some bad news too. A previous convert, Eóghan, was doubting his newfound faith, telling Pátraic he was about to return to druidism. Indeed, his argumentation was beginning to influence other believers.

"I cannot bring myself to believe that your God of Mercy would have such a place as Hell, where we spend an eternity. Our gods are mean and peevish, too, but they are not so punishing."

"Your gods don't exist," said Pátraic. "They are an invention. Your druids use them to threaten you. The God I have spoken to you about is a God of love. Hell is a place where souls are sent who never wished to go to Heaven. They refused to accept God's laws and gave no heed to being friends of God."

"Well, you even talk about a place called purgatory, a place where the souls of the dead suffer too."

"Yes, purgatory is a place of refinement and purification that enables us to be more perfect before we enter Heaven. You see, many are like a shining nugget that has dulled. But in Heaven everything must shine. The soul entering heaven must be as pure as the newborn baby. God sends us to purgatory to make us ready to join all the shining souls there, souls that exhibit no blemish. Everybody shines in Heaven. Everything is God's pure light. And the presence of Christ is felt in purgatory where grateful souls look forward to the joys of being with God forever."

"So then it is all right to sin a little bit. Purgatory cannot be so bad!"

"No, it is never all right to commit sin of any kind. On the other hand there are times when we sin with little heed of what we are doing. We can speak ill of our neighbor and not realize we may be hurting our neighbor's character. But that comes from thoughtlessness, and though it is against God's law, and we sin, it is not the same as if we were deliberately setting out to destroy that person's reputation. Just yesterday I heard someone speaking ill of another person, and at the end saying, 'Bless his heart!' That is a contradiction."

Eóghan was deep in thought. After a few seconds he remarked, "It is hard to believe what you are saying. You will have to explain more to me."

Pátraic was praying quietly to God asking Him to help save this man from relapsing back into his old paganism. Eventually he heard God's response.

"You see that lake there! It has a little island[146] with a cave. Let us get a boat and go out there."

"That's a chilly lake, and the winds are always bitter. Why do you wish to go out there?"

"With God's help I may be able to satisfy all your questions."

A short time later they had arrived at the island. They came to the mouth of a cave that was but a short distance from the shore. The cave was within a rock formation. To the naked eye it exhibited only darkness.

"See that darkness?" asked Pátraic. "No light there. The Son of God is the Light of the World. We who are His followers are expected to carry the Light of Christ anywhere we go. We are to light up the world. Darkness covers our souls if they are in any way, even the smallest way, separated from Christ."

Eóghan replied, "But what has the darkness of this cave have to do with what we are speaking about? Did you bring me out here just to show me a dark cave? I have been here before, and I have looked into that cave many times."

"Ah, yes," said Pátraic, "but you haven't given any thought to the darkness, have you?"

"Why?"

"Eóghan, you want to have it both ways. If you are to live in the light of Christ, then there will be no darkness in your life. Those who don't know the true God never experience true happiness or joy because they have nothing to live for. Their graves will swallow them. What then? Will there be any life after?"

"Our gods will take care of us," responded Eóghan.

Pátraic stared at Eóghan eye-to-eye.

"I invite you to crawl into the darkness of that cave. Go as far as you can. Then come back and tell me of your experience."

---

[146] This island now known as Lough Derg (Saint Patrick's Purgatory) has become famous as a place of pilgrimage not only in Ireland, but throughout other European countries. It is visited by thousands annually who spend three days there in prayer and fasting.

"So you brought me here to this island to crawl into a cave? I am not that young anymore, and I don't really want to crawl into the gloom created by a rock formation. Why would you want me to do that?"

"You'll see," replied Pátraic.

He stood and watched as Eóghan crawled through the opening, inching forward until he eventually disappeared in the darkness.

Within a couple of hours Eóghan emerged from the cave. He was trembling all over, and his face had paled almost frighteningly. Even before Pátraic could say anything, the shuddering man spoke.

"Pátraic, help me. I have seen hell, and there is no way I can tell you about it. There were flames and souls screaming in the midst of them. As I watched, trying to breathe in that atmosphere, I could see in the distance a sparkling golden gate. Pátraic, I never want to experience that place again. I cannot allow myself to fall into hell."

"You have not seen hell," said Pátraic. "You have been given a vision, and what you saw was not hell but purgatory. And believe me, if you were to experience a vision of hell you would most likely have died on the spot. What God allowed you to see was a place of passage from this life to eternal joy. Those golden gates you saw were indeed the gates of Heaven and they open frequently to allow the souls purified in purgatory to come through to the joys of eternal life."[147]

"I need to get myself together," replied Eóghan. "I am so glad God did not show me hell. I feel in need of a rest. I hope I can get this vision that I have just seen out of my mind. Yes, I believe in the One True God, and you may be sure that belief will carry me through life. Now I understand we must love God and each other if we are to gain the delights of the next world."

[147] Based on legend. The island in Lough Dergh became famous as a place of pilgrimage, not just in Ireland, but all over Europe. Most accounts go back to the twelfth century, although there is evidence that the pilgrimage had indeed begun in the time of Saint Patrick himself. The pilgrimage is known as Saint Patrick's Purgatory. See Wikipedia.

It was the end of the month of June, and the weather was accommo-
dating and even dry on the whole journey. Pátraic decided to travel
south to other areas where he visited his formerly established Christian
communities, as well as creating new converts.

And, of course, word got out about Eóghan's vision. Word always
spreads. The news of the little island spread far and wide, even to
the islands off Tir Connaill. A young man named Muiredach was
intrigued about the happening and came ashore to see Pátraic.

For both men it was a fruitful visit. Muiredach became a Christian,
joined Pátraic's group on their journey, and was of great help through
his enthusiasm and caring personality. He was new to the faith but
quickly became one with Pátraic's companions as they journeyed
south and west.

In a couple of days they had crossed amhainn na Sionnaine[148]
and found themselves close to the palace of the dynasty that once was
governed by Queen Maedb in Croghan.

Pátraic went to see his friend the seanachí once again—the man
who had shared with him so many stories and facts of Irish culture
and civilization. Eochaidh gave him his usual welcome and recalled
their journey from the north to the west in days gone by. Eochaidh
had aged considerably, but he was still the same Eochaidh that Pátraic
had known. So Pátraic and his companions were invited to stay overnight and were afforded a good meal. By this time all of Eochaidh's
family had become Christian, and it gladdened Pátraic's heart to know
that his old traveling companion and teacher no longer had to hide his
faith but could practice it with his family and was attending the cill
in the area that was filled every Sunday with many of his neighbors.

Following the visit to Eochaidh, Pátraic lost no time in heading
northwest to Máigheo and the mountain he wanted to climb. Within
a few days, he and his companions had reached the Atlantach bhord
farraige,[149] and Pátraic began immediately to look for An Cruach. As

---

[148] Shannon River.
[149] Atlantic seaboard.

they rode along on their horses they had cause to admire the beautiful landscapes into which they were riding, and suddenly, there was the mountain—right in front of them.

Pátraic told his companions they needed to find a friendly location in which to stable their horses while they were gone. They found a pleasant Christian farmer who was delighted to help them, so they started their journey to the foot of the mountain and then began the climb.

From the bottom, looking up, it seemed an almost impossible adventure. And the farther they got, the more they found the mountain to be covered with stones that would roll out of place and take them back a distance and possibly leave them lying on their stomachs. They were carrying the tents and the food for their time on the top of the mountain, and that did not help their climb. But worse was to come.

The mighty Atlantach sent in its weather troops to create havoc on these good men. It began to rain in copious heavy showers until their clothing was wet from inside out. But Pátraic led his men on, saying, "We must not allow these rains to prohibit us from carrying out the Will of God. Our struggle here is part of our pilgrimage."

Gradually they got to the top, covered with mud, saturated all over with the rains that continued to fall, and almost totally exhausted.

The view from the top was magnificent despite the heavy rains, but the drenched-to-the-skin missionaries had little interest in their surroundings until they could find a place on the very top where they could erect the two tents they had brought with them. These gave them some shelter from the rain, and Pátraic suggested they divest themselves of the wet clothes. And then he reminded them of his time in slavery at Slíabh Mis when he had to live without a tent and with no more coverage than the trees that went bare in the winter.

"God wants us to do this, and we will survive the elements. Let us rest as much as we can from our climb, and when morning comes we may be in a better position to examine our situation. We will light a fire when the rain stops and try to dry our clothes and have some food."

The rains did indeed cease a short time afterward, and the fire was lighted in accordance with Pátraic's directives. The fire took care of the wet clothing problem in no time at all.

Three of Pátraic's companions as well as Muiredach decided they would occupy one tent while Pátraic and his other priest could sleep with more space in the other. Pátraic was pleased to hear snoring coming from all around him, before a gentle sleep entered his own soul. It was a dreamy sleep, too, featuring rocks and water, and then the children of Foghill calling for him again.

The sun was out by morning. They offered the sacrifice of the Mass together, had a little breakfast, and then Pátraic announced, "I am going to find a site in which I can pray alone, and I invite the rest of you to find quiet places in which you, too, can join in my prayers. Keep in mind, we are praying for the people of Éireann for centuries and centuries to come, that they may remain faithful to the Lord who gave Himself for them."

Soon there was silence as the priests scattered to various locations where they could join their prayers with those of Pátraic and reflect on the love of the Lord.

The temper of the an tAigéan atlantach became more friendly, and after a week Pátraic and his companions had taken stock of the beautiful countryside surrounding them.

Pátraic remarked, "The beauty of this land has been given by God to a deserving people who are able to enjoy their surroundings. We need to give them the teachings of Jesus Christ. I feel as if we should stay here for as long as we can. I remember the Lord spent forty days in the desert praying for all of us, and I would like to imitate Him by spending forty days in prayer here."

One of his companions dissented, saying he would feel much safer if he could get out of the wind and rain, which were sure to come again, rather than remain such a long time in this wild spot.

Pátraic gently replied, "You can leave us and wait for us until we get back down to join you, but try to pray as much as you can when you get the shelter you are looking for."

The mild answer of Pátraic touched the heart of the somewhat unhappy priest, and he immediately replied, "Holy father, I will not leave you. I will stay here and pray with everyone else. I know that the Lord will help us all."

The weather was mixed, some days with constant showers that drove the men to their tents, even though it seemed to them that Pátraic was always the last one to arrive for shelter. However, they all continued to be in company with the Lord, and on the sunny days that came occasionally they used their time in more deep solitude and prayer.

After forty days, Pátraic announced, "We have now been imitating Our Savior for the forty days we had planned, and I know our prayers have come close to the Heart of the Lord. On this mountain I have prayed for the well-being of Éireann from now until Judgment Day. Indeed I have asked Him to protect the Celtic people here from the awesome calamities that will fall on the world at the end of time. I got a message that my prayers have been answered. Éireann will be smothered by an tAigéan atlantach and all its people drowned seven years before the final catastrophic event.[150] Let us now gather our belongings and trek back to our horses."

There was a smile on the faces of his companions because in truth they felt in their hearts it was time to get back to the typical world.

The band of missionaries was soon to find another challenge. As they tried to journey down the mountain they found even more danger than when ascending. It was a misty day, and the mountain stones were not kind to them. They had to be careful of their steps, and frequently, when they put forward their foot on a stone that seemed secure, the stone and those surrounding it quickly rolled downward, throwing them on their backs and developing within them a fear of

---

[150] From a fable.

injury to their bodies, especially their legs. The descent was dangerous, and they prayed together, and in the silence of their hearts, that
no one would be injured. After many falls, some very painful, they
reached the bottom. Pátraic had come to grief a number of times, too,
but he was unscathed and happy that he had been able to carry out
his resolution, and he knew his prayers were answered.

"We have spent time on this mountain in imitation of Our
Redeemer, and our prayers will be answered. Our climbing up and
down was part of our prayer, and I have no doubt God was with us
from the beginning to the end. And now let us rest for a while and
have something to eat before we begin our journey farther north to
An tAonach Beag."

All were aware that An tAonach Beag was very close to Pátraic's
heart, and they were quick to meet the farmer who had cared for
their horses and begin their way northward. This despite the farmer's
persistent invitation they stay the night and have a meal or two with
him. The farmer refused any compensation, and in the all-embracing
mists along the western coast of Máigheo, Pátraic and his companions
rode quickly toward their destination. They rested overnight with another Christian family, who were delighted to meet them, but before
they could leave in the morning a messenger came to invite them to a
hamlet that had never been visited by Pátraic himself. The place had
a well at which the druids celebrated their spring festival and came
there in hordes to begin a journey on foot to An Cruach to placate
their gods—the very same mountain at the top of which Pátraic had
prayed. Pátraic was receptive and curious in his answer.

"Where is this well?" he questioned. "Are you telling me the place
is overrun with druids every year?"

"Yes, it is indeed," replied the messenger. "The well is a gathering
spot for druidic rituals. They gather to placate their gods, and when
the rituals are completed, they then trek to An Cruach, walking the
journey to honor their gods."

"And they do this every year?" inquired Pátraic.

"Indeed they do, and they inveigle many villagers to walk with them. We all believe that if you, O holy man, would come and visit us, all of that would change."

"Very well," replied Pátraic. "I will come. Lead us to your hamlet."

In his heart Pátraic felt God with him. Now he had an opportunity to gather converts and turn the druidic ritual into a Christian prayerful practice.

Word spread quickly and reached the village that Pátraic and his group were coming to visit. On their arrival they were greeted by a large gathering of inhabitants who welcomed them profusely. Pátraic's first words related to Christian beliefs with emphasis on three Divine Persons in the One God. Then he inquired if anybody was present who was not yet Christian. To his surprise, quite a number disclosed they had not yet sought baptism.

"Is it because you are unsure of the new teachings? Or because you are afraid of the druids?"

One man spoke up and said, "I have been watching our new Christians, and I have come to believe that I want to be baptized. But I admit, too, that I fear the druids. They might seek revenge."

Pátraic replied, "Anytime, anywhere, a person accepts the call of Christ, there may be unknown consequences. Keep in mind the devil is always at work. Remember, too, that Christ Himself was crucified for His teachings. That was almost five hundred years ago. But look what has happened since! The Christian faith flourishes in An Európa. Yes, many have lost their lives, but they are now in Heaven forever."

There was a murmur among the crowd. Several persons eventually came forth to receive baptism. Pátraic conferred with his companions.

"We will stay here for a couple of days to instruct you, and then we will baptize you."

"There is a lake, not very far away, in which we could be baptized," advised one of the new recruits.

"That is correct," replied Pátraic, "but there is a well right beside us which we will use for the baptisms. We want all to know that the waters from this well have led people to eternal life."

"But," replied one individual, "this well belongs to the druids."

"Not anymore," said Pátraic. "This well belongs to the people of the One True God, who created Heaven and Earth and the spring for this well too. We will gather here in two days' time to perform the baptisms."

The next day, two local druids accosted Pátraic and his companions arrogantly.

"Who gives you the right to use this well for your deceptive message? We have been using this well for hundreds of years."

"Yes," replied Pátraic, "but that doesn't give you the well as your property. Can you initiate springs of water to create another well? No, you can't. And the springs that feed this well are created by the One True God who governs all things in heaven and on earth."

There was further confrontation, but eventually the unhappy druids departed with their heads down. They had no arguments to meet those of Pátraic.

"This man is destroying us," said the one, "and now we must share our well with his new Christians."

Two days later the inhabitants of the entire village were back again to meet Pátraic at the well, this time with a larger number asking for baptism.

"I will do it myself," said Pátraic, as he advanced toward the well.

One by one the aspirants came forward. Pátraic knelt with one knee on a hard rock to allow himself to cup the water in his hands and let it flow over the participant as he baptized. It didn't take long for him to feel his knee hurting. He offered a silent prayer that he would be able to get through this ceremony, and he kept administering for more than an hour. The pain in his knee seemed to abate itself minute by minute, until finally there was none.

At the end of the ceremonies he arose, and the onlookers saw an impression of his knee melted into the rock, which had softened like putty, but was now hardening once more.

Ballintubber Abbey as it appears today, having been restored in the last century. Patrick's Well is in a courtyard to the right of the abbey, located in southeast County Mayo.

Patrick's Well at Ballintubber Abbey, surrounded by the remnants of the original abbey destroyed c. 1643 by Crommel, the impression of Saint Patrick's knee still visible

By the time he and his associates departed the village,[151] they had left a contented and believing Christian community that would continue to flourish.

And flourish it would! And because of Pátraic.

"The druids have their celebrations here, and when they are over they climb the high mountain to placate the gods," Pátraic said. "Now I invite everyone who is baptized here to imitate the druids. Walk together in prayer to the same mountain, the very one that I have climbed. Climb it together in honor of the Most Holy Trinity, in whose name you were baptized. And climb it frequently if you can. Pray on the way up, pray at the top, and pray on the way down. The One True God will be pleased, and each of you will be blest."

The new Christians were nodding their heads. Now they had a real reason to climb the same mountain as the druids. And they would be in prayer all the while to the One True God.

At An tAonach Beag, they were welcomed with open arms by the many Christians who were already there and were offered wonderful hospitality. Within a short time Pátraic had added many more converts to Christianity. But Pátraic's heart burned with the desire to

---

[151] The place was Ballintubber, now a flourishing small town in southeast County Mayo, Ireland. The name comes from the Gaelic Baile Tobair Phádraig, meaning "The town of Patrick's Well." In many ways Ballintubber has a remarkable place in Irish Christianity. Rory O'Connor, last high king of Ireland, was defeated by the Normans c. 1169. However, it would appear his descendents continued to maintain the respect of the people. His son, Cathal O'Connor, invited the Augustinian order to maintain an abbey he had built there. Despite a great deal of suffering from the penal laws, the abbey survived until destroyed by Crommel c. 1643. However, it was always a place of veneration for the people and was restored in the last century. It stands as a tribute to Irish Catholic Christianity, and is probably the oldest abbey in Ireland with roots going right back to the time of Saint Patrick. The stone with the imprint of Patrick's knee is still to be seen.

get to Foghill once more, and he would forever hold the dreams of the children of Foghill in his heart. After all, it was because of these children he had come back as a missionary to Éireann. Foghill was just a short distance from An tAonach Beag, and Pátraic was very conversant with the surrounding area, so within a short time he and his companions found themselves trekking the well-known trail by the ocean and fording the Abhainn Mór to find themselves in a beautiful area, with wonderful people whom he remembered from days long ago. He felt that in many ways this was his second home, and he would have liked to have spent more time there were it not for his missionary endeavors throughout the rest of the country. But he was glad to be back once again.

His thoughts turned to Oona, the first and only girl in his life, who had ardently loved him and desired to marry him. In meeting her, he remembered his own love for her too. But God had different plans.

Oona was now happily married to a local farmer, and she and her many children, as well as her husband, were now Christian. The farmer for whom he worked had passed away, but his son, now running the farm, greeted Pátraic and his companions, and informed them that even though he could not accommodate any more than three persons, he would find lodgings for the rest in homes close by. So Pátraic, now in his senior years, accepted his offer, also telling him that he might be away from his beloved Foghill for a few days here and there to visit the surrounding seaside and the places with which he was familiar on his escape from his slave days. He wondered how his previous converts were doing, and he wanted to see if possibly more conversions had taken place.

Out of the blue another unexpected event happened, something Pátraic had prayed about over the past few years. A princely carriage was making its way down the well-treaded pathway in Foghill. Pátraic recognized this could be the opportunity he was waiting for, a chance to speak with one of the princes of Máigheo. He knew if he could convert the princes, they would support his efforts to win over the people under their jurisdiction.

It was a local prince, and he had come to oversee the land and to make sure that the people were loyal. Pátraic knew these visits were commonplace throughout all of Éireann. This prince served the king of Connacht and reported the attitude of the people—this to prevent uprisings or downright rebellion. Pátraic made sure to bow to the prince in recognition of his power and status. This was the first opportunity for Pátraic to speak on a personal basis to one of the princes of Máigheo, and he quickly availed of it. A conversation began, and he found that the prince worshiped twelve gods, and it did not take Pátraic long to explain to him the beautiful news of Christianity. The prince listened to Pátraic in a skeptical way but at the same time seemed to respect him and his efforts to change Éireann's beliefs to Christianity. He told Pátraic that his name was Brann O'Tuathil, prince of Tír Amhlaidh,[152] and that he would share Pátraic's tale of the One True God with his fellow princes throughout the area.

"Perhaps you might like to meet the princes yourself and share your story with them. Indeed, what you were saying needs a lot further explanation that conceivably might make sense to myself and all the other princes of Máigheo."

"It will make sense," said Pátraic, "and I would look forward to such a meeting."

"Would you care to join us at a get-together in Mullach Faraidh[153] at my own residence? I will send word to you as soon as arrangements are made. By the way, as you probably know, Mullach Faraidh is only a short distance from An tAonach Beag."

"I will have no trouble finding it," replied Pátraic.

"May the gods protect you."

"May our One God watch over you," replied Pátraic.

The prince smiled as he told his horseman to move forward.

---

[152] Tirawley, north County Mayo, including where Patrick was presently.

[153] In English now known as Mullafarry, County Mayo, northwest of Ballina.

Shortly thereafter, Pátraic got a message that all of the princes of Máigheo would be in Mullach Faraidh a week later. Pátraic was euphoric on hearing the news, and immediately sent word that he would attend.

After all, this was what he had been praying for.

Chapter 24

A Princely Meeting

I t was the month of August. Pátraic took a companion priest with him for support at the assembly of Máigheo princes. They had no difficulty getting there, as Prince Brann's quarters were well known throughout the neighborhood.

On arriving in Mullach Faraidh, Pátraic and his companion were welcomed by Prince Brann himself, and judging by the number of carriages outside, it was clear that there must be a full attendance. The prince led them into an ornate, well-furnished assembly hall that Pátraic guessed was used by the prince for all his important meetings. When the discussion began at the request of Prince Brann, Pátraic noted that all nine baronies of Máigheo were indeed represented here. Nine princes, many of whom did not seem very friendly, were seated at a large rectangular yew table. Prince Brann occupied the seat at the top of the table and invited Pátraic and his fellow visitor to be seated close to him.

At the opportune time, Prince Brann opened the conference.

"Pátraic would like to discuss his Christian religion with us. And, as you know, there are many Christians already in Máigheo, and most likely quite a number in the barony you, my friends, watch over. Possibly you are aware of some Christian beliefs that attract many of our people. Would anybody like to start with a question for Pátraic?"

"I am Cormac O'Ceallachain,[154] and, as you all know, the barony of Iorras[155] is my domain."

The speaker had a facial appearance of antipathy toward Pátraic that indicated hostility. It was going to be a rancorous debate!

"Let me state immediately, I am not impressed with the teachings of this bishop of the Roman Empire, spreading the influence of An Roimh among our people."

Pátraic retorted, "Christianity has been declared by the emperor of An Roimh to be the religion of all of the people, including those belonging to his army. My own father was a *decurion*[156] who was very involved in the religion that you are scorning."

This while staring O'Ceallachain straight in the eye.

"And I am Neill O'Muireadhaigh[157] from the barony of Carra. I would like to ask you, Pátraic, why you have been such an enemy of our druids. You have managed to weaken their functional ability, and they now get less respect from many of our people. This angers me since our druids believe and teach that we have twelve gods, not the one God you are proclaiming. I believe we have twelve gods, and I have no notion of how your Christianity reduces them to one. Tell me, Pátraic, how your one God came to be."

"How did your sun god come to be? Surely the sun itself is not a god, so where in the sun does your god live, or how did you come to know about that? From your druids, of course. Who is God? God is the Supreme Ruler and Creator of the world and all that is in it. If there are twelve supreme rulers, is that not contradictory? For example, there is a king of Connacht. Just imagine if there were twelve kings of Connacht. How would that work out? Twelve kings, all equal, in one small area. I am aware that you have gods of wind and water and the seasons and all the rest, but how do they manage not

---

[154] In modern English, Cormac O'Ceallaghan.
[155] Erris, a townland on the north coast of County Mayo.
[156] An officer in charge of a squadron.
[157] In modern English, Niall O'Murray.

to get in each other's way? Supposing your god of the seasons decides that your god of the sun does not allow enough light, and he is upset. Will they bring in the ten other gods to resolve the problem? Isn't that totally ridiculous? Christianity teaches that we have three Divine Persons in the One God."

"So now you are stating that you have four gods. How does that differ from our twelve gods? Have you not got the same problem?"

"We believe in One God whose nature is in the three Divine Persons, all of whom cooperate together because they are one, so there can be no division."

Pátraic, as was his custom, asked that a shamrock be plucked outside and brought into the meeting.

"See this little plant? How many leaves does it have on it?"

"Now you are asking us if we are able to count," said O'Maille[158] of the barony of Burrishoole. "I find your question offensive. What are you trying to prove?"

Pátraic replied, touching the shamrock with his hand, and breaking off a stem. "How many leaves do you see on this stem?" he inquired.

"Now you are taunting us," said O'Maille. "The stem you broke off the shamrock plant has, as we all know, three leaves."

"Exactly," replied Pátraic. "You see three leaves on one stem. All being nourished by that one stem, and so there are three Divine Persons in one God. One stem, three leaves. Our faith teaches us that the three Divine Persons are the Father and the Son and the Holy Spirit, and all three have the same Divine Nature. The Son became man, one of us, and assumed our human nature, so, in His case, we have the second Divine Person, now with two natures, human and divine, and it was in His human nature that He died and won for us the hope of joy for all eternity."

O'Muireadhaigh remained silent.

Then Brann spoke.

---

[158] In modern English, O'Malley.

"Now I understand what you are saying, and when you explain it like that, it all makes sense to me. You are right, too, about the twelve gods. How can they compete with each other?"

"Our God," said Pátraic, "is a God of love. He has chosen us as His children, and He treats us with wonderful compassion and forgiveness for our faults. Your druids do not teach love, compassion, or forgiveness. So, you see, there is an ocean of difference between our beliefs. Indeed, your druids offer human sacrifice to appease the gods. But tell me, has a druid ever offered himself for sacrifice? Of course not. Your druids, with pretended inspiration from the twelve gods, use your people to further their own ends."

In a flash, O'Maille jumped up, drew his sword, and put it to Pátraic's body right above his heart.

"You are trying to convince us," he screamed. "You already, with your Christianity, have done great damage to all of Éireann. Admit it, or I will drive this sword into your heart."

It was Brann's time to intervene with his own loud scream.

"O'Maille," he said, "how will you explain to the people, many of whom are Christians, that you murdered Pátraic, their leader? Put down your sword."

In a flash, Pátraic's fellow priest Cuimmín[159] leaped at O'Maille and succeeded in knocking the sword from his hands and to the floor. O'Maille's face showed shock and rage as he stared at the rest of the gathering. Looking at Cuimmín, he picked up his sword, sat down in his place, and retorted, "You, my friend, may taste the vengeance of this sword sooner or later."

There was a murmuring around the table as the rest of the surprised princes ingested what had taken place.

---

[159] Cuimmín (pronounced cummeen) appears to have been one of Pátraic's best leaders who helped Pátraic plan his journeys. In north Mayo there are at least two local areas that took their name from Cuimmín, the parish of Kilcummín is in northwest Mayo, with another locality named exactly the same as part of the parish of Lackan on the north Mayo coast, not far from the town of Killala (called Anabeg in this novel, the place from which Pátraic escaped to France).

It was Prince Brann's turn to speak.

"I am sorry this event has gotten out of order, and you, O'Maille, are the guilty party. You gave no indication you were going to be violent, and on behalf of the rest of us I apologize to Pátraic and Cuimmín. And, O'Maille, Pátraic has never created violence in Máigheo or anywhere else in Éireann as far as I know. He deserves our respect, the same respect he and his converts have shown to all of us here."

All heads around the table were nodding in support of Brann's statement. Pátraic and Cuimmín remained silent.

Then O'Maille replied, "I am sorry for my behavior and for threatening Pátraic. It was never my intention to pierce him with the sword. I am upset that he may be misleading this assembly and our people, but I am very sorry for what has just happened."

Brann spoke up.

"Perhaps, Pátraic, it might be best for you to explain your beliefs and how they came to be."

Pátraic agreed, first speaking about the three Divine Persons in the Blessed Trinity and told them the history of the Second Person, the Son, taking our nature and becoming man just like ourselves. He was given the name Jesus, and He was truly one of us. It took Pátraic quite a while to explain Christianity, and he finished with the Crucifixion of Jesus and His Resurrection. There was a very respectful silence as Pátraic spoke, and as he completed his address a remarkable momentary calm descended upon the hearers.

The silence was broken by Brann.

"What you said certainly is an extraordinary recounting of the person you call the Son of Man and the Son of God. But I have a problem with the Resurrection. You say that this Jesus of yours was crucified and buried and rose again. You also say that many of His followers saw Him after His supposed resurrection. How can we be sure that He really did rise from the dead? Oh, I know you said that He appeared to many people and that they passed on the word about this astonishing event having taken place. However, might it not be that the people who stole His body put out these stories to justify their new pretense?"

"Well," said Pátraic, "let me ask you a question. Would you give up your life for what you knew to be a fable?"

"Indeed I would not, and I am sure that nobody else in this room would die to maintain a false story."

"You are right," said Pátraic, "neither would I. In this case, however, His followers were certain He had come back from the tomb, so certain indeed that His twelve specially chosen disciples, with one exception John, underwent martyrdom for the cause … John was saved from martyrdom through Divine Intervention … followed by thousands of others in the Roman Empire who gave their lives and suffered greatly while doing so in order to uphold their beliefs. They knew that the Blessed Trinity was with them; they felt His presence at the time of danger; they knew their future in heaven with their Lord and God was certain, and the retribution they received now would be over in time, and then they would have an eternity of joy and happiness."

Quite unexpectedly the enigmatic O'Maille spoke.

"Yes, I agree with your reasoning, Pátraic. But how do we know that your story is true? I wish I had been a little more in control of myself earlier on, and I sincerely apologize once again, to both Cuimmín and you, for my bad behavior."

Pátraic quietly gave thanks to God for the progress he appeared to be making with these princes.

He then responded to O'Maille's question.

"It is like this. The chosen followers of Jesus, the Son of God, who were frightened to death and gathered in a room for fear of their enemies, were no longer afraid, as I told you, when the Holy Spirit came upon them. I told you also that they suffered martyrdom, and their beliefs were accepted by millions of people, of whom I am one myself, and so is Cuimmín, your fellow Máigheo neighbor. Do you think it is possible that all of those millions childishly approved of a myth? Many of those people gave their lives for what they believed. For more than three hundred years, the Roman Empire treated Christians as criminals. Don't you think it was amazing that an emperor of An Roimh became interested in Christianity and suddenly found himself on the Christian side? His name was Constantine, and one day in October in the year 312, while visiting his troops, he looked up and saw a bright cross in the sky. The cross was athwart the sun with the words written underneath, *in hoc signo vinces.*[160] Indeed it was through Constantine's influence that the first gathering of Christian bishops was called at Nicea to summarize Christian beliefs and outlaw falsehoods. Don't you think it was extraordinarily astounding that an empire that for three hundred years persecuted Christians, giving Christianity hundreds of martyrs, suddenly turned around with an announcement from the emperor that Christianity was now the chosen religion of the empire?"

"That is indeed remarkable," said O'Maille, and all heads around the table were nodding in agreement.

O'Maille continued, "You are indeed a remarkable man yourself, Pátraic. I had no notion about Christianity, but you have convinced me of the authenticity of Christian beliefs."

At the head of the table, Brann called for a show of hands seeking approval of Pátraic's Christianity. Contrary to Pátraic's earlier expectations all nine princes raised their hands. Pátraic breathed a sigh of relief, expressing his gratitude to God for the success He had given him. Standing at Pátraic's side, Cuimmín was smiling. It was the beginning of nightfall, and candles were being lighted on the walls around the room.

"It is high time we eat," said Brann. "We have been preparing a banquet for all of you irrespective of what decision would be reached."

He called a servant and told him to inform the kitchen staff that the guests would now be served dinner.

---

[160] In this sign you shall conquer.

Nine baptisms would, of course, be called for. For those who wished to have it done here and now, he and Cuimmín would participate in a special ceremony. And if some of the princes wished for a public baptism within their own barony, he would make arrangements to satisfy their wishes.

The encounter was over, and, once again, Pátraic had left his mark on another upper branch of Éireann society.

Chapter 25

The Wake

Pátraic and Cuimmín made the journey in darkness en route back to Foghill. In their hearts, however, there was no darkness, only a light that enshrined their hearts in joyous recognition of the success they had at the assembly of the princes.

It was long after midnight when they reached the accommodations where they were both hosted. As they walked into the little farmhouse, they were surprised that the man of the house had not yet gone to bed. He sat in dim candlelight by a dying fire.

He addressed them saying, "I was awaiting your return. My heart is broken. One of our neighbor's children, a child of eight years, was bitten today by a snake. The child is dead, and there will be a wake, according to our custom, tomorrow evening at his home. I have no doubt there will be a good turnout of the neighbors. Earlier this evening I purchased spirits to bring with me to the wake-house, and I am sure that many others will do the same."

Cuimmín spoke first.

"This is a terrible tragedy. Those snakes are growing in population, especially those that live in water. Was he bitten by a water snake?"

Their host nodded his head and said, "Yes, it was a water snake. I wish we could do something to get rid of all snakes, or many more people will die."

Pátraic stood in thought as he heard the sad news. A child of Foghill! Then he replied, "Certainly we must do something about these snakes, and I will ask our God to help me in devising a plan to rid Éireann of its entire snake population."

The man of the house nodded.

"You have an 'in' with God, and I pray that He will reveal to you a solution for the problem."

Pátraic responded, "I will pray, and tomorrow evening we shall accompany your family and you to the wake, pray together there in community, and bless the body of this little boy. In the meantime, it has been a hard day for all of us, so let's get some rest and place ourselves in the hands of the Almighty Father."

The wake was no new experience for Pátraic. He had attended quite a number since the beginning of his mission, but sadly this was his first time attending the wake of a young child. When they got to the wake-house they were led into a crowded living space, and thence to an adjacent room. There on a bed they saw the body of the dead child laid out in a white robe. Pátraic, with his group of fellow priests, made their way through the crowd to console the distraught parents standing immediately in front of the bed. Since the family was Christian, the visiting missionaries prayed over the body of the dead child, thanking God for his short life and now his dwelling among the angels. Turning once again to the parents, Pátraic extended to them a special blessing. Then he invited all present to join with him in common prayer for the family who had lost their child and in gratitude that this "little angel" had been called to the joys of God's kingdom in heaven. Joining hands, all prayed together for many minutes until Pátraic and his companions extended their blessings on all present. He then assured all of the mourners that he himself would be offering the funeral Mass next day in the cill by the bay, together with his priests, and he would also lead prayers at the gravesite. The visiting clergy then moved from the bedside to allow others to view the dead body. There were conversations all around; songs were being sung; stories were being told, and there was a great deal of laughing, which might have seemed to be contrary to the solemn mood of the occasion but that, on the other hand, elevated the atmosphere to more joy than sorrow, even bringing smiles from the grief-stricken parents. Well past midnight, a local seanchaí appeared on the scene. A large group of the mourners gathered around him in the kitchen. He sat by the fireside, holding a jar that Pátraic judged contained homemade spirits, reciting stories that totally absorbed the attention of his listeners. The Christian missionaries were among his audience, with their attention fully alerted to the stories he told, their minds diverted from the sad occasion. The seanchaí included the dead child among his stories, bringing back delightful memories of his young years and skillfully avoiding any kind of sadness. Dawn was breaking when the crowd began to disassemble.

While journeying home to get some rest, Pátraic and his missionaries discussed the events of that night, the mellow tone of the seanchaí, and the friendships expressed to the mourning family and to each other.

Pátraic responded with his own gentle summation.

"The custom of the Éireann wake is really an exposition of Christian love, and it existed long before our time. Somehow or other it is a gift given by God Himself to the people of this land. Our own attendance tonight amid the presence of so many neighbors illustrated that love is the heart and soul of Christ's teachings—and love permeates every action we perform."

On the morrow with the Mass set for noon, Pátraic addressed a community that overflowed outside the cill.

"Our Christian faith already tells us this child is among the blest. We are gathered here in his honor and to console his parents. We bless God for the short life of this child, and we pray particularly that God will be with this good family in their grief."

Then, addressing the family directly, he told them they would mourn for quite a while and remember their child all through their lives. That memory was a blessing in itself and would reaffirm their longing to be with the Trinity and their child in heaven.

The stillness of the cill was suddenly disturbed when a native druid shouted at Pátraic.

"You are telling falsehoods. Our gods created us for this world only. We offer our human sacrifices to the gods to placate them so that they will continue our existence here on this earth. They give us a long life or a short life. In this case one of our gods was obviously displeased with this family and ordered the life of this child to be taken in reparation."

The attendants had heard enough. A group of men pulled the druid from his place and took him toward the door of the cill. Pátraic raised his right hand in a gesture of peace.

"What is your name?" he inquired.

Showing lack of grief and with a haughtiness inimical to the occasion, the druid replied, "I am Lobhar Dearg.[161] I wanted to hear and see your ceremony over this dead boy. I simply have no time for the new beliefs you bring us. You speak ill-truths."

Pátraic quietly replied, "Friend, you have no business at this funeral other than to make trouble. If you sincerely wish to learn about Christians and our beliefs, I will be glad to talk to you after burial takes place. Now please leave and do not disturb this grieving Christian community. Go quickly, and no hand shall touch you."

Lobhar Dearg followed the advice, and turning, departed. Pátraic never saw him again.

The little congregation returned to prayer and the corpse of the boy lying within a wooden homemade box was removed to the grave-side close to the cill. With the lowering of the body of the dead child into the open grave, loud crying began. Smothering the silent tears of the many present, the *caoiners*[162] continued in their melodic wail through Pátraic's final prayers. The ocean nearby was almost at full

---

[161] No English translation. Pronounced "Lowver Jar-ug."
[162] Professional mourners.

tide, the sounds of its lapping water in harmony with the lamenting voices of the caoiners.

The gravediggers began their work closing the grave. The hollow sound caused by the clay thumping on the coffin created further heavy tears, with its heartrending message of a soul departed. Meanwhile, the caoiners contributed to the melancholic atmosphere by their wailing and loud weeping, quietly stealing away when the grave had been completely closed. Soon it was over. The gravediggers put down their shovels, and walking over to the grieving parents, extended to them a loving embrace. After the burial, neighbors visited with each other. Gradually the mourners began to leave the scene. The grieving parents were escorted to their home by their relatives and friends. Before long the graveyard was empty. The crowd had departed, and the clamor of the breaking waves against the rocks was the only intrusion on the graveyard silence.

The little boy would rest in peace, but the family would endure the torment of his loss for a long time to come.

Chapter 26

Snakes and Swans

Pátraic was now keenly aware of the growing snake population in the west of Éireann and especially in Máigheo. In his heart he grieved for the little boy who was lost because of the venomous bite of a snake. He had heard the complaints of so many people who wished that something could be done to rid the entire island of the treacherously dangerous reptiles. His new Christian converts had great belief in his relationship with the Blessed Trinity. He began to pray constantly about the problem, to the extent that his soul was totally captivated with the dilemma.

One evening, having contemplated the goodness of God and the graces He had brought to his life, again placing his quandary in the hands of God, he retired for the night. In many ways for Pátraic it was a night of wonderment, with a dream that he believed was a message from on High.

In the dream he was standing on the bluff by the oceanside. Reptiles of all descriptions surrounded him. They were but a short distance away, and he was unnerved by their massive numbers endangering his life. Snakes of every kind seemed to be slithering around him threateningly. In his dream he turned to God, asking Him to free him. Suddenly, at the raising of his hand in a gesture of *stop*, all the snakes crawled with alacrity over the bluff and fell to the saltwater below, where they drowned. All other vicious reptiles in his dream disappeared.

Pátraic awoke with a start. His heart was throbbing. He had been through a nightmare. He lay on his pillow with prayers on his lips. He began to wonder if perhaps this was a communication from God. He pondered and prayed.

"Could this be true?" he thought to himself. "Might it be possible that, instead of a nightmare, this was a message from the Divine Persons?"

He recollected that his mind had recently been engulfed by thoughts of snakes and the calamities they were causing. He had many followers beseeching his intercession with God, some even suggesting that through Divine help Pátraic himself would have the ability to rid the neighborhood of this plague. For a number of days Pátraic prayed and prayed over this conundrum. Then, one day, he watched a snake crawling up a tree. Instantaneously he decided that, yes, he could, and he would do something with God's help. He told his companion priests he was about to visit his Christians on the north shore of Máigheo, a journey that would take them as far away as possibly the shores of Oileán Achla,[163] farther down on the west coast. Pátraic remained silent that somewhere along the way he intended to perform a ceremony with the intent of ridding Éireann of snakes, once and for all. It would remain undisclosed until Pátraic identified a place and time. And so all the missionaries began their pastoral visits through Leacan[164] and onward to Baile an Chaisil.[165] Nearby, Pátraic observed a promontory with a deep fall into the ocean. As he viewed the setting, he decided this would be an ideal spot for his forthcoming prayer ritual that would ask God for help with the growing problem

---

[163] In English now termed Achill Island, on the west coast of County Mayo, reachable by bridge, and almost part of the mainland.

[164] Lacken parish is situated on the north shore of Mayo, about eight miles northwest of Killala.

[165] Ballycastle, County Mayo, the base word Chaisil in Ballycastle means an ancient stone fort.

of snakes. Just across from the bluff he beheld a great conical rock standing on its own, just a stone's throw from the mainland—a jagged piece of the earth's crust that had been undermined by the stormy ocean waves rolling in with the predatory and irresistible force that brought about this design of nature. Mother Earth still carpeted the top of the rock, now connected to the headland by a very narrow wooden bridge.

A lone figure gazes out toward An Dún from the mainland where Saint Patrick stood as he banished the snakes of Éireann to the sea.

Surely a piece of God's artwork that was a sight to behold, thought Pátraic to himself.

He felt immediately that here was the place God wanted him to hold his ceremonial prayer regarding the snake pestilence. It was time to inform his companions of his intentions. He planned to ask them to spread the news throughout all the neighboring Christian communities that in three days' time at noon he would pray with them at this spot, begging the Most Holy Trinity to send the snakes away. Until then he would focus on this problem in every prayer he made. But first he had to inform his missionary companions of his plans so that they would be the messengers who would spread the news near and far.

His associates, however, were disturbed by his plans.

"You mean you intend to banish all the snakes from this neighborhood?" asked Cuimmín.

"Yes, all the snakes from this neighborhood, but I have asked God not only to banish these local snakes but all the snakes of Eireann."

Ala[166] spoke up.

"Now you are preparing to work a stupendous miracle. And what if you fail?"

"*Fail* is not a word in my vocabulary. Why does it cross your mind that we might fail, especially if we ask with a faith-filled petition? Has God ever failed us in our mission before this time? And I say, to my companions from overseas, to recall our first major success on the Cnoc Shláine. Ala and Cuimmín, you were not present then, but let me tell you both that the rest of your cohorts were very fearful that they would be put to death by the high king. But God had a plan for all of us, and that plan came to fulfillment because of our faith and our courage. Indeed we have been in many dangerous situations since then, but God's angels have always protected us. We simply can't allow fear to obstruct our faith. We are going to go ahead with the plan, and we are going to spread the news far and wide of our meeting at An Dún Briste[167] at noon in three days' time. I would like you to decide among yourselves who takes which path to the various Christian destinations that surround Baile an Chaisil."

---

[166] Patron saint of the district known today as Killala. It is very possible that the name Alan so prevalent in Ireland has developed from Ala.

[167] Now termed Down Patrick Head. Technically an English translation would mean "the broken rock." See photograph above.

Muiredeach shook his head.

"You surely have strong faith," he said, "much more than we have ourselves. It would be wonderful to get rid of all the snakes of Éireann. But don't you think we are asking too much from God?"

Pátraic responded, "Nothing is impossible with God. At least we will pray about the snake problem, and if it be God's will, our prayers will be answered. We should not be afraid."

Then, before anyone else could reply, Pátraic said, "Cuimmín and Ala, you are natives of Máigheo. You know this area better than any of us. So I will let you two decide which Christian communities your companions and you choose for the announcement that we will gather here in three days' time to pray together."

Three days was a short time, but Cuimmín, Ala, and their companions managed to spread the news far and near. When the gathering took place, Pátraic was truly amazed at the numbers that showed up to be a part of the planned ritual of prayer. From where he stood, he simply could not see the borders of the crowd. He raised his mind to God in gratitude for the wonderful faith of these people. He prayed that God would exert His power to grant his request on behalf of not only those believers but all the people of Éireann. Then he began to pray aloud, first asking blessings on these Christians present, on all who had become Christian, and indeed on all of the people of Éireann, including the druids.

His prayer was unexpectedly interrupted!

The assembly were murmuring. There was a lot of movement. A tall man with a black beard was shoving and pushing his way through the gathering. He was creating a major disturbance. The bearded man began to scream. He got to the front of the crowd. He was holding something in his hand. It was a knife. He was heading toward Pátraic with abusive rants. Five or six men swiftly got to him. They shook the knife out of his hand. They held his arms fast. They asked him who he was.

"I am Crom Dobh. The people of this area know I am a druid.

This pretender," he screamed, pointing toward Pátraic, "is a fake. He tries to fool you. All druids were astounded at his influence over the high king. This man is destroying our profession and dishonoring our gods. He has turned thousands of people away from us. Just look at the numbers here today! I tell you he is an imposter and a hypocrite. Throw him over the bluff and drown him."

At that moment the sun came out as if throwing a spotlight on the occasion. The men holding Crom Dobh pulled him away a distance from Pátraic.

"He is a pretender, I tell you. And he is a liar. Destroy him! He gathered you together today under the facade that he would drive out the snakes. But where are the snakes? Do you see any snakes? The God that he preaches is but a reverie. Let us keep worshiping our own twelve gods."

By this time the rays of the sun had reached a clump of yew trees but a short distance from the gathering. There was a rustle among the leaves. Something was happening over there. Were more druids in hiding ready to attack Pátraic? Now there was a movement in the grass. All present witnessed an extraordinary happening. Thousands of snakes were crawling toward Pátraic, moving at a fast rate. They went in the direction of Crom Dobh. They slithered and crawled and hissed. The closer they got to him, the more frightened was he. In seconds snakes were crawling all over his body, some squeezing themselves around his throat.

"Help me! Help me!" shouted Crom Dobh.

Pátraic raised his hand as if in blessing. The snakes dropped from Crom Dobh's body, and they all went in the direction of Pátraic. Pátraic raised his hand again, and the snakes recoiled. Pátraic prayed silently. After a couple of minutes he spoke directly to the snakes.

"I command you in the name of the Most Holy Trinity to leave this land of Éireann and to crawl over this bluff and into the ocean below."

The crowd was filled with amazement as the snakes began to carry out Pátraic's orders. Within a few minutes, they were all drowned in the ocean. Pátraic turned to the assembly and spoke loudly.

"Oh, Lord God, we thank you for the wonders of this day. You have quietly gathered all of these snakes together unbeknownst to us. You had already listened to our prayers. We praise you, and we thank you. May Éireann never be troubled with a snake problem again. Praise be to You, O Blessed Trinity. Praise be to Your Divine Son, Jesus, who died for all of us that we might be saved for an eternal life of joy."

All present responded, "Amen."

They were almost in ecstasy at what they had seen, and promised each other they would never forget this day or the marvel Pátraic had worked.

Crom Dobh wasn't finished yet.

"You have allowed this sorcerer to invade your imagination. It was all a trick. You will still have snakes on your land tomorrow."

There was a rush at Crom Dobh.

"Throw him in with the snakes," was the cry.

Pátraic once more raised his right hand and said, "Do not interfere with Crom Dobh or cause him any harm. Our following of Christ calls for perpetual love of each other."

The on-rushers stopped in their tracks. Pátraic turned to Crom Dobh and said, "Go your way in peace."

The druid turned around and walked without hindrance toward the rock on which he had built his abode. He obviously felt a defeated man as he made his way from the mainland over the connecting wooden bridge to his home. Most of the assembly watched as he disappeared into his abode. Returning to their homes, all had a happy feeling that they had certainly witnessed a wonderful miracle.

For Crom Dobh, there still would be problems galore.

As the setting sun descended beneath the western waters, winds began to blow. The skies indicated that a storm was brewing. A storm to remember! By midnight the winds were howling. The fury of the waves was deafening as they threw themselves violently against the rocks. Cattle in the fields ran for shelter wherever they might find it. The population stayed within. Openings in the homes were barricaded. Smoke rising from each family quarters through the opening in the roof swirled into obscurity. The storm screamed louder than a thousand Crom Dobhs. For those immediately along the coast of Baile an Chaisil, a loud cracking and breaking reached their ears. Was a lightning storm approaching? Or had something horrible happened with one of their neighbors? Going out to investigate would be suicidal. There was little sleep for anyone throughout that night.

Before dawn the storm abated. The winds died, and mist blanketed the area. Through the mist a shrill cry pierced the air.

"Help me! Help me!"

Approaching the rocky walls of An Dún by modern-day kayak

The angry seas at An Dún

It came from the abode of Crom Dobh. His wooden bridge had been torn asunder by the storm. His small dwelling was almost demolished. Pieces of wood were scattered on the rocks beneath, some wood floating on the now-calm sea. He was a man alone and separated from his neighbors. There seemed no way of escape from his chosen dwelling on top of An Dún.[168] In due course the mist lifted, and Crom Dobh was standing piteously on his own, separated by a short distance from the bluff, a distance as far as he was concerned that could be a thousand kilometers. Neighbors came out to see him, many saddened by his plight.

"Where are his twelve gods now?" remarked one of the new Christian converts.

Before long, the onlookers were joined by Pátraic.

"Can anything be done to help this poor fellow?" he inquired.

"Well," said a bystander, "I know how his bridge was constructed. With help I could be able to work a plan that might enable that druid to be taken back to the mainland."

Pátraic, with his hand laid on the shoulder of the bystander to whom he had been speaking, turned around and shouted, "Does anyone else here know how this bridge was put together?"

Three men raised their hands.

"I saw how it was done," said one, "but it took weeks and weeks. I know something about it, and I have some ideas that might be useful."

Pátraic spoke again.

"God wants us to help this man. I appeal to all for help. Especially those men who might know something about how the bridge was built."

Four men came forward. They stood together with Pátraic's first adviser.

One spoke up and said, "I think we can get him off, but it will take quite a length of time before we can start the rescue. We have work to do."

---

[168] An Dún is a steep-sided, flat-topped very high rock, almost impossible to climb, divided from the surrounding plateau by great ice-carved trenches. See photograph.

Several hours later, planks fashioned from the local yew trees had been fastened together to reach from the bluff to An Dún. This process was repeated three times until eventually a walkway to An Dún had been erected. One rescuer crawled twenty feet out. He pitched a long rope that had been rolled up in a ball to the druid.

The man on the planks shouted, "Attach the rope around your waist, then throw the rest back to me. You can then lie on your stomach and crawl across the planks. We will be holding the rope for your protection."

The sun was setting as Crom Dobh began his hazardous crawl. It was slow and painful. Did he have the protection to prevent drowning if he were to make any movement that could cause him to lose his grip? He feared what might happen were he to slip off the plank. Would he be drowned or dashed against the rocks should his rescuers lose control of their grip on the rope that had secured him? He could see the powerful waves beneath him and the darkness of the deep and threatening waters that could swallow him into oblivion. It was the first time in his life in which he found himself in a perilous situation that could bring certain death. The evening chill was in the air, but for Crom Dobh it made no difference. The sweat of fear crept from his bones. He did indeed wonder if he would make it.

Lying on his stomach on the plank, he looked up and saw the large group of people with Pátriac standing almost on the edge of the cliff, urging his rescuers on. He thought to himself, *Only yesterday I wanted this man thrown into the sea. Here I am this evening relying on him to save me from a similar fate.*

He had a newfound courage and belief that Pátraic's God would save him. His body was tense. His situation was traumatic. Would he be saved?

He was!

He made it the whole way across without incident and it was an exhausted figure who was finally pulled to safety. The very first to stretch out his hand and help him get on his feet was Pátraic himself.

If this kind of love was part of Christian teaching, then he himself wanted to practice it too. He realized that the imposition of twelve gods on people was a sham. He would ask Pátraic for baptism to take him into the Christian faith.

The shadows were stretching. Twilight was at hand. But Crom Dobh would never forget this occasion on which he was born into a new relationship with the One True God.

Next morning was chilly and wet. A roar from the waves told of further stormy weather approaching. After the events of the last couple of days, Pátraic felt weary. The stormy seas brought poignant memories of his first voyage to the land where he now stood and where he had lived for the past several decades. He recalled, too, his many travels, the risks he took to convert the high king and to destroy the druidic system, and his altercation with the Bishops of Brittania following the martyrdom and capture of some of his little congregation away to the north. Just the same, he knew he loved the people of Éireann, and he knew, too, that they loved him. It was as if the entire image of his life was emerging before his eyes. He dropped to his knees, leaning against his bed, and prayed. His prayer was one of thanks, once again commending himself to God. Finally, his somnolence overpowered him, and his head gradually slumped onto his bed.

This was how Cuimmín found him when he entered the room. Pátraic's knees were still on the floor, with his head on the bed. He was in a deep sleep. Cuimmín had come to advise that the weather conditions were unsuitable for further travel today. Now Cuimmín finalized his decision. Bishop Pátraic was obviously unable to face the elements on the planned journey farther west. He spoke to Pátraic, who apologized profusely for having fallen asleep.

"I was communicating with my God. Unfortunately my tired body dominated me. I am glad you woke me."

Cuimmín replied, "I was coming to advise you that this is not a day for travel. I am sure you have looked out already and seen the threat of the elements. I think you should rest in bed, and we can determine tomorrow morning if we should ride farther along the west coast to visit our friends. You had decided, but let's talk about our plans tomorrow when you will be well-rested."

"Cuimmín, you have been a wonderful companion, and you have helped me so much in the furthering of our ministry over here in the west. I think it would be proper for you to stay here and watch over our Christian friends in this locality."

Cuimmín was unsure what Pátraic meant and replied, "You are going to leave me here on my own? That will be a difficult assignment."

"But you are a native of Máigheo. You know the people well. Yes, we are going to leave you here among your own people, and I will ordain you bishop this coming Sunday."

"Holy Father," said Cuimmín, "I have never expected separation from you, and when you leave me here, my heart will be broken. You have been my guide for so many years. You have shared your faith with me. I realize the sacrifice you are asking me to make does not compare with the sacrifices you have made all through your life. You have left home and relatives to share your faith in a strange land. I will be glad to carry out your wishes."

Pátraic nodded.

"Go and tell our companions to invite the rest of the Christian community. I will ordain you bishop on Sunday, and if they wish to join us for the ceremony, that would be a blessed circumstance."

Cuimmín replied, "May God's will be done! I promise you I will serve our people to the best of my ability. Holy Father, please pray to our Lord that I will be a good and faithful servant."

A much larger congregation than had been expected gathered for Cuimmín's ordination as bishop. There was much joy among the attendees, and it was very evident that Cuimmín was a happy choice. They knew their own Máigheo native was going to stay with them.

Only Pátraic's priest companions who took part in the ceremony noticed the developing frailty of their leader. His face had paled considerably, and he seemed to have lost his vigor. During the Mass he delivered a homily, but his voice was nowhere near the strength it once had. It did not take long for them to decide together that they must not allow the saintly Pátraic to journey any farther west. Instead they would advise him to return to his monastery at Sabhall, which had been established as their home for a long time.

That evening they gathered with Pátraic, who had been their constant inspiration down through the years. Sadly, on this occasion he appeared exhausted physically and emotionally. Pátraic readily accepted their advice. In his own heart he felt it would be a long and arduous trek back. He felt feeble and challenged by the distance he would have to travel. He did not know that these same thoughts permeated the hearts of his companions.

The following morning witnessed a calm ocean, but heavy showers frequently interrupted the tenor of the day. It had been Pátraic's ambition to journey farther west, even as far down as Oileán Achla. Today he was feeling fatigued due to the recent extraordinary happenings. The many converts were acclaiming yesterday's miracle, but in Pátraic's heart all that mattered was the proclamation of the Good News.

But his spirit was very much alive.

"I must at least journey as far as Iorras to visit our friend Mochua, and to find out what success he is achieving. I should ordain him a bishop. I may not be back this way again."

Pátraic's coworkers could do nothing but agree, although they feared because of their great leader's health. But they knew Pátraic's mind was made up. Since Iorras was not that far away, they felt they could probably make the journey within one day.

Mochua was surprised and excited at their arrival, and greeted them as long-lost brothers. He had good news for Pátraic. The Christian church was growing by leaps and bounds. He needed more priests in order to keep up with the large numbers of conversions.

"It shall be done," said Pátraic, "and you will be ordained a bishop so that you will be able to ordain the priests you need to keep the fires burning in this part of Máigheó. And I will ordain Muiredach priest so that he may stay in this area and help you."

Mochua immediately expressed his gratitude.

"I wish you would stay for at least a few days so that I may notify as many of our new Christians as I can. It will be of great advantage to me to be able to ordain more priests because we certainly need them in this part. And I greatly want your advice on something else."

"We will gladly help resolve any of your problems if we can."

"This is a major problem," said Mochua. "I will need to explain it to all of you. I don't really know what to do although I have strong feelings about the situation."

The small band of missionaries was sitting around a huge peat fire. Their main meal was over, and they were in a relaxed mood.

"We are all listening," said Pátraic, nodding to Mochua.

Mochua began, "It's like this. And I can hardly believe it myself, unless I had seen it for myself. Nine hundred years ago, when the Tuatha De Dannan were in full control of Ireland … after the Fir Bolg had been conquered by them, there seems to have been a great deal of witchcraft."

Pátraic interrupted.

"Witchcraft is from the devil, and it is not at all unlikely that the devil reigned—and still reigns—in places that are yet totally pagan. There are spells and devil worship in many places, not just here, but all over the world."

"I am glad you said that," said Mochua, "and now I have come across it. As I said, it is a nine-hundred-year-old story of witchcraft that extends to our own time. Hard to imagine that. Well … there was a territorial king living somewhere in the middle of Éireann nine hundred years ago. His name was Lir. He wanted to be high-king but he lost out to another king whose name was Bo Dearg. Since Bo Dearg wanted to be friends with Lir, he gave him his oldest daughter, Aoibh, in marriage. It was a happy marriage, and they had four children. The oldest was Fionnuala. Then they had twins, Conn and Fiachra, and a third boy was born to them, and they called him Aoidh. It was a very happy marriage altogether, and the children were growing up loved very much by their father and mother. They were gifted children too. They all could sing and dance, and they all loved each other. Well … didn't their mother Aoibh die … and didn't Bo Dearg offer another of his daughters to Lir, so there would always be peace between them? Lir was happy and agreed. He thought since his first wife was so loving and caring, her sister would have to be the same. The new wife's name was Aoife. Poor Lir was in for a surprise! Aoife was very jealous of the four children, and she didn't love her husband much either. She would have liked to have them killed, but who would want to kill the king's children? This Aoife was a horrible person. The name is quite familiar around here, too, and I can tell you every Aoife I have met is a beautiful lady. But not this one! She was mean and vengeful. So didn't she contrive a plot to get rid of the children?

"Well … you'll forgive me, but what I am about to tell you will shock you, and it's all true … it's a terrible thing … one day Aoife told the children they were going down to play by the lake, and she was coming with them. Now, the children were no fools! It was the first time Aoife had ever taken part in their playtime. Fionnuala, the eldest, was a bit suspicious, but she was concerned about her brothers so she agreed to go along. And while they were at the lake, splashing around as children do and having a lot of fun, what does Aoife do?"

"She drowned them all?" inquired a listener.

"No, she did not. She was a merciless person. She produced a wand and waved it over them …"

"This is a good story. Where did you hear it, and what's the problem?"

Mochua looked a little annoyed.

"This is for real. And I am not anywhere near finished yet. Aoife waved the wand and told the children they were being turned into swans. And ... they would have to spend three hundred years on Lake Derravaragh,[169] where they now were ... near their father's castle, three hundred years more on the Sea of Moyle[170] ... after that another three hundred years on the western sea at Iorras. Then she said something peculiar, and mind you it has come to pass. She said after that time they would hear a bell ringing, and the sound of that bell would be caused by a druid who had come from overseas. Pátraic, I think she was referring to you.

"Their witchcraft mother then told them she would leave them their voices; they would be able to continue to speak and to sing songs. Then she left her poor victims on the lake and went home. Now when the king arrived, he wondered where the children were ... so he asked his wife.

"'Down by the lake' she tells him.

"Lir was irritated that the children were out so late, and he went quickly down to the lake. He found the children all right, but they were now four swans. They spoke to him and told him of their plight. He begged them to return home with him, and he would try to have the spell removed. They followed him, but on reaching their home, Fionnuala spoke out.

"'Father, we are now swans. We have to live in water. We cannot go into the house.'

"Immediately, they flew away singing a song of sorrow. They had beautiful sweet voices, and their singing could be heard around that lake for three centuries.

"Now it was time for them to encounter the rough waters of the Sea of Moyle. Poor creatures, they were blown all around; they lost some of their feathers, but they survived the three hundred years."

---

[169] The actual location of this lake is unknown. It may have been in County Longford toward the middle of Ireland. Other scholars think it was situated in County Donegal.

[170] North Channel connecting the Celtic Sea and the Atlantic Ocean between Ireland North and Scotland.

"And you believe all of this?" interrupted one of the listeners.

"Yes, I do, and I am going to prove it to you," answered Mochua defiantly.

"They flew to Iorras from the Sea of Moyle to finish their condemnation of three hundred more years. Now you well know that the seas around Iorras are very stormy and terribly cold. Poor things, their feet would get frozen to the rocks when they sought shelter in the severe winters around here, and they continued to lose more of their feathers, something that didn't help them. Still, they continued to sing mournful songs, and the natives had a custom of going down to the seaside to hear them. They were by Inisglóra[171] not very far from where we are now. Those poor swans were afraid to speak to the people. They feared for their lives because they thought the onlookers would kill them if they spoke. So they stayed a safe distance from shore.

"Now listen carefully ... I have a little bell in my cill to call my people to prayer. One morning they heard the sound of my little bell, and it brought back the memory of what their stepmother had told them. A bell ringing out ... had the promised druid come from over the seas?

"At the sound of the bell, they swam to shore and as best they could flew and limped toward the place from which the sound was coming. Now I am sure it was by God's design that the first person they encountered was myself. I was totally shocked! Four swans in front of me ... and they started talking."

Another interruption!

"Mochua, are you sure you are all right? Has somebody cast a spell on you?"

Mochua made the sign of the cross on himself.

"Now I have come to the spot where I need help. And it's not for me. It's for the swans. Oh, yes! They even gave me their names ... that is why I was able to tell you at the beginning. And they told me the whole story I have just narrated to you. Hard to believe, isn't it? I

---

[171] Glory Island, off the northwest coast of County Mayo, Ireland.

was waiting for you, Pátraic, to help make a decision. They are swans, but they seek baptism!"

"Take me to them tomorrow morning," said Pátraic. "Will they speak to me too?"

"I don't see any reason why not."

In the midmorning, Mochua led Pátraic and his companions down to the shore. Four swans were huddled together as if awaiting them.

Mochua spoke first, placing his hand on Pátraic's shoulder.

"Fionnuala, this is our leader. We have been awaiting his arrival. I have told him your tale of woe. Would you speak directly to him?"

The swan began to speak. Her voice was low but gentle. It was the voice of a very old lady, and Pátraic had difficulty understanding, but with the knowledge he had gained from Mochua, he was able to put the words together.

"Please, sir, we would like to be baptized into your religion before we die. We have suffered greatly, and Mochua has told us of the wonders of your God. We want to be with Him, and we are certain we will die soon."

The onlookers were amazed.

"Fionnuala, I know all about you that I need to know. For you and your brothers' great suffering at the hands of witchcraft throughout all those years, the Most Holy Trinity will greatly compensate you. You have taken care of your brothers, you have kept all your family together, and I have no doubt God wants me to baptize you here and now. You will all die in God's love."

Mochua was excited.

"O, thank you, Holy Father. I am so glad that you are here and that you will administer the baptism yourself. I will fetch you a pail of the holy water."

The baptism took place. Immediately a very thin and worn-out old lady stood before them. Beside her were three aged men, bony with wizened faces, their heads bent to the ground, their backs in a stooping posture. Pátraic blessed them and prayed. Before his prayers were completed, they were dead.

Pátraic looked compassionately at the four lifeless bodies.

"Those poor victims of witchcraft deserve a respectful Christian burial. Now they are in a place that is timeless, and their new joys will never end. Instead of the light of the sun shining on the waters, they will enjoy the perpetual light of the Creator of all things."

Chapter 27

Going Home

Following the events of recent weeks, Pátraic's brethren decided this would have to end their journey. Because of the health of their beloved inspirer, any further journeying would have to be abandoned. The most important thing would be to get their now frail chief back to his monastery in Sabhall.

There was much resting and many overnights on the way home. At times his associates were fearful of his ability to complete the task of arriving home. It was a longer ride than their previous trips. Despite the tribulations of the journey, they reached their destination.

On seeing his monastery, a great peace and a sense of elation filled Pátraic's soul. He was home! Home to that place where it all began, once more in the familiar surroundings of his early missionary days. The place from which he had launched, through God's help, his conquest of the soul of Éireann. Pátraic appeared exhausted to his community brothers. Before they had a meal, they helped Pátraic to his bed. Supper was prepared and served to him.

Word quickly spread to his friends and neighbors that their beloved mentor and guide was back among them. When they attended Mass on Sunday, the congregation saw no sign of Pátraic, and just after the reading of the gospel they were informed of his health conditions. The presiding priest asked them to pray every day for Pátraic that he would be with them for a long time.

There was a groan from the congregation. They wondered and whispered to each other … was there something serious about Pátraic's condition … when would they be able to see him and hear him again … might his illness be fatal? After the ceremony, the priest was surrounded by an inquiring and disturbed throng, wanting to learn more about the apparent serious illness of the man who had bestowed on them such a wonderful knowledge of the One True God and who had brought so much peace into their lives. They were aware the druids still existed, but without power, and even nonconverts to Christianity were dismissing them as nonentities. The love of the people for their saintly leader overflowed, thereby demonstrating their concerns for him.

For the next two months, there was no change in the reports about Pátraic. He did not appear at any Mass or ceremony. The realization grew that his illness was terminal. His brother priests living in the monastery saw him fade away little by little. Then one day the news was delivered.

The beloved Pátraic was dead. It was March 17.[172]

The news of Pátraic's passing spread rapidly. Mouth to mouth it was passed on until within a very short time it reached the Christians of Árd Mhacha many kilometers away. Clergy and leaders there assembled to discuss the site of his burial. Surely it should be Árd Mhacha, the very place where Pátraic had established his first *deóise*.[173] It was to be the site of an *easbog*[174] who would have governance over the entire country. Árd Mhacha was the place they determined where their great leader should be buried. Was it not the *ard-dheoise*[175] of all Ireland? He should be buried in no other place than here!

---

[172] This would have been according to the Julian calendar, which was displaced by the Gregorian calendar in 1582. The date March 17 mentioned here, Julian calendar, may not be exactly precise with the Gregorian calendar. However, the difference in days would most likely have been within a couple of weeks.

[173] Diocese.

[174] Bishop.

[175] Archdiocese.

The people of Sabhall thought differently!

Sabhall was the place where he founded his first Christian community as well as his monastery. It was the place to which he returned for resting periods with his priests, and it was here he had died. Pátraic belonged to them! And among them he should have his final resting place.

A dispute was simmering! Both sides knew their blessed leader would not have wished for this disruption among his people. The man of peace should be buried in peace. They prayed together that God would somehow show them the way. A suggestion came from the Árd Mhacha side. Would the Sabhall people agree to allow two bullocks[176] yoked to an undriven carriage bearing the body to go forward? Wherever they stopped would be the burial place of their patron. If the bullocks passed Sabhall then they were bound for Árd Mhacha.

"A strange suggestion," complained one of the Sabhall monks. "You are leaving the animals to tell us where our leader should lie."

"No, indeed we are not doing any such thing. We are leaving it to God to lead the animals," was the reply from the Árd Mhacha side. "Many years ago did not Pátraic found the ard-dheoise for all of Éireann? It was the place where his Cathaoirchill was built."

"So you are expecting God to do wonders for us."

"God has already done wonders for all of us. Why should he not continue to do so? Remember the tale Pátraic told us how the first apostles of Jesus cast lots to find out who would replace the departed Judas? In other words they drew straws, and Matthias got the short straw. God had directed them to choose Matthias, and so they did. Now we are asking God to direct us where we should bury our own great apostle. He will direct us through the bullocks."

There was a murmur among the participants. The people of Sabhall finally agreed.

The dispute was over. Pátraic was waked for the two following days. Stories about the dead man were narrated. They were joyous

---

[176] Steer.

stories. The banishing of the snakes at Baile an Caisil was told and retold, mostly by people who hardly knew the location of that place. A seanchaí was of course among the mourners, and he brought forth stories of Pátraic's spiritual strength, his physical strength, and his dedication to all of his people. There was laughter, and there were tears. But everybody believed their teacher was now with his Lord. They knew, too, that his influence would remain.

The funeral cortege began immediately following the Mass. Fortunately it was a dry if somewhat windy day. The wooden coffin bearing Pátraic's remains was placed in a carriage decorated with daffodils. A herdsman started the bullocks on their journey, then retired to the large crowd following the remains. Many people wondered how far they could travel on foot if the choice of burial ground be Árd Mhacha.

They did not have to wait too long for the response. Right outside the little cill at Sabhall, the bullocks stopped. The herdsman walking with the crowd behind the carriage moved up front and tugged at the harness. The bullocks remained frozen to the ground. They simply refused to move.

For the next half hour, the effort to get the animals to go forward was repeated and repeated. It was a vain effort. Those bullocks had come to the end of their journey. This was where Pátraic would lie until the day of the never-setting sun. And so he was laid to rest in the little *reilig*[177] just outside the cill,[178] which had been erected so many

---

[177] Cemetery.

[178] The burial place of Patrick has an extraordinary history. First, the Cill of Saint Patrick was replaced by a cathedral founded by Saint Malachy in 1124, and run by the Augustinian order. Later the Benedictines took over in 1177 by order of the Norman John de Courcy. In 1538 the monastery was suppressed, and later destroyed by Lord Leonard Grey, lord deputy of Ireland (overseeing British occupation). Grey himself was executed sometime afterward for this destruction. An act of the British Parliament helped restore the ruins in 1790. By this time Catholicism had been outlawed in Ireland. The building now functions as a Church of Ireland cathedral for the Diocese of Down. The cathedral for the Catholic Diocese of Down and Connor is in Belfast, and named after Saint Peter.

years ago when his disciples and he set about bringing Christianity to Éireann.

Pátraic sleeps until the Light whose brilliance is eternal shines on everlasting day.

But his spirit is well awake in the land he loved. And his shamrock thrives aplenty.

The End
Crioch

Epilogue

The year of Patrick's death is not exactly known. Tradition has it that he died in 461 AD. However, a number of scholars make the date 464 or 465. Among the general Irish population, the accepted date is the traditional one of 461.

Does it matter? Not really. Without any doubt Saint Patrick is the saint of the Irish. Indeed the majority of Irish people will frown if reminded that Patrick was born in Scotland or in any foreign land. He is an Irish saint! He was canonized by popular acclaim a short time after his death.

He is the patron saint of Ireland, where he is commemorated with parades and a variety of celebrations on March 17 every year. No other country's patron saint is honored worldwide as is Saint Patrick. Nor is any other patron so well known. This phenomenon may be attributed to the Irish diaspora, who left their country in very large numbers in times past, and spread the story of their patron everywhere they went.

In my own memories, I still recall my first Saint Patrick's Day in the United States, fifty-six years ago. The first thing I saw outside, early in the morning, was two or three people walking their dogs. To my surprise, all of the dogs were wearing green ribbons around their necks. Saint Patrick's Day was being celebrated more than four thousand miles from Ireland!

The Saint Patrick's Day Parade in New York City is historical and draws the attention of national television news every year. In Savannah, Georgia, a parade and celebration is held that equals that of New York. Seattle, Washington, celebrates, too, as well as San Francisco and other cities throughout the United States. In Chicago, the Chicago River is dyed green for the occasion with oversight from city authorities and, of course, the approval of the parade committee. Thousands of miles farther away in South Korea, a major parade takes place in the capital, Seoul.

Patrick was made a citizen of Ireland almost sixteen hundred years ago.

Saint Patrick belongs to the Irish, and they have given him to the world!

Glossary

Aballava.

    Roman fort, south of Solway Firth, now Burgh by Sands, England.

Abhainn Mór.

    Now known as the Palmerstown River, located in the Killala area.

    Official name is the Owenmore.

Abhainn na Sionainne.

    River Shannon.

Ablatum Bulgium.

    Dumfries, Scotland.

adiutor.

    Deputy.

alaris.

    Prestigious horse soldier, noncitizen of Rome.

a-máw-ruck.

    Tomorrow, from the Gaelic amárach.

Ala.

    Patron saint of Killala, County Mayo, Ireland.

Alba.

    Scotland.

Amhainn na Sionnaine.

    Shannon River.

An Bhóinn.

    River Boyne.

An Bhreatain.

    Britain.

An Bhreatain Bheag.

    Wales.

An Cruach.

Known today as Cruagh Pátraic, or Saint Patrick's mountain or The Reek. County Mayo, Ireland.

an dún.

Steep, flat-topped, very high rock,

separated from surrounding plateau by ice-carved trenches.

An Dún Briste.

Now termed Down Patrick Head;

technical English translation is "the broken rock."

An Euróip.

Europe.

An Frainc.

France.

An Mumha.

Province of Munster.

An Roimh.

Rome.

An tAigéan atlantach.

The Atlantic Ocean.

An tAonach Beag.

Killala, County Mayo, Ireland;

named for Ala, a companion of Saint Patrick.

An tSionna. The Shannon.

Anabeg.

Now Killala, the place from which Patrick escaped to France.

Angias.

Wife of King Laoghaire;

mother of Lugaid Mac Lóegairi, a high king of Ireland.

Angleterre.

England.

Aogán.

Irish for Aidan.

Aongus.

Devout king of Munster 453–489, killed in battle c. 489.

ard-dheoise.

Archdiocese.

Átha Luain.

Athlone, County Westmeath, Ireland.

Atlantach bhord farraige.

Atlantic Seaboard.

Atlantique.

Atlantic.

Baie de Biscayne.

Bay of Biscayne.

Baile an Chaisil.

Ballycastle, County Mayo; chaisil means an ancient stone fort.

Ballintubber.

From the Gaelic Baile Tobair Phádraig,
meaning the Town of Patrick's Well.

Bar.

Where the River Moy and the Owenmore meet the Atlantic
Ocean, Killala Bay.

Béal an Átha.

Ballina, County Mayo, Ireland.

Beal Feirsde.

Belfast.

beansi.

In English, banshee, a preternatural spirit associated with death;
mythically cries with loud wailing before a family member dies.

Bhreatain.

England.

Blasius.

Anglicized Blaise.

Bré.

Bray, County Wicklow, Ireland.

Bréssal Bélach.

    King of Leinster.

Brian Echach Muigmedóin.

    Very famous king, who most likely became high king of Ireland.

Brian O'Dubpthain.

    In modern terms, Brian Duffy.

Bricius.

    Fourth bishop of Tours, 397–443.

Bristol Alveo.

    Bristol Channel.

Britannia.

    England.

Brú na Bóinne.

    Located on the River Boyne, about thirty miles north of Dublin.

bullocks.

    Steer.

Caledonia.

    Scotland.

Calpurnius.

    Name of Saint Patrick's father.

caoiners.

    Professional mourners.

Caolán MacMulruaidh.

    Name Caolán has fallen into disuse;

    MacMulruaidh means Mulroy.

Carmarthen Bay.

    Southwest of Swansea, Wales.

Carraig.

    Carrick-on-Shannon, County Leitrim, Ireland.

céad míle fáilte.

    One hundred thousand welcomes.

Céash.

    Keash, County Sligo, Ireland.

cill.

Small church.

Cill of Saint Patrick.

The small church founded by Saint Patrick where he was laid to rest.

Clydach.

Small village near Swansea.

Cnoc Shláine.

The Hill of Slane, along the River Boyne, in an area of historic sites.

Conchessa.

Name of Saint Patrick's mother.

Connacht.

Province of Connaught.

Constantine.

Emperor Constantine I declared Christianity to be the religion of the Roman Empire in 325.

Cormac O'Ceallachain.

In modern English, Cormac O'Ceallaghan.

Coroticus.

Minor king in southern Scotland or northern England; possibly acquainted with Patrick.

crozier.

Staff carried by a bishop at religious ceremonies; symbolizes the shepherd's staff.

Cruachán.

Croghan, County Roscommon, Ireland.

Cuan Toirneach.

The Hound of Thunder.

Cuchullain.

Famous warrior, directly translated "The Hound of Ulster."

Cuimmín.

Associate of Patrick; at least two local areas took their names in his honor: Kilcummin in northwest Mayo and Kilcummin in the parish of Lackan, on the north Mayo coast.

Deaglán.
> Saint Declan, son of a Déisi chief, founded monastery at
> Ardmore, County Waterford, Ireland.

decurion.
> An officer in charge of a squadron.

denarii.
> Roman coins.

deóise.
> Diocese.

diaspora.
> Dispersion of any people from their original homeland.

Dubhlinn.
> Dublin.

easbog.
> Bishop.

Éireann.
> Gaelic for Ireland.

Eithne.
> Wife of King Aongus, known as "the hated";
> died in battle c. 489 along with her husband.

Fir Bolg.
> Pre-Celtic invaders of Ireland;
> traditionally small in stature with a large stomach.

Foghill.
> Now Fohill near Killala in County Mayo, Ireland.

Hadrian's Wall.
> Defensive fortification in Britannia, begun in AD 122;
> extends from Newcastle on Tyne on the east coast of England
> to Carlisle on the west coast.

hurling.
> Gaelic game played with a specially made stick to strike a ball.

in hoc signo vinces.
> In this sign you shall conquer.

Inisglóra.

Glory Island, County Mayo, Ireland.

Iorras.

Erris, townland on the north coast of County Mayo.

Irlande.

Ireland.

La France.

France.

Laigheann.

Province of Leinster.

Lake Derravaragh.

Exact location unknown;

thought to have been in County Longford or County Donegal.

Laoghaire.

High king; name shortened to Laoire;

became disinterested in practicing his religion;

died in the Liffey Valley,

possibly the result of a curse by the druids, according to myth.

Leacan.

Lacken Parish, on the north shore of Mayo.

Lérins.

A Cistercian monastery on the island of Saint-Honorat;

founded c. 410 by Saint Honoratus.

Leucarum.

Located in the city of Swansea, Wales

Lia Fáil.

The Stone of Destiny;

used at the coronation of a high king of Ireland.

Loch Cé.

Lough Key, County Roscommon, Ireland.

Loch Cúan.

Strangford Lough.

Londinium.

London.

Londres.

>Londres.

>London.

Lough Derg.

>Saint Patrick's Purgatory.

Luguvalium.

>Located within Carlisle, on the Celtic Sea.

m'amie.

>My love, as addressed to a woman.

ma chêrie.

>My dear, as addressed to a woman.

ma chéri.

>My beloved, as addressed to a woman.

Máigheo.

>County Mayo in Western Ireland; means Plain of the Yew Tree.

March 17.

>Feast Day of Saint Patrick.

Martin of Tours.

>Bishop of Tours, France, 371–397.

Messe.

>Mass.

Míle buíochas.

>A thousand thanks.

Mise.

>I am, (followed by a name), in Gaelic.

mo grádh thu

>You are my love.

mon chaton

>My love, as addressed to a man.

mon cher.

>My dear, as addressed to a man.

Muaidh.

>River Moy.

Mullach Faraidh.

>Now known as Mullafarry, County Mayo, northwest of Ballina.

276

Na Déisi.

Historical tribe under King Cormac Mac Airt; relocated to the Province of Munster in Ireland, due to an attempt on the life of Cormac.

Na Fianna.

Group of ethical warriors; probably existed; feats became mythical.

Na Sí.

Mythological small people (fairies); can only be seen by moonlight.

Novatian/Novatianists/Novatianism.

Antipope in Rome;

early heresy in the church denying Mary's motherhood of the Divine.

Oileán Achla.

Achill Island, on the west coast of County Mayo.

Oisín.

Irish mythological character, pronounced Esheen.

Pátraic.

Patrick, as adapted into the Celtic language.

Pays de Galles.

Wales.

Penarth.

A town in the Vale of Glamorgan, Wales.

Pons Aelius.

Roman fort near Newcastle upon Tyne.

praefectus castrorum.

Third most senior commander of the Roman legion.

prêtre.

Priest.

raths.

Underground forts with mounds above ground.

reilig.

Cemetery.

Ross.

    Near Slane, County Meath, Ireland; a well-known junction
    on the Navan Dublin Road.

Sabhall.

    Location of Saint Patrick's monastery, County Down, Ireland.

Samhain.

    Gaelic festival;
    marks the end of harvest season and beginning of winter.

sár mhaith.

    In Gaelic, excellent.

Sea of Moyle.

    Between Ireland North and Scotland,
    connects the Celtic Sea and the Atlantic Ocean.

seanchaí.

    Irish professional storyteller.

sí rath.

    A fairy mound, sometimes called "the home of the little people."

slán abhaile.

    Safe home.

slan leat.

    Goodbye.

Sliabh Mis.

    Slemish Mountain, pronounced "sleeve mish,"
    located in County Antrim, Ireland.

Succat Maewyn.

    Patrick's name at birth.

Succata.

    Name Patrick was called by his slavemaster.

tablifer.

    Standard bearer.

Teamhair.

    Tara, ancient seat of high kings of Ireland, County Meath.

Tír Amhlaidh.

>Tirawley, north County Mayo, Ireland.

Tir na nÓg.

>Country of the Celtic gods;

>directly translated "The Country of the Young."

Tuatha De Dannán.

>Warring tribe; occupied Ireland after Fir Bolg and before the Celts.

uisce beatha.

>Whiskey.

Ulaidh.

>Province of Ulster.

Uláinn.

>Province of Ulster.

Bibliography

de Paor, Máire B. *Patrick. The Pilgrim Apostle of Ireland*. New York: Harper Collins, 1998.

Harkins, James J. *The Irish Matryoshka: A History of Irish Monks in Medieval Europe*. Ruskin, FLA: M&M Printing, 2007.

McCormick, Donal. *The Road to Downpatrick*. Lacken, Mayo, Ireland: Donal McCormick, 2016.

Reilly, Robert T. *Irish Saints*. New York: Avenel Books, 1981.

Tobin, Greg. *The Wisdom of St. Patrick*. New York: Fall River Press, 1999.

Edwards Brothers Inc.
Ann Arbor MI. USA
May 3, 2018